The Kangaroo Conspiracy

by Heidi Dolan

For additional copies, write or call:

Smiletime Publishing
P.O. Box 11614
Jackson, WY 83002
307 739-9872

Copyright June 2000

ISBN 0-9702565-0-7

This book is dedicated to the
individuals who are, or at anytime were,
a part of the Jackson Hole, Wyoming
Class of 2001!

To Phil, Tara, Patrick, and Jill

And

In loving memory of
Patrick Gildea,
Adam Harshman,
and Ben Roice,
three individuals who lived life to the fullest
and who left this world much too soon.
The memory of your warmhearted spirits
will remain in our hearts until we meet again.

Chapter One

Tomorrow would be Jeff Farnsworth's fourteenth birthday, but there wouldn't be any balloons or a cake or even any presents to open. Instead, Jeff would find himself alone, walking along a desolate stretch of California highway with nothing more than a plastic bag to shield himself from a driving, torrential rain. As for now, he stood in a dark corner of the bedroom, a room that he and his little sister, Sarah, shared with two other foster kids, unaware of what awaited him outside of these four familiar walls. Stuffing his duffel bag with the few personal items he had left, he rummaged through a dresser drawer for the last of his socks, underwear, and a few T shirts, hardly enough items to fill the oversized sports bag. He decided he'd wear his raggedy wool sweater under his fleece lined parka to provide some extra insulation against the frigid night air. He grabbed a flashlight, knowing that this final item would be essential to his success when making the descent down the mountain road's winding traverses. He tried not to think about the darkness that would envelop him as soon as he stepped outside or the possibility of an early season snowstorm. He was well aware of how unpredictable and unforgiving the late autumn weather could be and he only hoped it would stay clear at least until he reached the lowlands.

Checking the pockets of his jeans, he pulled out a crumpled, but crisp $50 bill and a random assortment of change. He wished he had kept more money aside from his summer of mowing lawns and doing odd jobs, but Mrs. Johnson had insisted that he deposit the bulk of it into a savings account. Now it was too late to make the twenty mile trip to town to withdraw the rest of his cash.

He chose one final item to stuff into the bag. It was an official NBA basketball, the last gift he had ever received from his parents on his eleventh birthday, three years ago.

1

The basketball made the packaging bulky and lopsided, so he reorganized the load for easier handling. As he zipped up the bag, he heard someone stir in the top bunk bed next to him. It was Sarah.

"Do you really have to go?" Sarah whispered in the darkness.

"Shhh! You'll wake Jamie and Harry," he whispered back, looking toward the other set of bunk beds where the children were sleeping. "You know I do."

"But what if I never see you again?" Sarah persisted, becoming teary eyed at the thought that her only brother was leaving her behind.

"You'll see me again, I promise. I'll send for you as soon as I get to Uncle Frank's."

"So, then why don't you just take me with you now?" Sarah suggested eagerly.

"Sarah, we've been over this. It just wouldn't be practical," Jeff reminded her.

"But what if you forget about me? You know how sometimes it's hard to remember what Mom and Dad were like, how they laughed and stuff." Sarah thought that her argument was gaining validity in her brother's mind, but she was mistaken.

Jeff turned and peered into his young sister's beckoning eyes. They were round and looked almost black in the dimness of the night. Her long, dark hair, brushed back from her forehead, framed her beautiful, little face with its freckled button nose and rosy lips. She waited impatiently for his response.

"That's different. We might forget things *about* them, but we'll never forget *them*. Don't worry, Sarah, I could never forget you," Jeff reassured her.

But Sarah couldn't contain herself any longer. She jumped out of bed, her feet making a loud thump as they hit the floor. "I don't want to take that chance," she announced. Even at eight years of age, Sarah was determined not to be denied this opportunity, at least not without putting up a fight.

She pulled out another dresser drawer, just below the one Jeff had just finished emptying, and hit him squarely in the groin with the corner.

Jeff doubled over, managing to muffle his reaction vocally as he cringed in pain. "Sarah," he whispered in an exasperated snarl, "get back in bed before we both get caught. Do you want me to get sent away? You know you'll be fine here with the Johnsons until I get settled and can send for you. So, please just let me get out of here."

"But what if they move *me* while you're gone? You won't be able to find *me*." Sarah thought she'd made a rather good point.

That was something that Jeff had not thought about, but he quickly dismissed the notion. "They're not after you. You're not turning fourteen. It's me they want. Don't worry, you know the Johnsons will do everything they can to keep you here. They love you."

Sarah knew this to be true. It was this truth, along with the lateness of the hour and the fatigue that plagued her petite body that ended the contest between Jeff and Sarah. For even in the shadowy darkness, Jeff could see the resignation in her limbs as she collapsed on the lower bunk bed in surrender.

"Okay, well then promise me one thing, no two things," she corrected herself, getting up again and taking a sterling silver cross and chain from around her neck.

"What?" Jeff, who was still recovering from his encounter with the dresser drawer, was now more anxious than ever to leave before anyone in the household was aroused by all the noise and commotion.

"First," she directed, holding up her index finger, "don't get in with any weirdos. If someone looks weird and they want to give you a ride, just say no. You got it? Even if it's raining or whatever, just don't do it!"

He wanted to ask her to define "weirdo" since compliance to her demand could immensely limit his choices for transportation on his 250 plus mile journey to the Los Angeles International Airport. Feeling pressured

3

to move on, he reluctantly agreed to her request and awaited her second commandment.

"And the second thing you have to promise me is that you'll keep this with you," she said softening as she tried to force the tiny necklace over his head without detaching the clasp. Gently, he touched her hand and retrieved the cross from on top of his head. His fingertip touched the inscription on the back of the cross as he stuffed it into the pocket of his jeans. He didn't have to read it. He knew that it was her name in large block letters. It, too, was one of the few remaining possessions that she had left from her parents, and Jeff knew that it meant the world to her.

"Thanks, Sarah, I won't let you down."Jeff gave his sister a huge hug that would have to last for who knew how long. "I love you, Sarah. Be good," he said.

Upon opening the window, he felt the brisk November air invade the room. "Do you want to get back into your own bed or do you want me to tuck you in right here?" He, now, too, had tears in his eyes as he looked at her tiny features and long dark hair for the last time.

"I'll stay in your bed. I want to smell you after you're gone," she murmured as she snuggled beneath the down comforter on his bed.

"What do you mean by that?" Jeff asked, puzzled by his sister's strange remark. "You mean you like the way I smell?" He smiled at the implications.

"Well, not all the time," she replied with a hint of sarcasm in her tone, "but since you're leaving I want to smell your pillow cause it smells like your hair and that'll keep you close to me."

With that final thought, Jeff kissed her gently on the forehead, tucked her in, and hopped through the open window. In a moment, he was gone.

Chapter Two

On the other side of the world at approximately the same time, another boy, who happened to be just about the same age as Jeff, was also preparing for a monumental journey. He, too, was packing his bags with his most valuable possessions, only the bags he was packing were made of the finest leather money can buy. He would also be bidding farewell to his family members, only he had been doubly blessed with nine year old twin sisters, a mother and a father. In the pocket of his jeans, there wouldn't be a keepsake or a memento from any of his family members, but rather a wallet, full of gold credit cards, travelers' checks, and United States currency, mostly fifty and one hundred dollar bills.

Not only was his departure lacking any sense of remorse on his part or on the part of the boy's young sisters, you might even call their reactions indifferent. They were perched on large, wooden kitchen stools stationed at the breakfast bar where they continued to watch cartoons for hours on end. Every once in awhile, they would glance out the immense picture window which framed the eastern Australian coastline as a gull passed by, but other than that the two girls seemed indifferent as to what was transpiring around them, the least of their concerns being their big brother's departure. They had decided long ago that their big brother wasn't worth the effort. He was self centered and conceited. It was obvious in his appearance and in his attitude. He wore his thick black hair slicked back off of his forehead. His Greek godlike features were tanned and he adorned himself with one earring and the most expensive pair of designer shades available to man. He spent most of his time alone in his room, listening to heavy metal bands from the early 90s, or out on the deck of his family's mansion catching rays. His time was his own and no one dared interrupt him in his lonely, self absorbed little world.

And why shouldn't he live this way? After all, he was Joshua Clayton Montgomery III, heir to the billion dollar computer empire created by his father, who was also known as the Wizard of Oz, not only in his homeland of Australia, but in all parts of the world, as well.

Just as the youth finished packing the last cashmere sweater on the pile, his mother entered the room, clutching a hankie and dobbing manufactured tears with it as she spoke.

"Oh, I'm going to miss you so much, Joshua," she wept as she reached out to her only son who was about to embark on an adventure as an Australian exchange student in America.

"I'd prefer it if you would call me JC, please," he retorted in his tangy Australian accent, ignoring his mother's attempt in conveying emotion towards him. "Besides, if you are so upset about me leaving, why are you making me go to Iowa, anyway?"

"It's Ohio, Joshua, and you know that it's all your father's idea. I think you're doing just fine growing up, but he thinks it would do you good to see what life is like amongst regular people."

"Mum, why should I? I'll never really have to live like regular people do. I could disappear off the face of the earth right now and live in luxury for the rest of my life thanks to the trust fund Grandfather left me."

His mother was speechless. It was true. Not only was JC the heir to his father's billions, but to the fortune his grandfather had left him, as well. And despite all of the efforts that JC's father and grandfather had made on his financial behalf, JC seemed not the least bit interested in following in their entrepreneurial footsteps.

"You may not appreciate all that your father has accomplished in his life. He earned every penny he has by working hard. He didn't rest on the laurels of his father's accomplishments. He did it on his own; he did it for you, to set an example. But he didn't do it to turn you into a lazy, spoiled brat."

JC shrugged off his mother's remark, turned away from her, and began fidgeting with the zipper on one of the bags.

6

His mother's tears of maternal concern turned to tears of anguish at her son's indignance. "Joshua, I didn't want to fight with you today. After all, you'll be away for more than seven weeks. We're going to miss you."

"Who exactly is going to miss me? If you are referring to yourself and to my father, I find that awfully hard to believe. He is not even here to say goodbye, now is he?" JC waved his arms in a horizontal circle around the room as if he was displaying the absence of a father figure there. "And for your information, Mum, I think you are a bit mistaken about his motivation. I happen to know that he made most of his money before I was even born, so he didn't do it all for me, he did it for himself. It's his passion and his pleasure. He does what he does because he loves it, Mum. He loves it more than he loves you or me or anybody."

Coldheartedly, JC picked up his leather baggage and made his way for the front door where William, the chauffeur was waiting.

His mother followed, ignoring the hurtful remarks that would sting inside for the next few days. She pulled herself together, as if making a pretentious show for the house staff was more important than addressing her son's selfish remarks or the inner turmoil she was experiencing as a result of the remarks.

"Now Joshua, you know we've had a computer and a fax machine installed in the home where you'll be staying. I don't expect you to call with the time difference being so great. You'd probably just wake us all up," she babbled on, almost as though she felt the need to explain to the servants that Joshua would not be calling. She chuckled as the smiling housekeepers and chauffeur nodded in agreement. "But do email us, Joshua, and let us know that you made it there safely. You'd better be going now. William, will you carry these out to the car please? Goodbye darling." Her voice had taken on an air of sophistication as it often did when her dignity was on the line or when other people were around.

7

Perhaps that was why JC had such an easy time turning on his mother the way he did. She tried to be there for him on an emotional basis, but she would get so caught up in her own aristocratic fantasy world at times that she couldn't even remember to call him by his self assumed nickname of JC, as he had requested she do thousands of times. He made it a point to go for the jugular when he sensed a false pretense in his mother's tone of voice, and he had done just that by dissing his father that day. Maybe what he said about his father was true, and maybe it wasn't. All JC knew was that he hadn't seen much of his father throughout his early childhood and now, as far as he was concerned, it was too late.

William opened the back door of the limo for JC and without looking back, JC Montgomery III, too, was gone.

Chapter Three

The road leading down from the summit of the mountain was a long and winding two mile descent. Jeff's toes were scrunched up all the way to the tips of his canvas sneakers as he trudged down the steep, gravel terrain.

He had been content living in the mountains again, although these mountains were uncharacteristic of the mountains in Wyoming where he had spent the first eleven years of his life. From a distance, these mountains looked like moss covered hills, blending all the shades of green together in the summer and creating a potpourri of color in the fall. This was not so with the mountains of Wyoming. The mountains of Wyoming were jagged and rocky, supporting boulders the size of Volkswagens. Or not supporting boulders, as had been the case on the day the accident had occurred, almost three years ago to the day.

Some said it was a freak accident. Others like Jeff's grandmother insisted that it was God's will, that it happened for a reason, and that someday they'd all understand why. Still others, like Uncle Frank, had trivialized what had happened while sucking down a cold brewski and saying, "Life's not fair, kid, that's all there is to it. There are no guarantees." This comment had been followed promptly by a vulgar belch that almost all of the people at the gathering after the funeral could smell, as well as hear. And that was that.

But Jeff didn't see it in any one particular way. All that he knew was that at the age of eleven, in the blink of an eye, his parents had been taken away and that he and his little sister, Sarah, were all alone.

Orphans. The first time that Jeff heard the word used in reference to Sarah and himself, it didn't sound real. Orphans were fictitious characters found in books. They didn't really exist outside of stories and movies, did they? Sarah and Jeff were living proof that they did.

So many things had happened since that chilly November day back in Wyoming when Jeff's parents had gone out for a casual excursion and had never returned.

Immediately following their parents' funerals, Jeff and Sarah had left their hometown in Jackson Hole, Wyoming and had moved in with their grandma in an even smaller, rural town in the southern Sierra Nevada Mountains. It was the same town in California where the Johnsons, their present foster parents, lived. In fact, the Johnsons had known Jeff and Sarah ever since their parents had died as they had brought the children's grandmother to Wyoming for the funerals and then had transported everyone back to California in their van.

Jeff and Sarah's grandma was the only living relative on their father's side of the family. The children felt secure living with their grandmother in the two bedroom trailer on the mountainside. Her strength was in her faith and even though she refused to tackle the tough questions like "why?" her words of wisdom were a great comfort to the children in the time of their great loss. She would tell them that they would be reunited with their parents someday and that God had not abandoned them. At times, it seemed to Jeff, that she went a little overboard in her steadfast, brick wall faith, never questioning what had happened to her only son and his wife or even shedding any public tears regarding their demise. Sometimes her strength was necessary in helping the children to cope, but at other times, the children could have used a shoulder to cry on. But she was family, and that in itself had been a comfort.

The only other living relative was on Jeff's mother's side of the family. Uncle Frank was so unlike his deceased sister that he would have to have died to have had even that one thing in common with her. Jeff's mother had been lighthearted and generous, while her younger brother was rather self centered and lazy. Jeff and Sarah had been relieved when they had heard they were going to live with their grandmother and not with Uncle Frank.

They had stayed with their seventy five year old grandmother for more than half of the first year after their parents had died. Then something began to happen.

Grandma started seeing things -little green men, to be exact. It all started one summer night when Jeff, Sarah, and Grandma were standing outside of the mountainside trailer, looking up at the stars. It was a breathtaking night with every constellation known to man basking in its own brilliance as the threesome gazed skyward. All of a sudden, a shooting start whizzed past their heads with a whoosh and then disappeared into the trees below the ridge. Its brilliance captured their attention. The children were in awe, but it sent Grandma scrambling into a frenzied tizzy. She shot up the steps and through the front door of the trailer in a flash, shouting, "Those darn aliens, they're back again!"

If she'd had a gun, Jeff and Sarah were sure she would have used it. They had never seen their grandmother react in such a way, but it was only the beginning of a series of unusual events that would eventually lead to Grandma burning down the trailer and landing herself in a new home away from home.

Following these unfortunate events, Jeff and Sarah were to embark on a whirlwind tour of California foster homes, ranging from inner city ghetto lodgings to real working cattle ranches. All of these temporary placements had not lasted for more than a month or two at a time, although they had ended up spanning an entire calendar year in the lives of the children.

Throughout this entire year, the Johnsons, a retired couple in their early fifties, had been appealing to the state to let the children come to live with them in their quiet home on the same mountain where their grandmother had lived. Finally, after much time floundering in the sea of red tape, Jeff and Sarah were granted permission to reside with the Johnsons. This had been a breath of fresh air to all concerned.

Up until one month ago, things had been going extraordinarily well for the children for almost a full year and a half. The Johnsons were wonderful foster parents whose own grown children provided an excellent extended family for Jeff and Sarah when they came to visit from their homes in southern California.

Sarah had been attending the local elementary school for the past year and Jeff had been looking forward to one more year of middle school before he would be eligible to try out for the regional high school basketball team twenty miles from home.

All had been going well until the day when Mrs. Johnson received a letter from the Human Resource Services Department for the State of California. It stated that Jeff Farnsworth would be relocated to another foster care facility on November 6th, the day of his fourteenth birthday. Somewhere in that same muddled sea of bureaucratic red tape, there was a stipulation stating that foster children who reached the age of fourteen would not reside in the same household as those who were under that age, regardless of the presence of siblings residing in that same household. The procedure, as the letter explained, was necessary to keep younger children separate from older adolescents who might have a negative influence on them. The bond that had kept Sarah and Jeff sane and hopeful throughout all of their trials was about to be broken.

The Johnsons were outraged by the news that Jeff was to be moved to another foster care facility and by the assumption that the human resource people had made in assuming that fourteen year olds were bad influences on younger children. Again, Mrs. Johnson went to war fighting the system, even opting to adopt the children to keep them from being separated. But all of these procedures would take time and one month was not enough time to procure any of the possible solutions. In Jeff's mind, this left him with few options, other than to strike out on his own.

He wasn't planning to disappear from the face of the earth. His plan was to contact his uncle who lived with his recently acquired bride in the frozen northeastern city of Buffalo, New York.

Even though Uncle Frank wasn't Jeff's first choice, or even his second, as a guardian, Jeff felt that his uncle was the only real hope that he had left to keep Sarah and himself together.

With this goal in mind, he trudged down the mountain trail. As he neared the bottom of the mountain, a black velvet veil of darkness surrounded him. His flashlight had gone out about twenty minutes after he'd left the house, so he had been following the sound of gravel crunching beneath his feet to find his way. The only other sounds he heard were those of furry, nocturnal critters and soft hooting owls. On several occasions, he almost jumped out of his skin when he glanced into the woods and mistook one tree trunk for a bear and another for a crazed maniac stalking his prey.

At times like these, when Jeff was all alone, his mind was prone to wander. To keep himself from thinking about what might be beyond the next bend in the road, he would get lost in his own thoughts.

Ironically, for a boy whose father had accused him of not thinking prior to the accident, it seemed that after the accident, it was all that Jeff could do. In fact, on the very day of the accident, his parents had hesitated in letting Sarah stay home with him for fear that he wouldn't *think* to call her in should it begin to rain or snow or that he wouldn't *think* to turn off the stove if he were to make hot chocolate.

"Don't you want to see where we're going to build our new house?" Jeff's mother had asked in an effort to coax the children into coming along for the ride.

"Is it in that meadow with the cottonwood trees?" Jeff had asked, dribbling his new basketball and taking an ill fated shot from the middle of the driveway.

"That's the place," his dad had exclaimed with unbridled enthusiasm. "It'll be the perfect spot for you and me to build the log cabin."

13

"I've seen it already," Jeff had replied smugly, successfully banking a shot off the backboard. "I'll see it again when we start to build."

In spite of further coaxing on the part of their parents, Sarah and Jeff had persuaded their parents to let them stay at home and shoot hoops with Jeff's new basketball and backboard, both gifts from Jeff's birthday only a few days before.

"We won't be gone long, Jeff. Don't let Sarah run into the street after the ball, okay?"

"Okay, Mom, don't worry. We'll be fine."

And so, as Jeff and Sarah were taking turns dribbling, shooting, and enjoying their first taste of independence, they hadn't really paid much attention to their mother when she rolled down her window and called out, "We love you!" for the very last time.

Thinking about that day and how it had changed his life had become almost a daily routine for Jeff. Oh, he thought about the same things that other boys his age thought about - like the sparse, but coarse stubble that was beginning to sprout from his chin. And he thought about girls. He thought about how he had grown about six inches in the last six months. And he thought about girls. He also thought about the crop of zits that kept erupting on his chin and forehead, regardless of how little or how much chocolate he ate or how often he washed his face. And he thought about girls. And finally, he thought about how his voice kept cracking at the most inopportune times while reading aloud in Mrs. Campbell's English class, as if he had swallowed a rubber squeak toy. Oh, yes, and he also thought about girls.

Perhaps the reason that he thought so much about so many things was because he had so many unanswered questions about the accident and about life.

Once, shortly after the accident had occurred, he had asked his grandmother about why it had happened. "Was God mad at my mom and dad or did Sarah or I do something wrong and that made God mad?"

His grandmother had told him that he wasn't supposed to question God.

He had answered innocently enough with, "I know I'm not supposed to question God, that's why I'm asking you."

After this, he pretty much kept his thoughts and questions to himself until Sarah got a little older and started asking them, too. Sometimes he tried to combine some of the theories that other people had about the accident into a tidy little package. "It was a freak accident that was God's will because life's not fair."

But as time went by and as he grew older, he started to formulate some of his own opinions about the accident. For one thing, the fact that his parents happened to be in the exact spot they were in when the boulder shifted from its perch and tumbled down the mountain, hardly seemed to be coincidental. He was no expert in mathematics, but according to his own calculations, the odds of that happening had to be about a bazillion to one.

In fact, he was beginning to think that maybe the accidents that people call "freak accidents" were really the only ones that weren't, freak, that is. In other words, for such bizarre events to occur at the precise moments they did, Jeff believed they had to be more than just coincidences.

Suddenly Jeff's thoughts were interrupted by two bright streams of beaming headlights that hit him squarely in the eyes. He raised his hands up to his eyebrows to keep from being blinded as the flatbed truck swerved slightly to avoid him. The sudden trip back to reality forced Jeff to realize that fatigue had taken over his body and that he was chilled to the bone. He knew he had to go on though, in spite of this. If he stopped now, he would be discovered lying on the ground by some local townsperson passing by and be taken back home. He had to make it at least to the main highway out of town before he stopped to rest. And the only way to do that was to get lost in his thoughts again.

"Did God cause it to happen or did He just let it happen?" he said aloud. This was something that he felt he had to know. Sometimes he would even answer his own questions as his own worst enemy. "What difference

15

does it make? It won't change anything or bring anyone back now, will it?"

But to Jeff, it did make a difference. In his mind, it was easier to accept what had happened if God didn't cause it. If it was something that just happened naturally and not something that God did, he would have no reason to blame God and he could be at peace. But the peace he longed to have always seemed to be short lived and soon he would find himself wrestling with his thoughts again.

Did things like this happen because of circumstances leading to them or were they simply destined to be by God ?

Sometimes he thought that he was losing his mind, just like his grandmother had, especially on nights like this when he was all alone and insecure about what the future would hold.

When he ran out of questions like these, his mind just naturally progressed to the next level of questions, questions that were pure torture for him. These questions were the "what ifs."

What if his parents had left an hour earlier or an hour later? What if all of the family had been in the car? Wouldn't that have been better? What if Sarah had gone along and he had stayed home alone?

Just as one thought always led to another, it was the same way with the "what ifs" which ultimately led to the one question which haunted him the most. It haunted him the most because it took the responsibility off of everyone else but him.

"What if I hadn't pleaded and begged my parents for twenty minutes to stay home? They wouldn't have been where they were when the boulder fell and none of this would have happened," he pondered aloud in the night.

That was the last thought that Jeff remembered having that night. The next thing he knew, he was riding in the back of a pickup truck that reeked of manure and hay. How he had gotten there was a mystery.

It was daylight now, but just barely. He glanced up

to locate the position of the sun. He was relieved to find that the truck was heading south.

Jeff turned around and knocked on the sliding glass window of the truck. The weathered man in the driver's seat turned, opened the window and announced that he would pull over so that Jeff could get into the cab.

"How did I get here?" Jeff asked once he was inside.

"About an hour ago when the sun came up, I saw you sprawled out on the side of the road about a mile shy of this highway. I thought you were dead at first, but you were breathing, so I picked you up and put you in the truck. Have you been drinking, boy? You didn't smell like you were, but I couldn't figure out why a young man like you would be sleeping along the side of the road. And then when I moved you and you didn't wake up, I thought you were in a coma or something. I was going to take you to the nearest hospital. It's only a few miles down the road from here, but then you knocked on the window and scared the bageebies out of me. Do you think you need to go to the hospital, son?"

"I think I'm okay. And I haven't been drinking. I guess I'm just exhausted. I've been walking most of the night. I'm trying to get to my uncle's house. I'm an orphan," he blurted out. The word still had a foreign ring to it when he said it aloud.

"Do you have any food with you, son?"

"Just some chips and a granola bar."

"You're never going to get your strength back without a decent meal," the kindhearted stranger remarked. "Why don't you come back to the farm with me? You can rest for awhile, grab some grub, and be back on the road at your leisure. You could even stay the night if you'd like. I could drive you out to the main highway in the morning. My wife makes a mean fried chicken dinner. Are you interested?"

"I don't know how I can say no to an offer like that, only I really need to keep moving. I'd like to try to make it to LA by tomorrow. Do you know how far we are from there now?" Jeff inquired, rolling down his window to escape the stench of his own sweat and the cow manure which had saturated his clothing.

"I believe we're just about two hundred and fiddy miles away from there right now. You could actually be there by tonight if you catch a ride with the right person," the man assured him. "By the way, the name's Mack. And you are?" Mack held out his right hand cordially.

"Jeff." He returned the introductory gesture and they shook hands briefly.

"It's nice to know you, Jeff. Now, what'll it be - back to the farm for farm fresh eggs and bacon for breakfast and later a fried chicken dinner or on to the main highway?"

"Throw in a daughter and you've got yourself a dinner guest," Jeff joked with the farmer, sensing that the kindly gentleman was no stranger to a sense of humor.

"Well, there's no daughter your age, but I do have a granddaughter. Unfortunately, she lives elsewhere."

"I guess I'll just have to settle for the home cooked meals then," Jeff replied wholeheartedly.

"You won't be disappointed, son, I guarantee," promised the wrinkled man as he turned right onto the dirt road leading to the farm.

And Jeff was not disappointed. For while, Joshua Clayton Montgomery III was dining on fried shrimp and oysters en route to his stopover in Hawaii, Jeff Farnsworth was happily gnawing on fried chicken, fresh corn, and mashed potatoes, a meal which had been preceded by a three and one half hour long nap on one of the farmer's featherbeds, and a breakfast of farm fresh eggs and bacon earlier in the day.

Chapter Four

By the time Jeff finished his scrumptious lunch, it was almost 3 o'clock in the afternoon. He was overwhelmed by a renewed sense of strength and energy. Even though part of him wanted to make himself comfortable and stay the night, maybe even drop a hint to the farmer's wife that it just happened to be his birthday, another part of him wanted to take advantage of the clear, sunny afternoon that beckoned him to travel on.

He listened to the more determined part of himself and decided to head out again. The farmer and his wife had been more than kind, having packed him a lunch to go and replenished his flashlight with new batteries.

The highway leading southwest was about fifteen miles from the farm, and the farmer had, as promised, delivered him to this destination. Jeff thanked the farmer and was on his way.

Sarah would have been happy to know that he had kept his promise to her, not having taken his first ride with a weirdo, not that he had had much choice in the matter anyway.

Jeff stood on the side of the road for about an hour before anyone even went by. The sun was setting quickly and storm clouds were rolling in from the west. He was beginning to doubt his decision to hit the road again. He thought about heading back to the farm for the night before he ended up stranded in the rain. He would give it a few more minutes and then start walking back if he had to. Just then it started to sprinkle, lightly at first, then in large droplets which pelted down with such thrust that they actually hurt when they bombarded his face. He saw a black, plastic garbage bag laying empty in the grass up ahead, so he picked it up and used it to shield himself from the cloudburst.

The sky was black overhead now. Night had not yet come, but the storm had stripped the day of any lightness it had left in it. Lightning slashed in the sky to the west and he counted five seconds until the sound of thunder reverberated in his ears.

Finally a small sedan approached. Jeff prayed that it would stop, but it zipped past him, the young female driver refusing to acknowledge his unfortunate predicament, in spite of the fact that he was waving the thumb on his outstretched hand wildly.

"Why didn't I stay at the farm?" he cried out in frustration as he turned around and started walking.

Just then, out of nowhere came a set of headlights behind him. It was a vintage 1967 VW bus. He wondered if behind its closed doors, he would find weirdos, the likes of whom Sarah had forewarned him. Maybe they would be aged hippies, leftover from a few generations ago, and they would offer him the chance to find peace and harmony through any number of hallucinogenic devices that they had in store.

As the bus squeaked to a halt next to him, Jeff braced himself for who and what were inside, expecting to be flooded by the aroma of burning incense or marijuana.

But instead, when the sliding door opened, it revealed a heavyset Mexican woman and two small children huddled together in the backseat and a toothpick of man in the driver's seat. Cigarette smoke poured out through the open door, and Jeff foresaw a suffocating experience ahead if he was to take this ride.

"Ola amigo," said the skinny chimney in the front seat, smiling just enough so that Jeff could see that his cigarette was wedged in a space where a front tooth should have been. "Vamos!"

Jeff obeyed his command and crawled into the middle of the van where the seat had been removed. The two youngsters, who looked to be about three and four years old, eyed him suspiciously from their mother's sides and buried their heads in her lap when he returned their curious gazes.

In rapid fire the middle aged woman asked, "Hablo Espanol?"

"No," Jeff answered. "Hablo Ingles?"

"No," she shook her head disappointedly.

That was all the conversation that transpired for about the next hour and a half. During that time, Jeff took out his flashlight and a crumpled map of California to try to figure out where to get off of this road and onto the next one that he needed.

Suddenly Jeff rose from his spot on the shag carpeted floor of the van and tried desperately to see out of the front window for road signs that would tell him if he had missed his connecting route or if it was still ahead. It was difficult to see since the ancient vehicle's windshield wipers barely scraped the surface of the windshield, doing little more than smearing the moisture and the dirt into streaks on the glass.

Just then, Jeff heard the tick, tick, tick of the turn signal and he could feel the vehicle veering to the right where there was a turnoff. Jeff squinted to see a small, detailed sign close to the road, but he couldn't make it out.

"I think I'd better get out here," Jeff stated much too quietly to be heard over the loud hum of the engine. "Stop!" he shouted, not wanting to go any further in what he thought might be the wrong direction.

The bus screeched to a halt and both the man and the woman began speaking rapidly in their native tongue, but since he was clueless as to what they were saying and it was too dark to see the accompanying expressions on their faces, he decided it would be best for him to make like an egg and scramble as quickly as he could.

"Gracias... and adios," he stammered as he fled from the smoky interior of the Volkswagen van. He slammed the door behind him and a puff of smoke from the exhaust pipe surged abruptly into his face as the vehicle chortled away.

"As if I needed to breathe in any more smoke tonight," Jeff coughed out sarcastically as he backtracked to the sign that he hadn't been able to read.

According to the sign, his departure at that precise moment had been crucial. The road he needed was just a few miles further up the highway. He thought he saw lights up ahead as he headed into the night. Maybe it was just a billboard lighting up the sky or perhaps it was a truckstop.

He wasn't really sure what he should do, at this point, other than to just walk toward the lights. He knew that it was too dangerous to try to hitchhike from where he had been let out since it would be too dark for anyone to see him, even with the aid of his flashlight.

Drawing in a breath of fresh air, he realized that once again his clothes were permeated with the odors from his most recent experiences. Wet dog came to mind as he caught a whiff of his damp denims. He must have picked up that scent while visiting the farm. Mack's golden retriever had insisted on leaning on him and nudging him from time to time on their ride from the farm to the highway. The stench of cigarette smoke and exhaust fumes saturated his hair and jacket, but now he noticed other distinct odors that were infiltrating the air.

He followed the aromas of diesel and fried food up a long narrow stretch of roadway which was leading straight to the lights at a truckstop coffee shop.

"Happy birthday to me," he responded, quietly rejoicing, having found a refuge in the middle of this desolate highway. There was little doubt in his mind that he would spend the night here.

Joshua Clayton Montgomery III had traveled first class nonstop all the way from Sydney, Australia and had spent several hours in a luxury hotel close to the airport in Honolulu. He would have liked to have stayed there indefinitely, swimming, and basking in the tropical sunshine, but unfortunately a representative of the airline was there to be sure he made his LA connection.

So, again, while JC was flying high over the Pacific Ocean, feasting on omelettes and French pastries, Jeff was sitting, crouched in a corner booth, trying to justify keeping his place by drinking cup after cup of decaf.

When the shift change occurred at about midnight, a new waitress came on board. She was in her early forties with shoulder length brownish blonde hair pulled back in a French braid. She stood over Jeff with a pot of the steaming brew, ready to pour at his command. But Jeff's eyes were closed, his chin propped up on the palms of his hands, his elbows resting on the table.

In spite of his unconsciousness, she poured the coffee, so that her boss would not see him taking up space without a reason. She also brought him a fresh cherry danish and set it on the table. The scent of the warm baked danish infiltrated his nostrils and brought him back to life.

He attempted to focus on the figure standing before him, but his vision and his consciousness were still blurry. "Mom?" he asked in a fuzzy disorientation.

"No, I'm not your mom, honey," the waitress answered soothingly.

His sudden awareness of the error he'd made startled him and he accidentally hit the plate with the side of his hand, causing the pastry to catapult off onto the table. "Uh, I didn't order this, did I?" he asked, still very confused and preoccupied with the physical appearance of the woman standing before him.

"No, honey," she responded, aware that she had inadvertently called him honey a second time. "It's okay, it's on me. You don't have to eat it if you don't want to. I just didn't want my boss to see you sitting here empty handed and make you leave. Are you here all by yourself?"

He continued to stare at her when he answered, "Yes. I'm hitchhiking to LA." He paused, realizing that in the dimly lit coffee shop, she did bear a slight resemblance to his mother. "Thanks for the danish," he continued, "and I'm sorry that I'm staring at you. It's just that you kind of remind me of my mom, and I haven't seen her in a long time. She was a nurse and that white uniform you're wearing and your hair really made you look like her when I first woke up."

"Are you a runaway?" she asked sympathetically.

"Well, sort of. I'm on my way to my uncle's in New York. I'm heading to LA to catch a flight out." In a way, he hoped that this response would satisfy the woman's curiosity and she would stop asking him questions. But in another way, he was enjoying talking to someone who reminded him of his mom.

However, his response did not terminate her questions and he continued to divulge more and more of his history to her. By the time the conversation ended, he had told her all about his parents' accident, Sarah, the Johnsons, and the social welfare people's idea to move him to another foster care facility.

"I've heard some sad stories in my day, but you are breaking my heart. I'd adopt you myself, but I can barely make ends meet for my own two kids and me."

"That's okay,"Jeff answered shyly. "You have kids, too?"

"I have a girl and a boy. My daughter is eleven and my son is sixteen. How old are you, about fifteen?"

For some reason, Jeff was flattered by the remark that she thought he was older than he really was. "I just turned fourteen today, actually yesterday," he corrected himself after looking at the clock on the wall. "That was the reason the state was moving me. They think that fourteen year olds are bad influences on younger kids or something."

"That's ridiculous," she said dryly. "What a rotten way to spend your fourteenth birthday."

"It hasn't been so bad, really. I've met some nice people and I haven't gone hungry, that's for sure.

"You seem really mature for your age," she replied. "I guess kids just grow up faster these days, especially when they have the weight of the world on their shoulders. My son, too, is mature for his age. He works twenty hours a week to help support the family. I don't know what I'd do without him. Both of my kids understand what I've gone through since their father left us and they've become very responsible. It's kind of sad, though, because I know they've missed out on a lot of their childhoods because of it."

"What can you do? You just have to deal with whatever cards you're dealt, I guess. Sometimes it doesn't seem like you have much choice in the matter," Jeff responded.

"Well, if I had it to do over again, if I could have had my same kids at a later time, I would have waited to get married and gotten my education, so that I could be doing something a little more lucrative and satisfying with my life."

"There's still time. You're not *that* old."

The waitress laughed at the insinuation that she wasn't *that* old. "It just gets a little harder to do when you have to be responsible for other people besides yourself. Anyway, I need to get back to work, but I think I might be able to line you up with a ride. Several of the truck drivers that stop here have routes that go right to LA. I don't see any of them here right now, but I'm sure one of them will be in sometime during the night. In the meantime, let me buy you something else to eat. This danish isn't going to take you very far. Take a look at the menu and tell me what you want."

"That's okay. I still have a sandwich left."

"No, I insist. You never know when your next real meal is going to be. Please, it's on me."

Jeff smiled and ordered up a deluxe hamburger platter and a chocolate milkshake.

Although his instinct was to wolf down the truckstop grub, he hesitated, thinking it best to make this meal last for as long as possible. A giant wall clock hung above the swinging door which separated the kitchen from the restaurant's dining area. Jeff watched the clock steadily for the next few hours, dozing off from time to time and then jerking back to reality when an unannounced snort interrupted him or when his head fell too far forward to support itself.

Every once in awhile, the waitress would wave or flash him a smile to let him know that she had not forgotten about him. Finally, she gave him a hopeful look with the raising of her brow when a mammoth, bulky trucker entered and sat down at the counter. His muscular bronze arms were decorated with tattoos of ship anchors, mermaids, and even a ferocious looking tiger. In spite of Jeff's anxiousness to get to LA, he hoped that this was not one of the truckers to whom the waitress had been referring. He looked too tough, too hairy, and just too plain scary. Not only were his arms decorated with works of art, but his face, too, was embellished with battle marks and scars from what Jeff assumed were remnants of night skirmishes on coastal harbors or brawls in bar rooms. The dark hair on his face connected his black bushy eyebrows from his forehead to his sideburns to his mustache to his beard.

25

"Please let it be someone else," Jeff whispered to himself under his breath, but he knew this gorilla was the man.

The waitress walked over to the burley hunk and laid her hand upon his shoulder, smiling and laughing throughout their conversation. Jeff watched as the trucker's eyes turned toward him and then without any change of expression gave his approval in the form of a solid nod.

The waitress was bubbling over with school girl enthusiasm as she relayed the news to Jeff. "He said okay."

Jeff started to get up to meet the man, but the waitress held up her hand to prevent him from doing so.

"Oh, don't get up. Wait until he's ready to go. I'll come and get you when it's time to go."

As Jeff listened to the waitress chatter, he wondered if Sarah would have considered this guy a weirdo. He couldn't concern himself with this now. The waitress had gone to all this trouble and he believed that she wouldn't steer him wrong.

"Are you sure it's okay? I mean I could wait for one of the other guys you were talking about."

"Oh, no, Bruiser will be happy to take you to just outside of the LA city limits. Besides, the other guys are kind of scary. Bruiser's just a pussycat," she giggled.

"The *other* guys are kind of scary?" Jeff mumbled inaudibly and shook his head in disbelief as the waitress went back to her duties.

When Bruiser got up from his stool, Jeff jumped into action, but once again, his friend in the apron motioned him back into his place in the booth.

"Bathroom," she whispered from across the room, mouthing the words excessively so that he could read her lips. "You don't want to go in there for awhile , trust me."

Jeff just laughed and gave her a wave goodbye as he headed outside to wait. The rays from the sun coming up in the east were mixing with the diesel fumes, creating wiggly streams of vaporized fuel in the air. The smell was making Jeff sick. Great, he thought to himself, all I need is to throw up in the cab of Bruiser's truck. That would go over really big.

"Good luck to you, Jeff," the waitress said as she stepped outside to wish Jeff well. "Now, don't worry, Bruiser will take good care of you."

"Hey," Jeff retorted as if he'd suddenly remembered something important. "I forgot to leave you a tip," he said as he dug into the pocket of his jeans.

"Don't worry about it. Remember, it was on me."

"Yeah, I know, but you've done so much for me."

"No, I haven't. I just did what I hope someone would do for my kids if they found themselves in a similar predicament. It's no big deal," she shrugged.

"Well, thank you. I really do appreciate it."

"I know. I can tell. Just be safe. If you ever get back this way, stop by and let me know how you're doing."

"I will," Jeff replied sincerely as he spied Bruiser coming out of the Little Boys' Room and barreling his way past the booths and lunch counter towards the front door.

Once Bruiser was through the doors, he whistled and gestured for Jeff to follow him, as if Jeff was some kind of a dog. But riding with Bruiser was not nearly as painful as Jeff had imagined it to be.

As it turned out, Bruiser wasn't as tough as he appeared. He had a wife and three kids in Portland, Oregon and he coached his son's pee wee football team. The scars on his face weren't the result of bar room brawls, but rather a serious motorcycle accident in which he'd been involved as a young man. And the tattoos, he explained, were leftovers from his days in the navy. Jeff laughed when Bruiser showed him how one of the mermaid's bellies grew when he flexed the muscle in his arm.

Being able to talk to someone on the road made the miles and the time fly by quickly. Before Jeff knew it, the semi was slowing to a stop on the shoulder of the road, letting Jeff know that it was time to depart.

Bruiser tried to explain to Jeff as best he could, how to get to the airport from this particular exit. Jeff shook his head as if he was following what the trucker was saying, but inside of his head, he was already lost.

27

Once Jeff was outside of the cab, he sauntered down the exit ramp and made his way toward the hazy outskirts of the city ahead. He heard Bruiser sound the horn as he drove off and Jeff turned to wave. Jeff was just thinking about how lucky he had been so far with the rides he had been offered. There had been no weirdos at all.

Just then, Jeff heard clicking sounds as a car pulled up beside him. He couldn't tell what make or model the car was since it was almost totally stripped of paint and parts. He thought it might be a Nova from back in the seventies, but then he couldn't be sure. At any rate, what was even more interesting than the car itself was what was inside of it.

As Jeff leaned over to peer into the open, passenger side window, he wasn't sure what or who he was seeing. Smog filtered rays of sunlight were coming through the dirty, front windshield, making it difficult for Jeff to see whether or not it was even a male or a female in the driver's seat. What Jeff did see was a figure with long blond hair topped with a colossal cowboy hat, and oval, wire rimmed shades propped upon a rather pointy nose. The mystery person was adorned with plastic beads around the neck and two lip rings, a nose ring, and three earrings in the right ear. Jeff finally discerned that the person was a guy when he looked down and saw the white tank top and green neon, lycra shorts that the individual was wearing. He held out an unopened container of beer to Jeff.

"Need a lift?" the voice was soft spoken and non threatening, but Jeff hesitated.

"Actually," Jeff replied, thinking of his sister's words before answering, "I'm just heading down to that convenience store down there. Thanks, anyway."

"Whatever," the driver sputtered, as did his unrecognizable vehicle as it sped away, leaving a trail of dust in Jeff's face.

Jeff was, for the most part, in the city now. He made up his mind not to take any chances, even if it meant that he had to walk all the way to the airport. It wasn't worth the risk. He was almost there.

Chapter Five

As fate or chance or divine providence would have it, JC Montgomery III's jet touched down at the LA airport at precisely the same moment that the car full of nuns, with whom Jeff had summoned a ride, pulled up to the curb and dropped him off.

He thanked them and they blessed him with the sign of the cross as he departed from their van. The automatic, sliding glass doors welcomed Jeff and he made his way through the crowded corridor of the airport terminal, blending in with the hoards of bustling travelers.

For some reason, he felt relieved to be off of the streets and in the midst of hundreds of strangers where he could maintain his anonymity. The first things he needed to do were to find a restroom and a phone, in precisely that order. Now that he was ready to travel, he had the confidence and courage to make the call to Uncle Frank in Buffalo.

Uncle Frank had been at the very least, hesitant, in the past to welcome Jeff and Sarah into his home. He based his excuse for not taking the children into his custody on financial reasons, the most valid of them being that he hadn't worked in years.

But now, Jeff hoped that his uncle would succumb to this request out of sympathy for the children's separation dilemma.

Jeff thought about calling him collect, but he was afraid that his uncle would not accept the charges. It had been known to happen in the past as it had one Christmas when Sarah had attempted to telephone him.

Digging into his pocket, he found less than a dollar's worth of change and his fifty dollar bill. He would have to get change for the fifty in order to make the call. He proceeded to the various eating establishments and shops along the concourse, but with no success. None of the merchants were willing to break the fifty unless he made a purchase. And even then, they refused to give him his change in the form of coins.

The only other alternative was to borrow someone else's calling card number and use it to make just this one call. He knew it wasn't right, but he didn't feel that he had any other choice right now.

He decided to look around for someone who appeared to be rich. That way, he rationalized, he wouldn't be hurting someone who really couldn't afford an extra dollar or two on their phone bill. He stood by the row of phones that were stationed along the wall, pretending to be engaged in conversation, so as not to arouse suspicion.

It was at this very moment that JC Montgomery III came into view. He was heading straight for the only available pay phone which happened to be directly next to Jeff.

Jeff sized up his over accessorized peer, contemplating just how easy this transaction might actually be. He began punching in his uncle's number methodically, so that when this young prince put in his calling card number, Jeff would be ready, as well.

Next to him stood JC, cool, collected, and cocky. Jeff watched as he slicked back his hair with his fingers and maneuvered his head back and forth so that he could catch a glimpse of his own reflection off the mirrored telephone casement. He seemed to be scanning the corridor for major league LA babes or perhaps just looking around to see if anyone was checking him out. When it seemed apparent that no one was giving him the slightest bit of attention, he attended to the matter at hand, making a phone call.

Jeff waited nervously for JC to punch in the phone number, followed by the calling card number. He watched as JC pulled out a voluptuous wallet and sorted through a number of credit cards in an attempt to locate his calling card. Peering cautiously over JC's shoulder, Jeff completed the sequence of numbers on the panel before him and turned away from JC.

The phone was ringing at Uncle Frank's house. Jeff waited. His heart was beating rapidly as he counted ring after ring after ring until eighteen successive rings had been completed.

"Come on, Uncle Frank, answer it, answer it!" Jeff commanded in quiet desperation through clenched teeth. But his persistent demands did nothing to change the situation. After twenty four rings, there was no answer.

Jeff gave up and placed the receiver back on the wall in its place. JC was still on the phone next to him and Jeff could hear him speaking as though he had gotten through to a machine and not to a person.

"Uncle Matt, I'm in LA. Pick me up at the Miami airport at 11:50 tonight. I have to make a bloody detour through Cincinnati to keep the stewardess from getting suspicious. I hope you get this message. Goodday mate," he ended the conversation with his thick accent beaming loud and clear across the corridor.

Jeff was just about to leave when he felt a hand on his shoulder. As he had turned away from JC, he had absolutely no idea whose hand it could be. Of course, he was fearing the worst, that it was the police or the social service people. His neck swelled scarlet with fear and his empty stomach churned queasily.

But when he turned around, although still quite disturbed, he saw that it was only the arrogant sounding boy who had been standing next to him.

"Would you mind taking your hand off of my shoulder?" Jeff reacted respectfully and cautiously toward this unknown entity who was becoming quite personal by touching him.

JC responded indignantly, "You want me to take *my* bloody hand off of *your* bloody shoulder, do you? Well, I was thinking that mates like us who have so much in common should stick together, don't you?"

Jeff was puzzled. The only thing that Jeff could think of that the two of them had in common was that they both had just tried to call their uncles. But how would this perfect stranger know that Jeff, too, had been trying to reach his uncle unless he had been listening when Jeff had cried out for his uncle to answer?

"Oh, you mean because we both just called our uncles?" Jeff replied innocently, still perplexed by the boy's assertiveness.

"Not quite, skank," JC sneered as he scanned Jeff condescendingly from head to toe. "We seem to have the same calling card number."

"Oh, that," Jeff felt his neck turning excruciatingly thermal again in embarrassment. "I'm sorry, man. Listen the call didn't even go through and my mind is so jumbled up right now that I couldn't possibly remember it to use it again even if I wanted to. Seriously, you aren't going to report this to the police or anybody, are you? I'm in a little bit of a jam right now, anyway, and if we get the cops involved, I'll be in deep, deep trouble. So, could we just forget about this, do you think?"

"Well, what if you're some sort of dangerous criminal and if I don't report you, I'll be endangering the lives of the people around you?" JC remarked smugly, although it was obvious by his tone that he didn't believe that for a moment.

"Trust me, I'm not. I'm just a guy who's trying to catch a break and get out of this state to get to my uncle's in Buffalo, okay?" Jeff was beginning to get exasperated by this conceited boy's persistence in grilling him.

"Let me guess, you are running away from home and you are going to stay with your uncle?" JC surmised.

"Well, you're on the right track," Jeff told him.

"Then, we do have something in common," JC exclaimed boisterously. "I'm not running away from home, but I *am* supposed to be on my way to Ohio to be an exchange student for the next seven weeks. I'm really not into it, so I've decided to go and stay with my uncle instead," JC stated emphatically.

"Where are you from anyway?" Jeff asked.

"The land down under," JC replied curtly.

"The land down under what?" Jeff asked blankly.

"Australia." JC gave Jeff a demeaning glare.

" Oh, so what are you going to do to get out of it?" Jeff was curious as to what type of plan this mini mastermind had cooked up.

"Once I get to Cincinnati, I'll ditch the stewardess and catch a flight to Miami. My uncle said he'll cover for me until it's time to go home."

"Won't the host family get suspicious when you don't show up?" Jeff questioned.

"I'll ring them up from here and tell them that there has been a crisis in our family and that I've had to cancel the trip. And I'll just call my parents from my uncle's house, pretending to be in Ohio. I figure I have at least a month or so until the phone bill arrives when they might notice where the calls are coming from. But most likely, with their busy schedules, they won't even notice."

"It sounds like a plan. I wish I had a plan like that."

"I just hope I can pull it off. I wish I didn't have to go all the way to Cincinnati, first, and then down to Miami, but it's the only way to keep the airlines off my back. If Joshua Clayton Montgomery III doesn't get off the plane in Cincinnati, there will be heads flying at the airlines. So, what's your story? You're going to your uncle's, too, eh? Won't your parents look for you there?"

"Not likely," Jeff answered confidently.

"What makes you so sure of that?" JC quizzed.

"They're dead."

"Oh, then I guess that won't be a concern." JC laughed, exhibiting a tinge of nervous self consciousness for the first time. "So, then who are you running away from?"

"It's a long story, but what it boils down to is that my little sister and I were living in a foster home here in California. They were about to separate us because of some stupid rule that says if you're fourteen you can't be in the same home as younger children."

"And you had a problem with that?" JC remarked sarcastically.

"I take it you have a little sister," Jeff surmised.

"Actually, I have nine year old twin sisters. I could care less if I ever see them again."

"Oh, you might say that, but believe me, you wouldn't feel that way if you'd been through what we have. I used to really resent my little sister, too, especially when she was first born. I was just getting to the age where I wanted my mom to go out and play baseball or shoot hoops with me and she never could because of the baby. When Sarah learned to walk, I'd trip her when no one was looking, just to see her fall."

"That's nothing," JC replied. "We live on the beach and one time I left both of my sisters stranded in a raft out in the middle of the ocean."

"Dude, that's pretty bad. I used to get in a lot of trouble for just tripping my sister. It made her tough, though, and now she bosses *me* around. And after my parents were killed, I was glad she was around."

"So, what about your uncle? Does he know you're coming?" JC inquired.

"Well, to tell you the truth, no, he doesn't. I was trying to get a hold of him to let him know. I was hoping that if I was already on my way, he would say it was okay. He doesn't work and he drinks a lot, but I figured if I could at least get him to take me in, maybe I could get a job, help pay the bills, and then send for Sarah. I know it's a long shot, but it was the only plan I could think of."

"Do you have a ticket to get to ... where is it that your uncle lives?"

"Buffalo, New York. No, no, I don't. I was going to search through the garbage for a used boarding pass or ticket and then try to pull a fast one when I went to board the plane, kind of like the kid did in Home Alone II when he bumped into the stewardess and sent the boarding passes flying."

"Too risky," JC commented, scrunching up his forehead as if he was formulating yet another plan. "All they would have to do is match up the people's names on the plane with the names on the tickets and you'd be busted before you even got to Buffalo."

"Well, it's not like I have a lot of other options here, unless you want to buy me a ticket to Buffalo," Jeff suggested halfheartedly.

"You know, that's not a bad idea!" JC lit up as another interesting idea was materializing in his head. "I have a little proposition for you, if you'll just hear me out. We both have some subtle flaws in our plans, am I right?"

Jeff nodded in agreement.

"You need an airline ticket and some cash that you could use to entice or shall I say sweeten the pot when you talk to your uncle about your coming to live with him, right?"

Jeff's head bobbed up and down in agreement, as he strained to follow the most recent plan that JC had concocted to save himself from having to take the flight to Cincinnati and to help Jeff get to Buffalo without a hitch.

"I, on the other hand, need a warm body to arrive at the Cincinnati airport this afternoon, so that I don't have to take that little detour on my way to Miami. I'd be willing to buy you a ticket to Buffalo and give you $1000 cash to flash in front of your uncle when you get there."

"You'd be willing to give me $1000 and buy me a ticket to Buffalo just so that you don't have to fly to Cincinnati first? That's very generous of you."

"Chump change," JC proclaimed irreverently.

"But won't the airline people know that I'm not you? We don't look anything alike."

It was true, they did not bear any resemblance whatsoever. Jeff had sandy blonde hair which usually parted itself in the middle or hung straight and fine just touching the tops of his eyelids. JC was dark skinned and had long, wavy black hair which he slicked back from his forehead, sometimes even sporting a pony tail if he let it grow out for a long enough time.

There was also quite a bit of difference in the boys' statures. At 5' 11" tall, Jeff's lean, muscular body towered over JC's 5'5" somewhat underdeveloped frame.

"They change responsible parties on each leg of the trip, so that the stewardess I had on the last flight will be replaced by someone new on this flight. All you have to do is pretend that you're me. Wait, that's it. I've just had another brainfart and this one is guaranteed to solve all of our problems," JC oozed with enthusiasm. "Okay, where is the first place that the authorities are going to look for you? At your uncle's house in Buffalo, right?"

"Pretty much, I guess," Jeff reasoned.

"And again, the obstacles that I might encounter within the workings of my plan are communication related. My parents might try to call me in Ohio. The Bakers, those are the people with whom I am to live, will tell my parents that I never showed up and then the whole world will be looking for me. Do you see where I'm going with this?"

"Are you saying that you want *me* to take your place in Ohio while you stay with your uncle in Miami?"

"It's the perfect plan!" JC was elated with the stroke of genius that had overwhelmed him and produced such a foolproof solution to both of the boys' otherwise flaw filled plans. "You need somewhere to hide out so that the authorities don't track you down and I need someone to be me in Ohio. I'll definitely make it worth your while. I'll give you my gold Visa card. It's got a $10,000 credit limit on it, so you can use it to buy things or you can get cash. When it's time to leave, just buy yourself a ticket to Buffalo, get whatever balance you have left on it in cash and flash some *real* money in your uncle's face. He'll be sure to take you in then."

Jeff couldn't believe what he was hearing. All that he could come up with as he sorted through the ideas that were being presented to him was that there must be something wrong, morally, ethically, or legally with this plan. But at the same time, it did seem to make sense. What did he have to lose?

"There's just one thing," JC added, "that you have to promise me if we go through with this."

"What's that?" Jeff had wondered all along if this proposition wasn't too good to be true and he feared that now he was going to be hit with a catch that would ultimately make or break the deal.

"You have to promise me that you won't tell anyone what we're doing."

At first Jeff thought that he would be able to comply with a request such as this quite easily. That is, until, he considered the implications of not being able to communicate with Sarah. She would be worried sick if he didn't contact her for over seven weeks.

"But what about my little sister? I have to let her know that I'm okay. Can't I just write to her and let her know that I'm alive?"

"It would be better if you waited awhile and you'd have to make sure that you didn't put a return address on it or mail it in the small town where you'll be living because of the postmark."

"Right," Jeff said and shook his head, realizing that he would have to be on top of things like that in order to pull this off.

"So, do we have a deal?" JC prompted him, holding up his right hand to become the recipient of a high five from Jeff.

"We have a deal," Jeff slapped JC on the palm to confirm the agreement. "So what do we do now?"

"The first thing we must do is to fill you in on all the details of my life. My name is JC Montgomery III. You already know that I have twin sisters. Their names are Lindsey and Katie. My mum's name is Mary Elizabeth and, of course, my father's name is JC, just like mine."

" My name is Jeff Farnsworth. What do you think I should have everyone call me?" Jeff asked.

"I'd go with Josh if I were you. That way, if I call you and I have to leave a message, I can still be JC and it won't seem weird that we both have the same name."

"Okay, that makes sense, I guess," Jeff decided.

"And this little book," JC instructed, "has all the information you'll ever need to pull this off, so don't lose it. First, here are my parents' phone numbers, fax numbers, and email addresses, but don't call them. I figure if you just email my father once in awhile, they'll figure out that I'm still alive and they'll pretty much leave you alone. This is my uncle's number in Miami where I'll be staying. Call me anytime. And here's the calling card that started this whole thing. You can use it when you call me, but don't use it to call your sister or anything stupid like that. This number is the pin number for the credit card I'm going to give you." He stopped talking and rifled through the pile of silver and gold cards until he came upon the intended one. "Sign this, so that your signature will match it, okay? You can get cash out of any cash machine with this baby anytime."

"That sounds good to me. Hey, what if the Bakers don't have a computer or a fax machine? Then what do I do to communicate with your folks?" Jeff wondered.

"Oh, they do. My father had a whole new system put into their house specifically for my stay, so don't worry about that. They are all set up. Oh, yes, and it might be good to know that my mum is a housewife. I guess you could call her that although she has maids and cooks to do everything around the house. And my father is in the computer business. And one more thing," JC babbled on, barely stopping to take a breath, "we have to do something about your speech."

"I have to make a speech?" Jeff looked flabbergasted at the thought of having to make a speech.

"No, no, I mean, we have to do something about the way you talk," JC insisted.

"What's the matter with the way I talk?" Jeff became a tad defensive.

"What's wrong with the way you talk is that you are supposed to be from Australia and you don't sound like it at all. You need to start practicing speaking as if you were from down under. Let's start with this. Goodday mate," JC instructed.

"Good.. day.. mate," Jeff repeated in broken, choppy English. "How was that?"

"It was positively dreadful. It's not good - pause - day - pause - mate - pause. It's goodday mate. It has to mesh, it has to blend, or else it's all wrong."

"Okay." Jeff tried again, improving just a bit. "Good day mate."

"That's a little bit better, but keep practicing."

"Do you guys really go around calling people mates all the time? I mean, don't some people take it the wrong way? I have to say I wasn't sure what you were up to when you kept calling me mate earlier today."

"Actually, we don't use it at all unless we're around Americans. We say it because you think we say it, when all the while we're saying it, we're really laughing at you. I think it all got started with one of those Crocodile Dundee flicks and it just sort of stuck."

Jeff couldn't tell whether or not JC was pulling his leg, so he dismissed any response that he might have made and reverted back to a more significant topic of discussion. "Instead of trying to talk Australian, can't I just tell everybody that I don't have a real thick accent because I spent so much time in the United States when I was little?"

"Do whatever works for you, but at least try to have a bit of an accent or I think people will be disappointed. What fun would it be to have an exchange student come from another country and then have that person sound exactly the same as everyone else? I'm telling you, they'll be very disappointed."

Jeff sensed a hint of sarcastic humor in JC's voice as he advised him on how to speak. "Well, what else can I do then?"

"Try dropping your h's. Instead of saying, 'he's not here,' say, 'e's not ere.' Can you hear the difference? And if you're saying something that ends in an 'a' like America, drop the 'a' and add an 'er' so that you pronounce it 'Ameriker.' That should help."

"I can do that, I think," Jeff sighed nervously, wondering if he could, indeed, pull this off. "I'll practice on the plane."

"Speaking of planes, I need to cancel my reservation from Cincinnati to Miami and make a new one straight to Miami. Here are your tickets to Cincinnati. You'll be flying first class and there will probably be some people with a sign at the airport to greet you when you disembark. There will be a limo to take you all back to their house. You'd better get going. The flight is due to depart in about fifteen minutes and you can bet your life that the airline people are frantically searching for me right now, as we speak. It's gate D-17. Thanks, Jeff. Call me if you need anything. Oh, I forgot, get my luggage. There are three leather bags that match this carry on bag."

In a flash, JC disappeared, toting the leather carry on bag with him. Jeff, too, was sprinting through the terminal, clutching the boarding pass tightly in his right hand and the lopsided duffel bag in the left as he headed for the gate.

Time had run out for Joshua Clayton Montgomery III for just as Jeff reached the gate, he heard a page come over the loud speaker, summoning an immediate response from the delinquent young traveler.

"Mr. Montgomery, paging Mr. Joshua Montgomery, please report immediately to gate 17," barked a harsh female voice.

"I'm Josh Montgomery," he stammered breathlessly, forgetting to use an Australian accent. "I'm sorry I'm late. I hope I didn't cause you too much trouble."

"Not at all, Josh," the woman's voice mellowed suddenly when she heard his heartfelt apology. "I was getting worried about you. The last flight attendant didn't deliver you to me as she was supposed to, but don't worry, your father will hear about this and she'll be reprimanded, if not suspended or terminated."

"Oh, no, don't do that," Jeff insisted. "It was my fault. I sort of tricked her and got away from her when I used the restroom. Don't get her in trouble. You see, I'm rather embarrassed about having to have a flight attendant accompany me, so I ditched her. Besides, she wasn't pretty like you." Jeff was amazed at the words that were coming out of his mouth. Pretending to be someone else was not half bad; he could say things that he'd never have been able to say otherwise. He was only saying what he thought the real JC would have said. But this part of the charade made him feel uncomfortable. If he was to do this, he was going to have to be himself in Ohio. After all, none of those people knew Josh, so Josh could be whoever he wanted to be.

"Well, thank you, Josh. You do go by Josh, don't you?" she asked, still basking in the compliment she had received from him and handing him back a portion of the perforated boarding pass.

"From now on I do," he replied and stepped lightheartedly through the door that led down the narrow corridor and onto the plane.

Chapter Six

As the plane touched down in Cincinnati, Jeff practiced saying "goodday mate" Australian style and dropping his h's in a variety of words. He also readied himself to take on his new identity. Starting now, he would no longer even think of himself as Jeff Farnsworth, but rather as Josh Montgomery.

Butterflies fluttered within the walls of his stomach. He wasn't sure if it was due to the sudden change in altitude or from the realization that he was about to embark on an adventure into the unknown.

"How bad could it be?" Josh said to himself, trying to convince himself and calm his nerves. "I've been through worse things than posing as a rich kid. Nothing could be as bad as what Sarah and I went through in some of those foster homes. The rats in the attic used to come and nibble at us while we were sleeping. All I have to do here is be an exchange student for a little while and then follow through on my original plan to go to Uncle Frank's. It'll be a piece of cake."

His legs were stiff when the captain finally turned off the FASTEN SEATBELT sign and Josh got up to leave. He still had his tacky duffel bag to retrieve from the overhead compartment. The stewardess continued her obligation to Josh by opening the compartment and handing the bag to him. Then she led him down the aisle ahead of all the other first class passengers and out through the exit ramp.

"As soon as we find your party, you'll be free from me," she declared.

Freedom did not smell as sweet to Josh as did the scent of her perfume. He wouldn't have minded if the limo carrying the Bakers had gotten stuck in traffic on the way to the airport and he had to wait for hours with this young beauty at his side.

His eyes searched the corridor of people who were awaiting the arrival of loved ones, or in his case, awaiting the arrival of a total stranger.

41

As he scanned face after face in the crowd, his infatuation with the airborne hostess was soon overshadowed when he caught a glimpse of another. She was the postpubescent version of the girl next store with sun streaked strands of shoulder length hair and large emerald eyes, intensified by soft defining lashes. She was wearing flared jeans and a ragwool sweater, similar to the one he had on.

She and another youth, a boy with dumbo ears and a dandelion colored, spiked coif, stood holding a large sign that read, "WELCOME JOSH MONTGOMERY."

Whatever the boy was saying must have been amusing as the young girl smiled and tilted her head back in laughter.

"Maybe this isn't going to be so bad," Josh said to himself as he pointed to the sign. "There they are," he told the flight attendant, forgetting to use his accent.

The stewardess didn't seem to notice anything unusual, but did seem rather anxious to be relieved from her duty as babysitter. She whisked Josh over to the waiting teens and asked, "Will you be able to get your bags by yourself?"

Josh answered positively.

"And I take it that you two rode here in the limo to pick Josh up. Is that correct?" she continued.

The yellow haired boy assured her that the motor was still running.

"Then I guess my work is done here. Good luck to you, Josh, and enjoy your stay in Cincinnati." Her voice sounded as professional as if she was still addressing passengers over the loudspeaker on the plane.

The threesome was left standing alone in the airport. That was when the dandelioned haired boy came to life.

He held out his hand, greeting Josh with an even phonier, more exaggerated accent than Josh would have ever been able to manufacture himself. "Goodday mate!"

"Goodday," Josh replied with his own less than authentic Australian greeting.

"I'm Patrick and I'll be your host for the next seven weeks. Welcome to the lifestyles of the dull and restless!" he verbalized in the phony accent, shaking Josh's hand vigorously like a politician on a campaign trail.

Josh was a little overwhelmed by this guy's enthusiasm, but instantly realized that he was simply trying to be funny.

"You must be Josh," said the girl who had taken Josh's breath away at first sight. "I'm Jennifer and this weirdo is my cousin, Patrick. He's really harmless. He's just really excited, that's all."

Before Josh could respond, Patrick interrupted again. "I brought you something - to make you feel, well, you know, a little more at home." Handing Josh a shoebox wrapped in aluminum foil, he added, as if it mattered, "Sorry about the wrap job, mate, but I was pressed for time."

Josh held the box in his hand, pondering whether or not it was safe to open.

"Go on, open it," Patrick coaxed him, grinning from ear to ear. "I promise nothing will explode or anything." Patrick continued to badger him, "I know what you're thinking. You feel bad cause you didn't bring me anything. It's okay. Just open it!"

Josh ripped off the aluminum foil and removed the lid.

"BOOM!" Patrick thundered.

Josh and Jennifer flinched reflexively from Patrick's outburst .

"Ha!" Patrick hacked. "Sorry," he apologized, still reeling in his own comic antics.

Peering cautiously into the shoebox, Josh was intrigued by the contents it contained. What he saw was an eleven inch fashion doll, wearing a yellow polka dot bikini, an unlikely gift, he thought, from one fourteen year old boy to another. On top of the doll was something pink and slimy. As Josh looked more closely, he could see that it was a piece of shrimp.

Before Josh had time to think about the unusual gift, Patrick's voice reverted back to his phony Australian dialect and he blurted out spontaneously, "I just thought you might like a little shrimp on the barbie! Get it? Shrimp on the barbie!"

In spite of the confusion, Josh looked over at Jennifer and grinned. He now realized what he was dealing with here - a total moron.

As promised, there was a limousine, compliments of Josh's father, waiting outside of the airport terminal to transport the three teens back to Patrick's house.

Of course, Patrick did not let the opportunity to fidget with all the buttons and accessories in the backseat pass him by. He turned the stereo up full blast, stood up through the open sunroof, and proceeded to serenade the other highway travelers. As they rode down the highway en route to the small town some thirty miles away, Josh watched his energetic peer revel in endless exhilaration and marveled at the spontaneity that gushed forth with each new adventure that presented itself. Josh could not even remember a time when he had felt free enough to do anything even remotely as spontaneous as this.

Josh and Jennifer watched from the leather seats below and found a more civilized way to enjoy the ride. Pouring the contents of a can of ginger ale into two champagne glasses, the couple clinked the fine glassware together in a toast to Patrick in his glory.

"Is he always like this?" Josh inquired, remembering to eliminate the 'h' to maintain his accent.

Jennifer stopped for a moment to observe her cousin whose left leg was now halfway out of the sunroof and whose right arm was dangling down in front of them.

"Pretty much," she said, nodding, as if she was remembering all of the things he had done in the past.

As the limo rounded the corner to the street where Patrick lived, Patrick managed to pull himself in, just before his mother and father caught a glimpse of his sprawled out body on the roof.

"That was some ride you had there, kids!" Patrick's father commented as the limo pulled into the driveway and the mischievous grinning threesome was anxiously escorted out by the frazzled limo driver.

"You have no idea," Jennifer mumbled under her breath, glancing at her derelict cousin whose wind blown hair was standing straight out in all directions.

"It was awesome, Dad! Can we get one of those?" Patrick bubbled.

Patrick's father ignored his son's remark and went on to formally introduce himself and his wife respectively as Dean and Linda Baker.

"You'll have to excuse Patrick," apologized his mother. "He's a little excited about you coming here."

"Excuse nothing," announced Patrick's little brother, Amos, who suddenly appeared from out of nowhere to greet Josh. If Patrick was the dandelion haired kid, then Amos was the freckle faced, strawberry patch headed, carbon copy of Patrick. "He's always like this," Amos retorted. "Cool car," he exclaimed, focusing his short attention span on the limo that was idling in the driveway. "Can I go for a ride?"

"No, I'm sorry, Amos, it's due back at the rental agency by nine o'clock and it's darn near close to that now," Dean replied as he checked his watch and handed the limo driver a tip of an undisclosed dollar amount. "That was quite generous of your father to rent the limo . We would have been happy to have picked you up at the airport, but when Patrick heard about the chance to ride in a limo, there was no stopping him."

Josh was about to say something about what a great guy his father was, but Linda interjected her own comment before he had a chance to respond. "You're probably used to riding in limos all the time, aren't you, Josh?"

"Yeah, cause you're rich!" Amos blasted precociously.

"Amos!" his mother reprimanded him curtly. "You'll have to excuse *this one*, too."

It was obvious that Dean and Linda were embarrassed by their eight year old son's outburst from the way that Dean attempted to usher him into the house, holding one hand over his mouth as they entered.

"Josh, Josh," Patrick rattled, "you've got to come inside. I've got to show you what I'm doing in science class tomorrow." He spoke as if he and Josh were lifelong buds.

Josh started to think that posing as "Josh" was going to be easier than he thought. So far, he hadn't been able to get a word in edgewise, other than in the limo with Jennifer on the ride home.

Linda, Jennifer, and Josh each picked up a piece of the luggage that was strewn along the driveway and followed Patrick's lead into the house.

45

Once inside, Patrick flew to the refrigerator. "Check it out! Check it out!" he shouted, holding out a tiny dish, covered with plastic wrap.

As Patrick lifted the plastic, Josh could see the shape of a frog on the plate. Looking more closely, he observed that the image he was seeing was not a real frog at all, but rather a giant dill pickle that had been carved into a frog's likeness.

"It's a pickle shaped like a frog," Josh confirmed, squinting to examine the specimen more closely to see if he was missing something.

"It's my science project," Patrick announced proudly.

"What are you going to do with it?" Josh asked, glancing at Patrick's mother and Jennifer who were smiling and shaking their heads.

"Well, I'm going to begin to dissect it, and then just as I'm cutting it up, I'll stop, pick it up and eat it," Patrick informed them proudly.

Jennifer interrupted, "Patrick, how do you think that's going to go over with Mrs. Grouse?"

"You mean Grouchface? She'll be fine. She'll get over it; she always does. Deep down I think she likes me. Otherwise, I would have gotten suspended a long time ago." Patrick's confidence overshadowed any concerns he might have had over the ramifications of his actions.

"You *were* suspended," his mother reminded him. "And don't you need to get at least a C on this project to try out for the basketball team?"

"Part of the project is based on originality and I figure I'll score at least 80 points for that alone. Besides that's not my real project, anyway. Once I get a good laugh, I'll bring on my real project."

"And what might that be?" his mother asked suspiciously.

"This," he responded, picking up a baby food jar filled with clear liquid and a glob of something pink and white floating inside. "This is my *real* project. It's the growth that my dad had removed from his leg last summer."

"I think I'm going to be sick," Jennifer decried as she eyed the floating debris.

"That's not the growth from your father's leg," Patrick's mother exclaimed adamantly.

"I know, but it looks just like it. I saw it at the hospital," Patrick assured them.

"What is it then?" Josh asked.

"It's the same thing that I gave to you. It's a piece of shrimp, but no one has to know that. I'll just tell them the whole story about Dad's leg and I'm sure to get an A."

"I was wondering what happened to the shrimp I bought. When I was cooking it up for dinner tonight, I thought it seemed like there were a few pieces missing," Mrs. Baker remembered.

"Sorry, Mom, it went for a good cause," Patrick explained.

Just then Amos entered the kitchen, having been dismissed from the father/son talk in which he and his father had been engaged. "You are too weird," Amos accused. "Mom, I'm going to have to go to same school as he goes to in a couple of years and I'm going to have to prove myself as being normal to all the teachers who will already think of me as 'Patrick's little brother.' It's not fair. I'm doomed." Amos pretended to shoot himself in the head with his trigger finger.

"You're just afraid that you won't be able to live up to your legendary brother's reputation," Patrick teased.

"Am not, dipwod," Amos retaliated.

"Boys," Linda interrupted, visibly annoyed at her sons' lack of manners, "we have company. Can't you at least save some of this until after Josh has been here for awhile. What is he going to think?"

Both Patrick and Amos shrugged as if they hadn't thought anything of their obnoxious behavior.

Now that there was a lull in the action, everyone's attention turned toward the unassuming stranger who had inadvertently put an end to the brothers' bickering.

"So," Mrs. Baker inquired with a typical maternal inquiry, "are you hungry or thirsty, Josh?"

"No, actually I had a great meal on the plane. And in the limo, there were drinks and stuff."

"Your speech is different than I thought it would be," Mrs. Baker observed. "I thought you would have more of an accent."

"It comes and goes," Josh fumbled for an explanation. "I spent a lot of time in the United States when I was just learning to talk."

"Oh, really, whereabouts?" Mrs. Baker questioned.

"Mostly Wyoming and California."

"Oh? Do you have family there?"

"I used to, but not anymore," Josh agonized his way through these few simple questions. He wished he had spent a little more time with JC to find out more about *his* family and *their* background, so that he wouldn't have to rely on his own history for answers. He decided to take the initiative to change the subject and get the attention off of himself and onto something else. "Patrick, did I hear you say that you are trying out for the basketball team?"

"Yeah, why? You play?" Patrick mumbled as he looked up from the kitchen table where he was devouring a freshly made peanut butter and jelly sandwich.

"I'd like to, but there weren't any teams until you got to high school back where I used to live," Josh explained.

"So, I take it that basketball isn't real big in Australia like it is here in the states?" Mr. Baker reappeared and pulled up a chair next to his son at the kitchen table.

Josh had no idea whether or not basketball was big in Australia; he had been referring to his school in rural California where there simply weren't enough students in the lower grades to form teams. So, in order to avoid further discussion, he simply nodded in agreement with Mr. Baker's assumption.

"You should try out, you've got the height," Mr. Baker remarked encouragingly. "Hey, guys, it's getting a little late and tomorrow is a school day. Patrick, after you finish that sandwich, you and Amos can take Josh's bags upstairs. Jennifer, it's probably time that we took you home, too."

"Why do I have to carry the bags upstairs?" Amos whined at his father's request.

"What did we just talk about Amos?"his father asked.

48

"We talked about how I have to think before I speak and help my mother out by not being difficult," Amos replied, reiterating the lecture he had just been given.

"Yeah, A Mouth," Patrick blasted him in a demeaning tone.

"Patrick, that goes for you, too," his father reprimanded.

"I'll take you home, Jennifer," Mrs. Baker sighed. "It'll be a nice little break for me."

"Bye you guys," Jennifer said with a smile. "I'll see you tomorrow at school."

The women left and the men headed upstairs to settle in for the night. Luckily for Josh, Amos and Patrick did not share a room, saving Josh from being in the middle of a verbal battlefield which seemed to ensue whenever the brothers came into contact with one another.

Patrick's room was typical of most other boys' rooms his age. There was an assortment of sporting equipment scattered throughout the room. Baseball bats and hockey sticks were propped up in one corner while a snowboard was propped up in another. Posters of basketball players, football stars, and scantily clad super models adorned the white walls. Not only were a TV set and a portable CD player part of the room's accessories, but also a phone, a fax machine, and a larger than life computer setup.

"Wow!" Josh exclaimed when he eyed the sophisticated software and the glut of recreational paraphernalia. "You've got a lot of cool stuff. Do you snowboard?"

"Not as often as I'd like. Do you?"

"I used to all the time back in Wyoming," Josh began and then stopped himself, deciding to change the subject to something he knew even less about. "Do you know how to send email?" he asked, pointing to the computer.

"Yeah," Patrick answered indubitably. "How about you?"

"I haven't really spent too much time playing with computers, but I should probably email my dad to let him know that I got here okay," Josh said nervously, sitting down and staring blankly at the black screen.

"You should probably turn it on," Patrick advised, unable to believe what he was seeing. Here was the son of one of the most influential software masterminds in the world and he didn't have a clue as to how to activate the system.

"Oh, yeah, and that would be where?" Josh asked, trying to appear somewhat computer literate. "This system is a little bit different than the one I have at home."

"Here, let me show you," Patrick volunteered, hitting the "on" switch and then punching in commands. "What's the email address?"

"Oh," Josh floundered and retrieved the little black book that JC had given him. "Right here." He directed Patrick's attention to the email addresses.

"Which one?" Patrick was becoming more and more suspicious of Josh's computer competency.

"Oh, this one, I guess," Josh answered, feeling totally inadequate.

"Let me show you how to do all of this, so that you can do it by yourself from now on." Patrick led Josh through the procedure of going online. "Now, just go ahead and type your message, and then I'll show you how to send it," Patrick instructed patiently.

Patrick's expertise in this area impressed Josh, shedding a new light on his roommate's mentality. Maybe there was more to this guy than air for brains.

Josh really didn't know what to say as he began to type, so he decided to write from the heart, as if he was writing to his own father.

"Dear Dad," he typed. "I arrived here safely. The Bakers seem really nice. Thanks for sending the limo. Tomorrow will be the first day of school for me and I'm thinking of trying out for the basketball team. What do you think? Say hi to Mom and the twins. I love you and miss you. Thanks for all you've done for me." He started to type Jeff, and then backspaced to type Josh over it. I've got to remember that I'm Josh, he thought to himself.

"I'm ready to send it now," Josh stated nervously as he summoned Patrick's assistance once more.

Patrick looked up from the <u>Sports Illustrated </u>he was reading. "Swimsuit issue," he replied with a raised eyebrow and a mischievous grin on his face. "I don't leave home without it," he bragged. It looked as if he really hadn't left home without it, including times when he'd gone out in the rain. It was wavy and bloated from excessive water damage.

"Press this and here," he said returning to the keyboard. "Your message has been officially launched into cyberspace."

"Thanks, Patrick," Josh said humbly.

Just then there was a knock on the door. "It's just me," Patrick's mother said from the other side. Patrick welcomed her in. "I just wanted to make sure that you boys are settled in. Josh, we're happy to have you here. I hope you'll feel very much at home. I know it's pretty modest compared to what you're used to, but I hope you'll be comfortable. Let us know if you need anything, okay dear?"

"Okay, Mrs. Baker. Thanks for having me here. I'm sure I'll be more than comfortable," Josh answered sincerely. The lack of sleep from the previous night was starting to take its toll on him and he was anxious to hit the sheets. He waited for the cue that would tell him that it was time to go to bed and let him know which bunk bed was reserved for him.

Patrick climbed into the top bunk, letting Josh know that he could now retire down below.

As Mrs. Baker was leaving the room, a voice from the room next door bellowed out with loud clarity, "Suck up!"

"Amos!" Mrs. Baker scowled at her young son's obnoxious remark.

Patrick looked down at Josh from the top bunk and the two of them just laughed.   It was the last thing that Josh remembered hearing that night before his head hit the pillow and he was in a deep, contented sleep.

Chapter Seven

Morning seemed to arrive prematurely as Josh and Patrick were shocked into consciousness by the obnoxious buzz of Patrick's alarm clock. As if it were routine, Patrick whipped his copy of Sports Illustrated down from the top bunk, hitting the alarm clock squarely on the top to silence it.

Neither boy moved. Josh was somewhat awake, but he was still groggy and waiting for his new roommate to make the first move.

"Patrick," his mother said, peering in through the half opened door, "are you boys up?"

"Does it look like we're up?" Patrick mumbled, slobbering into his pillow and then trying to suck it in again as he gained awareness of the wetness around him.

"Good morning, Mrs. Baker," Josh said as he saw her glance his way.

"Good morning, Josh. Did you sleep okay?" she asked, scrounging for dirty laundry throughout the room.

"Yes, thank you, I did," Josh answered politely.

"I wanted to let you know that you can use the bathroom down the hall to shower if you'd like. There are towels in the cupboard for you and anything else you might need. Just help yourself."

He thanked her and waited for her to leave the room before he got out of bed. He decided that he would take her up on that shower. He lifted up his right arm and leaned in to take a whiff. He pitied the Bakers for having had to tolerate his nauseating stench for the last ten hours. Without wasting another precious moment, he glanced around the room for his equally smelly jeans. He had worn them initially when he'd plopped down on the bed the night before, but he'd removed them shortly after when they'd become too uncomfortable to sleep in. But they were nowhere to be found. Mrs. Baker must have confiscated them when she was picking up clothing just moments before.

Josh panicked. They were the only pair of jeans that he'd brought, mainly because they were the only pair of jeans that he owned at the time.

Without his jeans, Josh felt naked standing in his briefs. He peeked around the corner to see if the bathroom door was open. Seeing that it was unoccupied, he grabbed some underwear from his own duffel bag, this time choosing boxers for maximum coverage, and made a mad dash down the hall for the bathroom. Soon he was enjoying a soothing hot shower for the first time in what seemed like an eternity.

Afterwards he again scoped the hallway for Bakers and dashed back to Patrick's room.

As he entered the room, he saw Patrick standing shirtless before the mirror, combing his hair and chanting, "Sexy man, sexy man, combing his hair like a sexy man can!" Then seeing Josh, he added, "How can I be so darn sexy?"

Josh just closed the door behind him. With a grin and a shrug, he uttered a simple, "I don't know."

"Hey, look, I'm getting some chest hairs," Patrick exclaimed, rubbing his fingers over his bare chest. "No, no, I guess it was just lint," he said disappointedly when the fuzz disappeared. "Well, anyway, goodday mate!" Patrick had rediscovered the phony accent again.

"Goodday," Josh said self consciously, getting down on the floor to open up one of JC's suitcases.

"You can use that dresser over there, mate," Patrick continued cordially. "It's empty."

"Thanks," Josh replied, frantically searching through the contents in search of pants.

There were sports jackets, khaki pants, button down shirts and classic ties. Josh wondered if JC's mother had packed this one. He zipped up the suitcase, finding nothing suitable for him in it.

Opening the second one, he didn't feel as though he had done much better, finding an array of footwear, ranging from Airwalks to loafers - all at least two sizes too small.

In desperation, he sought bag number three. Alas, there were some casual threads - a pair of jeans, some sweats, swimtrunks, and the cashmere sweaters.

He picked out a red sweater that looked cozy enough, grabbed a T shirt from his duffel bag and started dressing.

53

But the moment he picked up the pair of jeans, he panicked. From the looks of them, they were going to be at least a couple of inches too short and maybe an inch or two shy in the waist. And to make things worse, they weren't baggy, they weren't loose fitting, they weren't even boot cut, they were slim fitting straight leg jeans. But since the only other pair of pants that fit him were in the hands of Mrs. Baker, he attempted to put them on.

"Hey, it's true, you rich dudes *do* put your pants on one leg at a time just like we do," Patrick teased.

"That's very funny," Josh replied, holding his breath and sucking in his gut as he attempted to slide the legs of the pants up. With a little luck, he might be able to convince them to zip up and snap shut.

"You sure do wear your pants tight in Australia," Patrick said with a grin. "And short, too."

"You mean you don't wear them tight and short here in Ameriker?" Josh pretended that this was indeed the style in Australia.

"If I wore my pants that tight I'd have to let stinkies out of my belly button."

With the deliverance of this remark, Josh couldn't help but let out a snicker, causing the snap to pop open without warning. "No more comments, please, Patrick," Josh laughed. "It's hard enough to breathe in these as it is."

"Boy, I guess," Patrick said, rolling his eyes at Josh as he headed out of the room and down the stairs.

Josh followed, pulling on the backside of his jeans to avoid getting a wedgie. He wondered how he was going to get through the day, trying to remember to use his phony accent and holding his stomach in to keep his jeans from ripping apart at the seams.

At the breakfast table, the Baker brothers were back on the verbal warpath.

"Do you think you could chew any louder?" Patrick said, losing orange juice out of the side of his mouth in anticipation of criticizing his younger sibling. Amos was eating some kind of sugar sweetened flakes without any milk to soften the sound of the crunching.

Amos was ready with a comeback. "Are you getting any of that orange juice in your mouth?"

"As a matter of fact, I am, A Mouse," Patrick replied condescendingly.

"Mom, Patrick is making fun of my ears again," Amos tattled.

"Patrick," his mother yelled up from the basement where she was doing laundry, "be nice."

Josh, who was taking all of this in had forgotten how hungry he had been when he first woke up. The tight pants had stifled any real desire to eat and he settled for a half of a bagel and some orange juice. He was just considering going back upstairs and changing into the sweats or khakis when Patrick announced that it was past time to go.

Once outside in the daylight, Josh was able to see the makeup of the neighborhood around him. It was an older neighborhood with tree lined streets, although the trees were barren, the brisk winds of autumn having stripped them of their orange and golden leaves. Most of the houses had brick fronts and displayed magnificent front porches with wide stairs leading up to them. Wind chimes, hanging plants, front porch swings and rockers adorned many of them. Uneven diagonal sidewalks erupted along the way as a result of the ancient roots of trees exploding beneath the surface, challenging the pedestrians to watch their steps as they strolled.

The day was clear and the air was brisk and clean. All of the leaves were off of the trees, but they no longer crunched beneath their feet. Instead they were now compressed into damp piles on the brown lawns and in the gutters.

"Do you walk everywhere in this town?" Josh inquired, adjusting his pants with every three or four strides that he made.

"Just about. It's not very big. After school, I'll show you the town. We've got a bank, a movie theater, some office buildings, and a donut shop. I'll show you where that is in case you ever need to find a cop. Are you okay?" he asked, when he realized that Josh had not reacted to his cop joke and was still squirming painfully in his jeans.

"I must have packed the wrong pants. They're not usually this tight or this short," Josh tried to explain.

"Yeah, right. Maybe you just had a growth spurt on your way here," Patrick suggested sarcastically. "You should have said something. We're about the same size, you could have worn a pair of mine."

"Now you tell me," Josh grunted under his breath.

They continued on until suddenly Patrick stopped and gasped. "My science project! I forgot my pickle and my shrimp! Wait here, no, go on ahead. It'll take you longer since you have to deal with those pants. It's two blocks up and then make a left. You can't miss it. Wait for me on the steps. I'll see you there!"

In a flash Patrick disappeared, jumping over fences and rocketing past dogs in backyards to find the shortest route home.

Josh followed Patrick's directions and found the school exactly where Patrick had said it would be. He felt mortified when he approached the clumps of students huddled on the grounds in front of the school, especially when he felt the scrutinizing stares and heard the sneers of students as they sized up his apparel.

The uneasiness continued until he recognized a familiar face in the crowd. It was the angelic face of Jennifer. Unlike many of the other female students who were wearing baggy pants and slovenly sweaters, Jennifer was clad in a plaid, pleated mini skirt and a white cotton sweater.

Just as she made eye contact with Josh and was about to greet him from the school steps, another boy intervened from behind her.

"Don't you look preppy today?" he teased, putting his arm around her shoulder.

"Oh, I just thought I'd wear something different for a change," Jennifer said, turning her attention to the dark haired young man at her side. "There's someone I want you to meet."

"Oh really, who?" he said, squeezing her shoulder and grinning.

"Josh!" Her face lit up when she caught his eye again. "Hi!"

"Hi,"Josh said, sizing up his competition. He was muscular, tall, and good looking, but so what. What did he have that Josh didn't have? His arm around Jennifer, for one thing.

"Bull, this is Josh," Jennifer said, ignoring the sudden change of expression on Bull's face that would have told her that he was not interested in meeting the new guy in school.

"Hey," Bull mumbled and then turned to go.

"Wait, don't go," Jennifer begged and grabbed him by the arm. "This is the exchange student from Australia that I told you about. He's staying with Patrick. Hey, where *is* Patrick?"

"He forgot his science project so he went back home to get it," Josh explained, giving up on striking up a conversation with Bull.

"That sounds like Patrick," Jennifer replied with loving endearment in her tone.

But Bull's comment was less than endearing, "What an idiot. I hope he drops it on the way and steps on it. Then he'll get an F and he won't be able to try out on Friday."

"Oh, Bull, you don't mean that," she joked, making light of his negativity.

"I don't think he has what it takes to make the team this year anyway. The coach wants to see serious players out there, not clowns. Let's go Jennifer," he insisted as the first bell rang.

"You go ahead, Bull," Jennifer replied. "I don't want to leave Josh out here all alone."

"Fine," Bull answered curtly, turning on Jennifer like a cat on a canary.

"See ya," Jennifer responded sweetly, denying the obvious chill in his attitude.

Josh hated to see that. It reminded him of Uncle Frank and how he had treated his first wife. He despised Bull for having the audacity to treat Jennifer that way and he felt sad that Jennifer seemed innocently indifferent to it.

Just then Patrick came into view. He flew across the schoolyard, having heard the bell ring from a distance. His gait was lively and his form displayed evidence of genuine athletic ability. If he was as agile on the basketball court as he was on that lawn, Bull would be in for a big surprise at tryouts on Friday.

When he reached the steps, he didn't stop for Jennifer and Josh, but simply crashed through the door en route to Mrs. Grouse's first period class, prompting Josh and Jennifer to follow.

The late bell sounded as the threesome breathlessly entered the classroom.

"You're late," the gray haired lady growled, not even looking up from her wire rimmed glasses which were perched halfway down her nose.

"Our exchange student is here," beamed Jennifer, waving her arms as if she was presenting Josh to the class as some sort of a game show prize.

"Oh, how wonderful!" Mrs. Grouse's tone changed, reflecting pure joy. "Welcome Joshua Clayton Montgomery the third!" she bellowed.

"Thank you, maam," he said sheepishly as he stood in front of the roomful of strangers.

"We've been so looking forward to your arrival," Mrs. Grouse continued.

"Speak for yourself," Bull grumbled almost inaudibly, but loud enough for Mrs. Grouse's sensitive teacher ears to detect.

"Mr. Bull, did you have something to share with the class?" She was used to his utterances and was quick to put an end to them.

"Not really," he said bluntly.

"Then I suggest that you keep your mouth shut." She looked back at Josh, softening again to say, "So, tell us Josh, how do you like America so far?"

Maybe it was the roomful of silent, staring peers or the realization that he really was impersonating JC Montgomery that caused Josh to freeze where he stood. Not only did he freeze, but a lump, the size of a tomato, formed in his throat, making it almost impossible to breathe, let alone speak.

He shook his head and managed to squeak out, "I like it a lot," his voice cracking on the last word.

Laughter filled the room and Josh could feel crimson creeping up his neck, his face, and settling in the tips of his ears.

Jennifer quickly reflected the attention off of Josh's unfortunate squeak by speaking up. "Josh has spent a lot of time here already. He used to have family in, where was it, Wyoming or California?"

"It was both," he concurred, feeling a little less nervous, knowing that he had at least one person he could count on in the classroom.

"Does anyone have any questions for Josh about his homeland or about himself?" Mrs. Grouse seemed oblivious to the panic attack that was making Josh excruciatingly uncomfortable as she prompted the students to ask questions.

When no one raised his or her hand, Mrs. Grouse carried the ball. "We've been studying about weather patterns and climates around the world this semester. Can you tell us what the climate is like in Australia this time of year when we are heading into winter? What season are you heading into?"

Josh's first inclination was to say that they were heading into winter, too, but then he realized that there must be a catch. His second inclination was to say something like, "Well, if you've been studying weather patterns around the world, then you tell *me* what season it will be." But neither of these responses seemed to be appropriate, so he held back and waited for Mrs. Grouse to continue.

"Isn't it true that you are really just heading into summer while we are heading into winter?"

"Yes, that would be correct," Josh stated with a false sense of confidence.

"Are there any other questions?" Mrs. Grouse asked when Josh failed to elaborate on the climate of Australia.

"I have a question," said a plain looking girl wearing glasses in the front row. "What kinds of animals do you have in your country?"

Josh thought to himself, I think I can handle this one. "Let's see," he said, forging the inadequate Australian accent in spite of his ongoing panic attack, "there are kangaroos, of course, and uh, horses and cows, and uh, koala bears." He was satisfied with that answer and he hoped that the class would be, too, and that that would be the end of all of the questions. Unfortunately, it was not.

Another girl in the same row shook her painted fingernailed hand vigorously in his face. "Don't you have wallabies there, too? What's the difference between a wallaby and a kangaroo?"

"Is this a trick question?" he bounced back at her, trying to hide his ignorance by making light of the question. He didn't have a clue as to what the difference was between a wallaby and a kangaroo.

Patrick seemed to sense his uncertainty and started waving his hand wildly, bopping up and down in his chair. "OOOH! OOOH! I know!" he gushed.

"I guess I'll let Patrick answer this one," Josh said with relief.

"Wallabies are smaller. Am I right, Josh?" Patrick looked for assurance to the person who should have been the expert.

"That's right mate!" Josh figured he had nothing to lose by agreeing.

"Do male kangaroos have pouches?" came a voice from the back of the room at precisely the same moment as another person blurted out, "Have you ever seen the Great Barrier Reef?"

"One at a time, please people. Raise your hands," Mrs. Grouse directed.

Josh was relieved to have been hindered from answering the simultaneous questions which had been asked of him. He had no idea whether or not male kangaroos had pouches nor did he even know that a place called the Great Barrier Reef existed.

Hands around the room were flying up now as the clock ticked and his heart raced. Mrs. Grouse chose a wiry, brainy looking kid with braces and glasses to pose the next threat to Josh's composure.

"Can you tell us anything about you father's business?"

"Well, that's kind of a difficult question," Josh stammered, digging deep to remember what JC had told him that his father did for a living. With the pressure of all of these eyeballs upon him, he could not remember a thing. "He's a farmer," he blurted out finally.

"A farmer?" Mrs. Grouse gasped. "What kind of a farmer?"

Judging from the wide eyed, open mouthed expressions on most of the students' faces, Josh realized that he must have said something wrong, so he decided to go another route with this.

"Well, he's a kangaroo farmer." He stared into a crowd of blank faces who were waiting to be enlightened. "You see he raises kangaroos for shows and stuff. They're not like the wild ones, they're more like pets. Lots of people want them."

Mrs. Grouse, determined not to be taken for a ride on the gullible express, squinted her eyes and fired a shot, "Josh, I was under the impression that your father was in computers. In fact, I was under the impression that he was some sort of a computer genius. Wasn't his picture just recently on the cover of TIME for the fourth time?"

"He was on the cover of TIME?" Josh gulped. "I just meant to say that kangaroo farming is his true love. I thought that everyone knew he was big in the computer industry. I thought they might like to hear about what business he has on the side, you know, the kangaroo farm?" Josh's eyes pleaded with Mrs. Grouse to put an end to the question and answer session.

But before Mrs. Grouse could do anything one way or the other, Bull decided to put his two cents in. "Hey, Mr. Kangaroo Man, does it rain a lot where you're from? I was just wondering because of those pants that you're wearing. It looks like you're expecting a flood."

A dull rumbling of laughter flooded the room. Again, Patrick came to the rescue. Josh wasn't sure if he did so to defend Josh's honor or simply to keep Bull from having the satisfaction of having one up on him.

"Haven't you ever seen these pants before?" Patrick said belligerently. "It's what everyone who is anyone wears down under. You're such a doofus, Bull!"

"That's enough, boys," Mrs. Grouse growled. "We have time for just one more question."

The girl with the colorful fingernails raised her hand again. "Wouldn't it be cool if Josh could have his dad like send us one of the kangaroos and we could like have it as our school mascot or something?"

"No, I think that would be stupid," protested Bull from the back of the room. "Our team's name is the Rockets. What do kangaroos have to do with rockets?"

"Well, actually," another girl spouted from the back row, "I'm in student council and we've been considering changing the school's team name to something else. We feel that the name Rockets is a little outdated."

"What's outdated about Rockets?" Bull chimed in again. "What do you want to call the team, the Computer Chips, the Floppy Disks, the Hard Drives?" Actually, he thought the Hard Drives wasn't half bad.

"What's outdated about the Rockets is that the team was given that name back in the sixties when the factory in town was given a contract to build some parts for the Apollo space program. When the project ended and the factory closed, we were stuck with the name. Don't you think that it's time to move on and lose the Rockets?"

Everyone just sat there. Then Jennifer spoke up.

"It would be kind of neat. If we really could get a real kangaroo, maybe we could change the name of the team to the Kangaroos. Think about it - they're quick and they're agile. And they're cute."

The girl from student council looked directly at Josh. "If you really think you could get us a kangaroo, I'll bring up the idea of changing the team name to the Kangaroos at the next meeting."

"Well, what do you think, Josh? Is such a thing possible?" Mrs. Grouse inquired, impressed with the students' sudden spark of enthusiastic school spirit.

"I'll see what I can do," Josh promised, feeling a bit uneasy about the challenge before him, while at the same time reveling in the fact that his presence here was having such an impact. "I'm beginning to think that anything is possible."

"Very well, Mr. Montgomery, see what you can do. Now on with today's class. There are several of you who have not yet presented your projects to the class. Patrick, you are next," Mrs. Grouse commanded.

"Right, Mrs. Grouch, I mean Grouse," Patrick stammered, picking up a shoebox and carefully carrying it to the front of the room. Josh took Patrick's vacant seat and waited for the pandemonium that was likely to ensue once Patrick's presentation got underway.

"Mrs. Grouse, you might want to move to the back of the room for this. It smells pretty bad. I had to use that stinky stuff that you use to preserve dead frogs. What's it called?"

"Are you referring to formaldehyde?" Mrs. Grouse asked, taking a few steps toward the back of the room.

"That's it, frogmaldehyde," Patrick agreed, mispronouncing the word. "Anyway, this is my pet frog, Kermie," Patrick stated, slanting the dish with the frog shaped pickle, so that the class could see it. "Well, it *was* my pet frog before I, well, you know..." Patrick imitated slashing the frog's throat by slicing his hand across his own throat and making a scratchity sound.

Aahs of concern for the little frog impersonating pickle went up from the classroom. With the cellophane wrap still in place over the dish, no one had yet discovered the frog's true identity.

"It's okay. He didn't feel a thing. I gave him a little beer first," Patrick assured his classmates. Most of the class laughed.

"Mr. Baker, need I remind you that you are being graded on this?" Mrs. Grouse interrupted.

"I know, that's why I'm going into such great detail about what this frog has been through for the sake of scientific research," Patrick contended, setting down the dish and removing the cellophane in preparation for dissection.

"Please continue, Patrick, with only the facts that are pertinent to the dissection. That is your plan, isn't it, to dissect it?"

"Well, it is now, but originally I was just doing an experiment on the alcohol tolerance level of a frog. I sort of got the idea from a commercial I saw a long time ago.

There were these three frogs sitting on rocks or lily pads saying, 'Bud...wise...'"

"Mr. Baker!" Lazer beams of rage shot out from Mrs. Grouse's eyes at Patrick.

"Okay, okay. Anyway, I gave him too much beer and he croaked. Hey, I just made a little funny, Mrs. Grouse, did you get it? He croaked! Not like he made a frog sound - croaked, you know, like he died - croaked. When a word has a double meaning like that, isn't that an oxymoron?" Patrick rambled on.

Bull yelled from the back of the room, "No, but you're an oxymoron!"

Jennifer spoke up to correct her cousin's misunderstanding of the definition of an oxymoron. "An oxymoron is when you put two words together that are complete opposites. They don't really sound like they should go together even though they do. Like jumbo shrimp or sweet revenge or awfully good or civil war."

"Oh, I know what you mean," Patrick said excitedly, "like cool teacher, that's an oxymoron if I ever heard one."

"Class, there will be no further outbursts. Do you understand?" Mrs. Grouse yelled.

The laughter that had infiltrated the room softened and Patrick pretended to get serious about his project once again. "Sorry, Mrs. Grouse," he apologized.

He proceeded to take out his pocket knife, flip open a blade, and then retrieve a tiny two pronged fork from the pocket of his jeans. "I wondered what was poking me," he said, eyeing the counterfeit corpse as if he was trying to decide where to make the first cut. Finally, he lodged the fork into the dried out pickle, saying remorsefully, "Sorry, Kermie," as he began to carve.

"Can you tell us what you're doing, Patrick?" Mrs. Grouse asked, seeming to have gained her composure again.

"Well, first I'm cutting off its arms and legs and then I'll show you its innards."

"What are you going to do with the arms and legs?" the visually challenged girl in the front row asked.

Patrick stopped what he was doing and looked at the girl. If he had planned to have someone ask him that very question at that exact time, he couldn't have timed it any better than this. It was as if she had read his mind, setting him up for his next move.

"Well, I don't know. I guess I could EAT them!" He popped the fragmented pickle pieces into his mouth, chewing and swallowing them in one gulp.

Several girls gasped, while other students just broke up into laughter, realizing that the whole scenario was just another of Patrick's practical jokes.

"Mrs. Grouse, wait!" Patrick yelled, seeing his teacher fiendishly coming toward him with a frenzied, crazed look in her eyes. "It was a pickle, see? I only did it because I didn't want to kill my real pet frog, Kermie."

Josh leaned over to Jennifer and asked, "Does he really have a pet frog?"

"No," she replied, keeping her eyes fixed on the raving madwoman approaching her cousin. "I don't think Mrs. Grouse is buying it either."

"It's not even my real project. See! See!" he groveled, backing away from her and producing the jar with the floating shrimp in it from out of nowhere.

But his pleads for mercy went unnoticed by Mrs. Grouse. She picked him up by one ear, so that he had to stand on the tips of his toes to be escorted out of the room.

The entire class could hear her barking at him, even from behind the closed door. "You are to report directly to Mr. Webber. He shall decide your fate and your punishment!"

"Should I go with him?" Josh asked Jennifer.

"We're all going with him. Most of us have Coach Webber for P.E. next hour," she answered, standing up in anticipation of hearing the dismissal bell ring.

When it did ring, the hostile teacher was still pointing her finger furiously, verbalizing her outrage towards Patrick whose back was pressed up against some lockers. Josh waited patiently, watching Jennifer and Bull walk hand in hand down the hall. When the verbal fire was extinguished and Patrick was released, he caught up to Josh a few yards away.

"I think I might have really done it this time. She said that if she ever catches me taking part in another prank, she'll see to it that I never play basketball in this school or at the high school next year."

65

"Can she do that?" Josh asked.

"I'm not sure. I have to talk to Coach Webber right now. Taking away the right to play basketball, that's brutal. Maybe I can talk him into just suspending me or something," Patrick replied.

"Way to go, Moron!" It was Bull, anxious to throw his over opinionated and underinformed two cents in. "It won't be the same without you on the team this year. We might even have a chance to win the league. Let's go, Jennifer." He tugged on her arm to coerce her into following him.

"What does she see in him?" Josh just had to ask Patrick once the couple was out of earshot.

"I'm not sure. I asked her a couple of weeks ago when they started going out and *she* didn't even know. He's a good athlete. He played football and was pretty good at that, but other than that he just has a big mouth and an even bigger ego. His family has a lot of money. Maybe that's why she likes him. It sure isn't his personality. He's a dip."

"Jennifer doesn't seem like the type who would like someone for his money. I just don't like the way he treats her. Even if he treated her good, I'm kind of surprised she would like someone who treats other people the way he does. If a girl like Jennifer liked me, I'd never treat her like that," Josh declared.

"I think she just likes the idea of having someone like her. She hasn't been her normal self ever since they started going out. She's been acting pretty weird."

"What's her normal self like?" Josh inquired.

"Well, she's nice, but she's strong, not sicky sweet like she is when she's around him, like she doesn't have a backbone in her body."

"I think she's pretty cool," Josh defended her.

"She's okay when she's not around him. I just can't believe she follows him around like a puppy. Do you like her or something?" Patrick finally surmised.

"What's not to like?" Josh grinned.

They continued walking down the hallway towards the locker room.

"Did you bring any shorts?" Patrick asked, seeming unconcerned about reporting directly to Coach Webber.

"No, but I wish I did, these pants are killing me," Josh admitted.

"You're in luck. I got these for you when I went back to get my science project." He pulled a pair of his own jeans from his backpack. "These should fit you. We can look in the lost and found for some shorts that you can wear for PE."

The boys dressed for class and joined the other boys and girls who were shooting hoops in the gym.

"Hey, Patrick, how's it going?" Coach Webber greeted one of his favorite students with a hearty slap on the back.

"Not very well," Patrick confessed, hanging his head low to convey his need for a sympathetic ear to hear his side of the story. "I got into trouble again with Mrs. Grouse. She told me to come and talk to you."

"What'd you do this time?" Coach asked.

Patrick's voice sounded woeful as he told his version of what had transpired, including the part about not wanting to kill his fictitious frog.

"So, the bottom line is that you blew your chance to get a passing grade, thus making you ineligible to try out for basketball on Friday. That puts me in an awkward position, Patrick. Can you see why?"

Patrick squinted at the coach as he shook his head no.

"As the basketball coach, I want to see someone with your talent on my team, but as your disciplinary advisor, I have an obligation to uphold Mrs. Grouse's decision to fail you on the project and to punish you for playing yet another trick on her."

"Well, shouldn't I get something for originality? It *was* one of the categories for the project."

"Dissecting a pickle is original, but no, I don't think it warrants any points."

"Well, what if I make it up tomorrow? Could you talk her into that?" Patrick pleaded to his coach, who was now looking beyond him at the action taking place on the floor.

"Why should she?" Coach raised his voice to compensate for the accelerated noise level in the gym with all of the bouncing balls.

"Well, she touched me. She grabbed my ear when she took me out into the hall. I could sue her for that!"

"Patrick, I think you've been watching too much court TV, but I'll talk to her and see what we can come up with. I have to say that I do agree with her - anymore pranks and your basketball playing days are over." Coach turned his attention courtside again. "Who's that? he asked, pointing to Josh who was engaged in a little one on one with Bull beneath the hoop.

"That's Josh. He's the Australian exchange student staying at my house."

Coach blew his whistle and instructed the other students to take ten laps around the gym while he made his way toward Josh.

"Hi, I'm Coach Webber. I understand you are Josh. Welcome to Westbrook."

"Thanks, it's nice to be here," Josh replied, remembering to use his accent.

"So, you're from down under," Coach remarked. "Do you play a lot of basketball there?"

"Yes, sir. I love basketball, but I've never played on a real team before."

"I don't know if Patrick mentioned it to you, but tryouts for the eighth grade boys' team is on Friday. We'll be holding practices all week long right here after school. I think you'd have an excellent chance of making the team if you're interested."

"Oh, yeah, I'm way interested," Josh assured him.

"Is there any way you can get a permission slip signed by your parents by then?"

"I can fax one to my dad," Josh explained.

"Great, you can pick one up in my office after class and we'll get you signed up."

The rest of class and the rest of the day went well for Josh. In spite of the fact that Patrick was on pins and needles awaiting his fate from Grouchface, Patrick managed to introduce Josh to other students and faculty members and got him registered for classes in the office during lunch.

Josh decided to ease up on the accent and just tell people that he had visited the United States quite often throughout his formative language years. That seemed to satisfy everyone and it made life a lot easier for Josh.

Chapter Eight

Ten minutes before classes were dismissed for the day, there was a knock on the door in English class. It was Mr. Webber holding Patrick's destiny in his hands. Anxious, yet fearful of the fate to be revealed, Patrick somberly met Coach in the privacy of the hallway.

"I've never seen you look so pale," Coach noted cheerily, trying to lighten the load for Patrick. "Are you ready for this?"

"Go ahead. Let me have it. I suppose I deserve it after all of those pranks I've pulled - putting the cherry bombs in the aquarium, putting sugar in the saline solution right before we did an experiment and locking Grouchface in the closet."

"You were the one who locked Grouchface, I mean Mrs. Grouse in the closet?" Coach Webber was dumbfounded.

"Oh, that's right, you never found out who did that, did you? But I wasn't the one who flushed the key to the closet down the toilet. That was someone else. Maybe I'd better just shut up and listen, " Patrick concluded before he made matters worse.

"That might not be such a bad idea," Coach agreed. "I spoke with Mrs. Grouse last hour. She's a little more than fed up with your behavior. She wasn't willing to barter much. She had to take a sedative to calm herself down."

"Did you mention the lawsuit?" Patrick asked.

"The lawsuit?" Coach had forgotten about the ear pulling incident.

"Yeah, for pulling me by the ear."

"Let it go," Coach suggested nonchalantly.

"Okay," Patrick said dejectedly.

"I'll give you the good news first. Mrs. Grouse has conceded to giving you another chance in science. I don't know why. Maybe it's because she knows how much you love basketball or she's afraid that you might turn to bigger and badder pranks if you are deprived of playing."

"All right!" Patrick blurted out, not expecting to hear the list of conditions accompanying the second chance.

"These are the conditions that go along with your chance for redemption," Coach began. "In order for you to obtain eligibility for tryouts, you must do the following. First, you must hand in a ten page report on the scientific topic of your choice, typewritten, doublespaced, due tomorrow."

"Due tomorrow? You've got to be kidding! That's not fair!" Patrick objected, but then succumbed to the demands after seeing Coach's raised eyebrows. "Okay, go on."

"The report must contain factual information from at least five different sources. Only three of the sources can be internet sources. It must include a complete bibliography. And it must be worthy of a B or better gradewise."

"Why do I need to get a B or better on my report, if I only needed a C on my science project?"

"She'll be averaging it with the zero that you received today. Luckily, you have some very high quiz and test scores mixed in with those low homework scores, so you may be able to eek your way into a C with a very strong report. That's not all," Coach continued. "In order for Mrs. Grouse to even consider accepting the extra credit work, you must commit to three hours of volunteer work at the science club's booth at the Christmas carnival."

"Give me a break," Patrick pleaded.

"That's what we're doing by giving you this second chance. I suggest you decide on a topic and then beat feet to the library as soon as the bell rings. You're going to need to get started on this right away."

Patrick spent the remainder of the afternoon in the school library and most of the evening at home hacking away on his computer, going online in order to canvas the various websites pertaining to his topic.

At about 8:30, his intense concentration was disturbed when his bedroom door opened. It was Josh.

"Where have *you* been?" Patrick asked, stretching his arms up over his head and leaning back in his chair.

"Shooting hoops in the gym after school and then Jennifer took me downtown to the donut shop to meet the local law enforcement agents."

"It's actually more of a coffee shop, isn't it?" Patrick admitted and Josh nodded in agreement. " I just say it's a donut shop, so I can use the cop joke, you know?"

"I know." Josh smiled. "Then Jennifer's mom picked us up and took us to a drugstore so that I could get some school supplies."

"How did you manage to get Jennifer away from Bull?" Patrick asked.

"Well, the girls' basketball team was practicing on one end of the court and the guys were practicing on the other end. When practice was over, Jennifer just told Bull that she was responsible for taking me home since you were busy doing your report."

"Did he get all mad?" Patrick asked.

"He seemed to be a little bent."

"And did Jennifer try to back down and listen to him?"

"No, actually she didn't. She didn't seem to care," Josh explained, sitting down on his bed and removing his shoes.

"That's good. Maybe she's coming to her senses."

"I wonder if it had anything to do with what I said to her?" Josh speculated.

"What did you say?"

"Well, one time Bull said something rude to her while we were playing ball. I don't even remember what he said, but I turned to her and told her that she was too pretty and too nice to be treated that way. And the next thing I knew she was taking me to the coffee shop."

"All right!" Patrick held up his hand for Josh to slap.

"So, what are you doing your report on?" Josh inquired.

"How to make a bomb. I got all the information I needed right off the internet," Patrick divulged.

"I don't doubt it," Josh concurred.

"No, actually, I didn't do it on that. I was just messing with you. I did it on telecommunications and satellite technology. I started out researching the space program and how it all started out as a race to the moon and how now most space exploration is linked to satellites and telecommunication businesses."

71

"That sounds like a good topic," Josh acknowledged.

"I've got about eight pages so far and I haven't even really scratched the surface. Anyway, how did you like school today?"

"It was interesting. I'm pretty psyched about playing basketball."

"Yeah, me, too." Patrick's comment was cut short with the arrival of his mother at the bedroom door.

"I've got some laundry for you two," Mrs. Baker announced. "And I found this at the bottom of the washing machine. Is it yours?"

It was the necklace that Sarah had given to him.

"Oh, yes, thank you. One of my sisters gave it to me before I left."

"Oh, isn't that sweet? I wish Patrick and Amos got along that well. What did you end up doing your report on, honey?"

"The mating habits of the yellow bellied sap sucker," Patrick lied.

"That's nice, dear," she said, rolling her eyes and closing the door behind her.

Josh was eager to talk, but as soon as Patrick's mother left, he realized that Patrick's attention had returned to the task at hand. For the next hour and a half, he typed up the next two pages to complete his final draft. Josh waited patiently until he noticed the printer spewing out page after page of the edited copy. He would give Patrick a few moments to get organized before he sprung the next question on him.

"Hey, Patrick, I know it's late and everything, but do you think that tomorrow morning, you could show me how to fax the permission slip to my dad?"

Maybe Patrick was a little frazzled from having done homework for the last seven hours straight or perhaps he was just stressed out from his trying day, but irregardless of what the reason was, he just couldn't let it go this time.

"I thought it was weird when you got here last night and you didn't know how to email your father when he just happens to be one of the most innovative computer entrepreneurs in the world, but I didn't say anything. Then I thought it was a little strange when you opened up your suitcase this morning and your pants were three sizes too small, but I still didn't say anything. Then I noticed that your accent didn't seem to be quite as strong today as it was when you first arrived. And then I noticed that it actually seemed to be wearing off more and more as the day went on, but I let that go, too. Okay, then in science class this morning, there were a couple of things that didn't make sense. They were just little things, but they still bothered me. When Lucy Geiger, the geek with the glasses in the front row, asked you about what kinds of animals you have in Australia, you said koala bears."

"Yeah, so?" Josh retaliated, realizing that Patrick's mounting suspicions could lead to the demise of his human counterfeiting plot.

"They're marsupials, they're not *bears!* The only people who call them bears are stupid Americans who don't know any better. A true Australian would know that a koala is a marsupial. Then when Lydia asked you about wallabies, you drew a total blank, and then when you didn't even know what your dad did for a living, that's when I was really about to lose it."

In spite of the fear of what this conversation could lead to, Josh was impressed with Patrick's deductive reasoning. But was Patrick's intuition far more superior to other people's or was Josh's impersonation as Joshua Clayton Montgomery III even more pathetic than he had previously thought it was? He had thought that he was doing okay. No one at school seemed to think he was anyone but the billionaire's only son, and he thought that he had explained the sporadic accent sufficiently enough to everyone. He even thought that in spite of a few trying moments, he had channeled the questions in Mrs. Grouse's class fairly well. Obviously, Patrick saw it differently.

"And now, not only do you not know how to use a fax machine, but there's also this." Patrick pulled out a profile sheet which read Joshua Clayton Montgomery III. There was a list of facts about Josh, ranging from information about his family to his favorite sports, foods, hobbies, movies, and music. "We got this profile about a week before you arrived. It's kind of a courtesy thing, so that the host family can make the exchange student feel at home by making him his favorite meal or something. They also sent you a profile on us, so that you could get to know us, right?"

"Sure," Josh agreed.

"Wrong, Kangaroo Breath! They only send it to the host family," Patrick repudiated Josh's statement.

"So, what are you getting at?" Josh challenged.

"On the profile sheet, it doesn't say anything about you liking basketball, but I saw you on the court today - you've obviously been playing for awhile. And this," he said holding up the necklace, "my mom showed it to me earlier to see if I knew anything about it. I thought maybe Sarah was your girlfriend or something, but then when my mom came in to give it to you, you said it was from your sister!"

"It *is* from my sister!"

"Then why does it say Sarah on it? Your sisters' names are Lindsey and Katie according to this sheet!" Patrick tossed the profile sheet in Josh's direction.

Josh plopped down on the lower bunk, perplexed about where to go from here. It was obvious that Patrick knew that something was up and Josh was out of explanations in his own defense.

"Well?" Patrick continued the interrogation, "What's the deal?"

"Patrick, how can I say this?" Josh lifted his head from his hands and then seized the shoebox where Kermie had lain. "I guess you could say that I'm a little bit like Kermie was."

"What are you telling me - that you're a pickle impersonating a frog?"

"In a way, I am," Josh said, testing the waters as to what Patrick's reaction might be.

"I don't know what you're talking about, dude. All I know is that you don't know jack about Australia or computers, you don't have an accent and you think your multizillionaire father grows kangaroos!"

"When I said that I was a little bit like Kermie, what I meant was that I'm not who I appear to be."

"Are you saying that you're *not* Josh Montgomery?"

Josh nodded in agreement.

"Then who the hell are you?" Patrick demanded. "And what did you do to the real Josh?"

"I didn't do anything to him. It's nothing like that. He's a friend of mine, sort of. I met him at the airport in LA. Now, if you promise not to tell anyone, I'll tell you the whole story, okay?" Josh pleaded.

"All right, I won't tell anyone," Patrick promised.

"There's really not much to tell, on his end anyway. He was going to ditch you guys and go to stay with his uncle in Miami for the next seven weeks and just pretend to be staying here with you. Then he realized that there were some loopholes in his plan, since his parents might call here and you guys would say he never arrived and then everyone would be all worried. So, he came up with the idea that I could come here and be him."

"Yeah, but who are *you* ? Don't you have a life or a family somewhere who is looking for you?" Patrick asked suspiciously.

"Not really. My sister, Sarah, is the only real family I have left, except for my Uncle Frank. I was on my way to Buffalo, New York to find him when I met JC in the airport," Josh explained. He went on to tell Patrick all about how he had lived with his grandmother and later the Johnsons, and how the state of California was getting ready to move him to a new foster care facility, prompting his departure.

"So, what happened to your mom and dad?" Patrick asked, taking off his jeans, climbing into the top bunk, and then propping his head on the pillow so that he could look down at Josh.

"Well, it's kind of a long story. You up for it?"

"Sure, I doubt if I'm going to be able to sleep now."

"We used to live about fifteen miles outside of a small town in Wyoming. Everyday when we drove to town, we had to pass by a spot on the mountainside called Boulder on the Shoulder. It was called that because there was a gigantic boulder perched on what looked like a person's shoulder. Almost every time we'd pass it my dad would say, 'there's the over the shoulder boulder holder.' He got that from the Three Stooges - that's what they called

75

bras - over the shoulder boulder holders."

Patrick laughed and then waited patiently for Josh to continue.

"The Snake River was on the right and Boulder on the Shoulder was on the left. Anyway, one day they were on their way to look at some property they were thinking about buying. Just as they were passing the spot below the Boulder on the Shoulder, the boulder dislodged from its perch and hurled down the mountain directly into the path of their car. The police said that they died on impact, but the boulder came down with such force that the car plunged into the river. So, even if they hadn't died when the rock hit, they would have drowned."

"That's a bummer, Josh," Patrick sympathized. "How long ago did this happen?"

"What's the date?" Josh asked.

"If it's after midnight, it's the ninth," Patrick replied.

"I can't believe I almost forgot about it. It was today, three years ago today that they were killed."

Both boys were quiet for a moment.

"Do you still want to fax your dad, I mean Mr. Montgomery?" Patrick asked delicately, unsure of how he should refer to this man who Josh was calling his father.

"You can call him my dad. Even though my real name is Jeff Farnsworth, you're still going to have to call me Josh. So, we may as well just be consistent and play along with it all the time. It's kind of fun pretending to have a dad again, anyway. It's late, I'll just fax the permission slip in the morning."

As usual, morning came quickly, but Josh was up before the alarm went off to get a jump on his email.

"Dear Dad,

How are you, Mom, and the twins doing? I miss you all very much, but the Bakers are making me feel very much at home. Guess what? The coach saw me practicing and asked me if I'd like to try out for the basketball team. I'll be faxing you a permission slip. I hope you will let me play. The students and teachers are really nice. Thanks for sending me here. I think it will be good for me. There's just one more thing I need to ask you before I go. This may sound weird, but I sort of promised the kids at school that I'd ask you if you could send us a kangaroo. We would use it as a mascot for the team and they are even thinking about changing the team's name to the Kangaroos. I would need it a week from Friday, but if it's too much trouble, it's okay. I understand. Thanks for everything. Love, Josh"

Josh launched the message into cyberspace, remembering each step that Patrick had taught him. He would have to wait until Patrick woke up before he could fax the permission slip.

He felt relieved, having disclosed his deep, dark secret to Patrick, but at the same time, he realized he had broken his promise to the real JC. All he could do now was to hope that Patrick wouldn't inadvertently or purposely reveal the truth to anyone else.

He waited patiently for Patrick to show signs of life or for the obnoxious buzz of the alarm clock to arouse him from his slumber. Finally, it did sound, and Josh dodged the flying magazine as it hit its target on the clock.

After the fax had been sent, the boys went through the usual rituals of preparing for school, including Patrick teasing Amos at the breakfast table and the boys gathering up books, reports, and other necessary items for school.

The second day at Josh's new school went surprisingly well. He had his own jeans on and was definitely more comfortable physically than he had been the day before. He began getting assignments from his teachers and encouragement from other potential basketball team members who had seen him play.

"Look at that," Patrick said to Josh, pointing to the girl with well polished fingernails and the plain looking girl with the glasses. Both girls were wearing short, above the ankle, skin tight jeans, copycatting the misfitting jeans that Josh had worn the day before.

"Who would have thought?" Josh responded, shaking his head in disbelief at the realization that he had become a trendsetter in fashion.

"It's a good sign, though, when you think about it," Patrick mused. "It proves that you fooled some of the people here at school."

Just then Lucy and Lydia spotted the boys and rushed over to get an update on the kangaroo situation.

"Did you ask your dad about the kangaroo?" Lucy gushed, sporting one hand on her hip in an effort to display her new pants.

"He emailed him this morning, girls," Patrick interceded. "We'll let you know as soon as we hear, okay?" Patrick was beginning to sound like a Hollywood agent. "Now give the guy some space, will you?"

Lucy retorted with a scowl, "All I did was ask, Patrick."

Once the girls were out of earshot and no one else was around, Patrick inquired, "What *are* you going to do about the kangaroo?"

"What more can I do? I emailed my dad this morning and I guess I'll just have to wait and see if he comes through for me."

"Wait and see? Listen, Josh, if you have any kind of inkling, like I do, that your credibility is on the line here, you'd better figure out a way to come up with a kangaroo by the time we play our first game!"

"You think?" Josh asked unassumingly.

"I don't think, I know!" Patrick stated adamantly. "If anyone else has the slightest suspicion that you are a fake, the true test will be in whether or not you come up with a kangaroo. After all, you told a roomful of people that your billionaire father is a kangaroo farmer. How are you going to explain it if he doesn't send you one?"

"Well, what else can I do? I already asked him."

"I have an idea, but I don't want to tell you anymore about it until I think it through a little bit more. Tonight after practice, we'll work on a plan to save your butt."

"Sounds like a worthwhile cause to me," Josh agreed.

During English class, Josh noticed Patrick jotting down notes, only he knew that the notes were not related to class since the teacher was showing the classic movie, To Kill a Mockingbird.

Again, with only ten minutes of class left, there was a knock on the door. And again, it was Coach Webber, summoning Patrick.

"I've got good news for you, Patrick. You got an A+ on your report. You're eligible to try out on Friday, so I expect to see you at practice today."

A zealous shriek of enthusiasm reverberated in the hallway as Patrick learned of his redemption. "Thank you, Coach, thank you, I won't ever let you down again."

"Well, Mrs. Grouse is the one you should be thanking. She's the one who gave you the second chance."

"I will, I will. I'll send her flowers or something. Yahoo! Baby, I'm back!" Patrick shouted in jubilation.

The entire class was snickering when Patrick reentered moments later. "Oh, could you guys hear that?" he asked innocently, causing giggles to rise again.

Within a few minutes the dismissal bell rang, releasing the youths from their confinement in school. Patrick closed the notebook and stood up to meet Josh at the doorway.

"What were you writing in your notebook?" Josh asked.

"Just some ideas on how to get our hands on a kangaroo. See." Patrick opened the notebook again.

"While you were out in the hall, Bull grabbed it and was reading it."

Patrick was horrified. "He was?" He quickly scanned over the notes that he had written to see what vital information might have been divulged. "I don't think he'll be able to decipher this," Patrick said, pointing to a box labeled ZOO and then a little truck parked at the corner of Elm and Maple with a line and an arrow from the zoo box leading to it. Coming from the drawing of the truck were bouncy lines, representative of a hopping kangaroo, leading to another box which read MY HOUSE. Also, written on the page was the name Jethro and Thursday night - 11:30 with a question mark beside it.

Almost shoving the notebook diagram into Josh's face, Patrick asked desperately, "Can you figure out what this means just by looking at it?"

"No." Josh shrugged his shoulders. "It just looks like it could be a map giving someone directions to your house from the zoo, but there aren't any other streets on it, so it really doesn't look like anything."

"Phew!" Patrick sighed, somewhat relieved, that at least for now, he had nothing to worry about. "Let's go to practice. I'll explain this to you later."

Within minutes the boys and their fellow basketball players were in the gym, placing themselves strategically around the floor to take their best shots.

"You *can* really sky!" Patrick exclaimed, seeing how close Josh had come to touching the rim on his last layup. "Where did you learn to jump like that?"

"From the brothers," Josh replied, wiping the sweat from his brow with his wrist.

"From the brothers?"

"In LA, when I was in a foster home, I played a little street ball."

"Seriously?" Patrick was impressed. "Cause you jump like a darn kangaroo, you know?"

"Thanks, I guess," Josh said humbly, not sure whether or not the remark had been meant as a compliment. It had.

One of the other players had overheard Patrick's comment and agreed, "He does jump like a kangaroo!"

Soon others joined in and by the end of the practice, the players had nicknamed Josh, Kangaroo because of his unparalleled agility in jumping so high.

"So, how do you like your nickname, Kangaroo?" Patrick asked as they left the stale, humid warmth of the locker room and made their way out into the frosty night air.

"I think it's a great nickname for a guy from down under," Josh admitted. "Plus, I have hopped around from place to place a lot in the last few years. By the way, what's your idea for getting a real kangaroo?"

"Did I ever tell you about the guy who used to be the janitor at our school who quit and went to work at the zoo?"

"No, I don't think so."

" He said that he took the job at the zoo because the animals were nicer and easier to clean up after than the kids at school were. Anyway, he and I were pretty good buds. We used to keep in touch by emailing dumb blonde jokes and redneck jokes back and forth to each other, but

I think I hit too close to home for him with one of the redneck jokes and we sort of lost touch. I was thinking that I could call him and maybe just ask him if we could borrow one of the zoo's kangaroos for a little while."

"But won't everybody know it's from the zoo if your friend delivers it?"

"No one has to know that. That's where the diagram comes in. I'm hoping that Jethro will be able to deliver it to us at the corner at 11:30 on the Thursday night before the first game and then all we'll have to do is get it to school on Friday morning. Then after everyone sees it, we can just say that your dad promised this one to someone else and that we have to get it back to the delivery driver. Jethro can just pick it up back on the corner of Maple and Elm on his way to the zoo in the morning at about 8:30."

"Do you think that'll satisfy everyone, just having it there for a few minutes?" Josh asked.

"We can tell them that your dad is still working on getting us a permanent one - we can say they're really in demand right now. The kids in my class are gullible; they'll believe just about anything you tell them."

"It sounds like a good idea, but what makes you think that Jethro will do it for you?"

"To tell you the truth, he kind of owes me one. He started a fire in one of the trash cans at school with a cigarette one day. It wasn't a big deal, it was contained and everything, but the fire department came. I figured he would get fired if they knew that it was his cigarette that started the blaze. He's got a wife and a little kid and I didn't want to see them out on the street. No, seriously, I didn't want to see them out on the street, you should see his woman - kind of scary, not something you'd want to run into on a late evening jog in the park. So, I told Mr. Webber that it was mine. I was only in sixth grade then, so it wasn't like I was on the basketball team yet. I got suspended for two days, but at least Jethro didn't get fired."

"That was nice of you," Josh said, bracing himself against a gust of wind that whistled past him.

Both boys were becoming more and more ravenous and more and more chilled, so they decided to sprint the rest of the way back to Patrick's house.

The Bakers were just sitting down to feast on an aromatic chicken and mashed potato dinner when Josh and Patrick arrived.

After dinner, Josh and Patrick wasted no time in getting down to the business at hand, securing a kangaroo. Patrick made the call to Jethro. Finally, after going through the formalities of "how are the wife and kid?" and "heard any good ones lately?" Patrick hit him up with the proposition to borrow a kangaroo.

Jethro agreed to meet the boys with a kangaroo at 11:30 on the corner of Elm and Maple one week from this coming Thursday . No questions asked.

Patrick hung up the phone and had that mischievous grin on his face, just like the one he'd worn prior to the pickle prank.

When Josh saw that look, he remembered what attempting this prank could mean to Patrick. "Are you sure you want to go through with this? If you get caught, you'll probably be kicked off the team."

"I'm not going to get caught. It'll be a piece of cake. It's a no brainer," Patrick assured him.

Or so he thought. Bull's rage against Patrick and Josh was increasing by volumes. Not only was this newcomer setting fashion trends, he was becoming extremely popular and influencing important decisions to be made at school, such as what the team's new name should be. Along with this, he was posing a real threat to Bull's relationship with Jennifer. Bull knew he had to do something to stop this guy. But what? He knew the diagram must mean something, but he didn't know what, just yet. He would keep his eyes and ears open and take advantage of any opportunity he could find to ruin Josh's reputation and to put an end to Patrick's reign of obnoxiousness, as well.

Chapter Nine

Tryouts took place right after school on Friday as scheduled. Bull and Patrick seemed confident as they warmed up, doing layups and shooting foul shots from the line. Josh was a little more nervous than the others as this was the first time he'd ever tried out for anything. He was wrapped up in self absorbing tension until something happened that changed all of that.

It was Jennifer. She burst through the doors of the gym, carrying a basketball in one hand and pulling up one of her socks with the other hand. She was wearing her girls' basketball uniform with the royal blue shorts and matching tank top which displayed the bright gold number 11 on the front and back.

Bull stopped what he was doing and stormed toward her. "What are you doing here?" he demanded.

"The same thing that you are. I'm trying out for the team," she said, aware that she was about to open up a big can of worms.

"But you're a girl and you're already on the girls' team. This is the guys' team. You don't belong here," Bull quibbled.

"Why not? I'm better than some of the guys trying out."

"What makes you think that?"

"Josh said so."

"ERRRR!" Bull growled, cursing Josh with his fists held high in the air. "I should have known that *he* had something to do with this. He has the power to make people do whatever he says."

"He didn't tell me that I should do this. I was just thinking about it the other night when the guys and the girls were both practicing. It's like a form of segregation by keeping the girls and boys on separate teams, just like it would be if we had a black team and a white team. I think I'm good enough to make the boys' team, so I'm going for it."

"Oh, so then you're just going to do it to prove something to yourself and then you'll go back to the girls' team, right?" Bull pressured.

"If I'm good enough to make it, why should I?"

"Why should you? Because you're taking away some guy's chance to play."

"No, I'm not. A guy could play on the girls' team," she reasoned, realizing as the words came out, how outraged Bull would be at this remark.

"No self respecting guy is going to play on the girls' team!" Bull raved.

"Then they should change it to an A team and a B team, so that boys and girls could play on either one."

"You're more messed up in the head than I thought. And it's all *his* fault," Bull backed away, pointing toward Josh who had witnessed the entire confrontation from a few yards away.

Coach Webber had caught wind of the encounter, as well, and approached Jennifer. "What's going on?" he asked.

"I'd like to try out for the team, Coach," she stated confidently.

"What about the girls' team?" he inquired, not being quite sure of how to handle her request. "Aren't you already starting for them?"

"Yes, but if I make this team, I'll quit the girls' team."

"You know, Jennifer, here you might not be playing as much as you would if you were on the girls' team."

Jennifer scanned the assortment of eighth grade boys who were scattered throughout the gym. In her estimation, Josh, Patrick, and Bull were the only three who possessed all three necessary components of height, coordination, and natural ability in regard to the game. She had surpassed most of the other boys her age in physical maturity by the end of the fifth grade and most of them had not yet caught up. She figured that this was it, though. By next year, even the late bloomers would have blossomed into at least partial physical maturity. However, she knew that most of them would have a ways to go before they reached mental maturity, and she laughed at her own revelation.

"I'm willing to take that risk. I believe that I can compete adequately with the boys my age. I feel I will be an asset, and not a liability to the welfare of the team."

"That was an impressive speech, Jennifer, but can't you see that you might be ruining the chances for another boy to play ball this year?"

"That's what I told her," Bull yelled, obviously eavesdropping from center court.

" Yeah, I know, but look at it from my perspective. This is probably the last year that I'll be able to compete with guys my own age. By next year, most of these guys are going to have growth spurts and I might not be able to compete with them. Can't I just play against them now when my physical maturity will give me an edge, possibly for the very last time?"

"I see your point, Jennifer. Okay, go out there and show me what you've got," Coach exclaimed as he added her name to the tryout roster. He knew what she'd said about the other boys growing taller and stronger throughout the course of the year to be true, but he doubted that any would surpass her in regard to the drive and enthusiasm that she possessed.

Josh flashed an encouraging smile her way, while Patrick pulled her aside.

"Normally I would be the guy saying 'what's a chick doing on the court with us?' but since it bugs Bull so much, it's okay with me," Patrick teased.

"You pig!" she laughed in his face, knowing that both of their chauvinistic remarks were made in jest.

Tryouts seemed to last forever. Coach was obviously having a difficult time making the decision about who to cut. He was the kind of man who would have put everyone on the team if he could have. During the previous season, he had put the leftover players to work as scorekeepers, managers, and water boys.

Finally, after three hours of grueling play, the coach announced his choices for the upcoming season. "Baker, Bryan, Bull, Dorian, Gaitan, Hand, Haworth, Kellen, Kreiner, Miller, Montgomery, Shelby, Watson."

"Yes!" Jennifer exclaimed under her breath when she heard her last name, Watson, called.

"Would the boys whose names were not called please stick around for a few moments, so that we can talk about some non player positions available for you," Coach announced.

As Coach finished his speech, Bull slammed his towel down on the bleachers and got up to leave.

"What's your problem, Bull?" Patrick asked. "*You* made the team."

"So did she," Bull retaliated coarsely. "No girlfriend of mine is going to play on the same basketball team as me."

"Fine," Jennifer stated matter of factly. "Then I guess I won't be your girlfriend anymore."

"Bull!" Coach interrupted after witnessing Bull's deliberate protest. "There are six other guys over there who would pay to have a spot on the team. In my opinion, an average player with a good attitude is worth far more to me than an allstar athlete with a bad one. In order to play on a team, you have to accept your teammates, whoever they are, and put aside any prejudices that you may have had in the past. Have I made myself clear?" Coach was visibly aggravated, yet he kept his cool in dealing with Bull's total lack of maturity.

"Yeah," Bull mumbled and continued walking toward the locker room, lacking the class to even raise his head to acknowledge Coach face to face.

Coach shook his head disapprovingly and then focused back to other matters at hand. "Josh, before you go," he said, motioning for Josh to stay momentarily, "congratulations on making the team, but I still need that permission slip so that you can actually play."

Josh had forgotten all about it. "I'll get right on it," he promised, wondering why he hadn't heard from his father thus far.

Jennifer decided to join the boys for pizza at the Bakers' house after tryouts.

"How'd it go?" Mr. Baker asked as the threesome walked through the front door and into the living room.

"You're not going to believe this, Dad, but Jennifer tried out for the guys' team and made it!" Patrick exclaimed. "Can you believe that she beat out Sam Levin?"

"Well, I think he would have made it if he wasn't flunking math," Jennifer replied in defense of her competition. "He's great at the line."

"Maybe so, but you're pretty sweet at the line, too," Josh concurred.

"That a girl," Mr. Baker congratulated his niece. "I'm not surprised, though, I've seen you play. Did you hear that, Linda? Jennifer made the boys' team!"

"Good for you," Mrs. Baker said, carrying a trayful of drinks into the living room for the parched players. "Your mom told me you might try out for the boys' team when I talked to her this morning. Congratulations!" She set the tray down on the coffee table, so that she could hug her sister's daughter. "How did you boys do?"

"We didn't make it," Patrick said dejectedly. "They replaced us all with girls. Now, can we please order a pizza? We're starving to death."

Everyone laughed at Patrick's sarcastic wit.

Jennifer, Patrick, and Josh spent the rest of the evening wolfing down pizza and sharing highlights of the tryouts with Amos and Patrick's parents, including when Jennifer broke up with Bull.

Before too long, the threesome was bloated from too much pizza dough, exhausted from tryouts, yet hyped up from the flow of too much adrenaline and caffeinated soft drinks. So, the boys thought it best to walk Jennifer home and then retire upstairs to bed.

"How can I tell if I have any email?" Josh asked Patrick when they had returned to Patrick's room.

"You don't. I'll let you know if you do," Patrick replied confidently, as if he'd been checking for Josh regularly. "You never got your permission slip back, did you?"

"No, I didn't. I wonder why my dad never sent it back or why he didn't at least email me to let me know that he got it."

"Maybe he didn't get it. Do you want to fax it again? Or I could just sign it for you?" Patrick offered, forgetting that even the slightest deviation off the straight and narrow path could be considered a violation of his agreement with Coach and Mrs. Grouse. "Wait a minute!" Patrick gasped. "Something is not right here! There is something all over this fax machine! It looks like dried on chocolate!" Patrick bent down and took a good whiff of the substance. "It *is* chocolate!"

Without hesitation, Patrick zoomed into the next room where Amos was sound asleep. Switching on the light, Patrick barked ferociously, "Stay out of my room, Amos, and stay away from my stuff!"

"What's going on in here?" Mrs. Baker came flying in from her bedroom. "It's after midnight!"

"There's chocolate all over the fax machine, Mom. Josh was expecting a fax from his dad. Amos probably took it!"

"Amos, did you take a fax out of Patrick's room?" Mrs. Baker asked her younger son who peered out of squinty eyes at his mother and brother.

Groggily, he replied, "What's a fax?" and then drifted immediately back into la la land.

"It's this!" Patrick exclaimed, scooping up a piece of paper from the floor. "Here's your permission slip!" He handed the sheet to Josh, who had come in behind Mrs. Baker. "Let's go, Josh! Amos, stay out of my room!"

Josh and Patrick scurried back to their room, leaving Mrs. Baker behind in the dust. But she wasn't the only thing they left behind in Amos's room that night. Along with the permission slip, there was a crumpled letter under the desk from Josh's dad that neither Josh or Patrick would ever know existed.

It rained most of the weekend, so Patrick and Josh did nothing but sit around and watch TV most of the time. Josh did take time to email his fictitious father to thank him for signing the permission slip. He thought it strange that the man still had not communicated with his only son in any way, shape, or form. He also thought about calling his uncle, but decided to put it off for awhile. If he didn't confront his uncle, his uncle wouldn't have a chance to turn him down, thus, hope would remain.

Besides, he was enjoying himself so much here that reality was quickly escaping him. He liked being the popular, trendsetting basketball player that people referred to as Kangaroo. He thought it ironic that he finally felt as though he'd found himself, but that it was in someone else's identity. Still, there was one part of his past that couldn't be forgotten, not even for seven weeks of playacting. That missing part was Sarah. He wanted to call her, but was afraid that somehow the authorities would be able to trace his call to the Bakers' residence. He couldn't take that chance, not until he was ready to move on. And that was still over five weeks away.

As slowly as the weekend had passed, the week at school flew by, with practices every single day and the team's first game scheduled for Friday afternoon.

Before Josh and Patrick knew it, it was Thursday evening. Josh had still not heard from his father in response to his request for a kangaroo, but since Patrick had reconfirmed his date to meet Jethro at the corner later that night with the borrowed kangaroo, Josh decided to leave the matter alone.

The boys pretended to go to bed at about nine o'clock, hoping that this would prompt Patrick's mom and dad to retire early, as well. The sooner the Bakers were asleep, the easier it would be for Josh and Patrick to sneak out of the house at the designated hour. It seemed to take forever for Patrick's parents to turn off the TV and lock up the house, but eventually they did so, trudging upstairs to their bedroom for the night. Josh and Patrick found themselves dozing off from time to time during the two hour waiting interval, their minds and bodies fatigued from the past four intense days of basketball training. But at just a few minutes past eleven, they managed to come to life to meet the challenge before them.

Unbeknownst to either one of them, Bull had been going out of his way all week long in an attempt to find out what was going to transpire on Thursday night at 11:30 at the corner of Maple and Elm. He had staked out the location on the previous Thursday night, since the diagram had not specified which Thursday night the plan was to take place. When nothing had happened that night, Bull had almost given up, starting to believe that the diagram he had seen was meaningless. That was, until the following Friday afternoon, the day of tryouts, when Bull had been hiding in one of the gym lockers, just waiting for Josh and Patrick to come in and change.

89

"Are we still on for next Thursday night?" Josh had asked Patrick, as the two boys readied themselves for the grueling tryouts ahead.

"You mean with Jethro?" Patrick had answered. "Yeah, as far as I know, at 11:30."

That conversation was all that Bull had needed to convince himself that something pranklike was in the making. He knew that if he could catch Josh and Patrick in the act, drastic consequences would result for both of them. Patrick would lose his basketball privileges and Josh would lose his blemishless reputation.

Bull had not planned to act alone in his endeavor to catch Josh and Patrick in their soon to be discovered scam. He had recruited a short, stocky, smart mouthed youth known as Pudge to help him. Not only did Pudge possess stronger deductive skills than Bull did, but he was also more adept at thinking on his feet than was Bull.

"I never trusted the guy from the get go," Pudge boasted, as Bull attempted to boost Pudge's buttocks up the tree trunk. "He didn't know nothing about Australia on that first day of class," Pudge went on, seeming unaware of the effort Bull was putting forth in getting him into the tree.

Bull didn't really know anything about Australia either, so he had been easily fooled that day. All he wanted to do now was to get even with Josh for ruining his life.

"Are you sure this is the right night and the right place?" Pudge questioned, finally situating himself on a sturdy branch, so that Bull could begin his own ascent.

"I'm sure. I heard it with my own ears..." Bull began, but then stopped short when he heard footsteps coming from down the street. Within seconds, he scaled the tree trunk and was sitting next to Pudge in the tree at the corner of Maple and Elm.

Two shadowy figures approached in the darkness and stationed themselves just below the branches where Bull and Pudge's bodies were balanced. Like clockwork, a large, white delivery truck with illegible lettering on its sides rolled up behind them and slowed to a stop.

"Hey, buddy," Patrick's voice came out of the shadows to greet his long lost friend. "Do you have it?"

"You betcha!" Jethro confirmed, maneuvering his two hundred and fifty pound torso out of the front seat and around to the back of the truck where he pulled up the rolltop door.

"Drugs!" Bull speculated in a whisper to Pudge. But before Bull was able to speculate any further about the felonious activities that were taking place, he and Pudge witnessed a huge, steel cage being lowered down the truck's ramp. There was a thumping sound that plunketed over and over against the steel bars on the sides of the cage.

Before the cage had even reached the sidewalk, a set of headlights from an oncoming car threatened to expose its contents.

"Quick!" Patrick yelled, while the vehicle was still a few hundred feet shy of them, "Get it back into the truck!"

Jethro pushed the cage back up the ramp while Patrick and Josh pulled it up from inside of the truck. Jethro pulled down the door to close it and the three found themselves alone in the dark with the kangaroo.

Patrick asked, "Is it going to keep jumping around like this all night?"

"I gave her a laxative on the way over," Jethro explained. "It should be kicking in any time now and that should settle her down."

Startled by the remark, Patrick erupted, "You gave her a laxative! What did you do that for? She'll be pooping all over the place!"

"Did I say laxative?" Jethro chuckled. "I meant sedative. I gave her a sedative which will knock her out for the night. But you'd better get her home quickly. She'll feel heavier in the cage once she's dead weight."

"What's that smell?" Josh asked, waving his hand before him in disgust.

"It wasn't me," Patrick defended himself. "Jethro, was it you?" Patrick clicked on his flashlight and shined it in his face.

"It might have been the kangaroo. I had to bribe her into the cage with some Raisinettes. They might be giving her gas," Jethro said, defending himself against the accusation that Patrick had made.

"It smells like you gave her the laxative," Patrick retorted. "I hope no one catches wind of this. Get it? Catches *wind* of this?"

Jethro and Josh first rolled their eyes at Patrick's latest lame attempt at humor and then rolled the truck's door up to see if the coast was clear. Seeing that the car had passed and that the street was quiet once again, the threesome carefully wheeled the cage down the ramp. This time, Josh and Patrick wasted no time in transporting the cage down the street, into Patrick's driveway, and then into the backyard.

Patrick had propped a piece of plywood on the steps leading down to an old fashioned cellar door in preparation for the events that were to take place that night. It was a little awkward rolling the cage through the soggy grass, but once they had the steel structure in place on the plywood ramp, it rolled easily down into the dark dampness of the basement hideout.

"We did it!" Patrick exclaimed as he closed the cellar doors from inside, not taking the time to secure the latch. "We'll have to get up about 6 to get it out of here. We can put it on the front lawn and tell my parents that your dad sent it."

"If we're going to tell them about it and show it to them, why did we have to put it in the basement tonight?" Josh asked as he and Patrick tiptoed up the basement steps.

"They might think that it was weird for someone to have delivered it this late at night. It makes more sense for it to arrive in the morning. Besides, we couldn't leave it out in the cold. It might die or someone might come by and take it."

Josh agreed and the two boys snuck cautiously back up the stairs to Patrick's room for the night.

While Patrick and Josh had been struggling to move the now nauseated kangaroo to its temporary spot down under the house, Bull and Pudge had been struggling to keep up with them without being noticed.

"So, what do you make of all this?" Bull asked Pudge from their prickly hideout in the evergreen bushes on the side of the house. Bull was trying to put the pieces of this puzzle together, no easy task for a boy who Patrick always said had a brain the same size as the Grinch's heart.

"Well," Pudge surmised, "I get the feeling that Josh wasn't able to come up with a kangaroo from home, so he and Patrick managed to get one from Jethro at the zoo."

"So, what good is knowing this if we can't do nothing with it?" Bull asked, standing up and looking towards the cellar door.

"Who says that we can't?" Pudge contested slyly, climbing out of the bushes and watching the light go off upstairs in Patrick's room. Bull followed, anxious to hear Pudge's brilliant idea. "What's your objective here, Bull? Do you want to just shake things up a bit or do you want these guys to get kicked off the team?"

"I don't know. I guess I'm just getting sick of 'oh, let's change the name of the team to the Kangaroos,'" Bull exclaimed, changing the pitch of his voice to make himself sound like a girl. "And, 'oh, Josh, you can jump as high as a kangaroo!' I don't really want them off the team because I'd be cutting my own throat, but I guess I just want people to stop thinking Josh is so wonderful. Do you know what I mean?"

"Yeah, I guess. Well, you don't have to figure it out yet. Maybe you'd just like to play a little practical joke of your own on them, eh?" Pudge suggested.

"What do you have in mind?"

"Well, I have a couple of ideas. Right now, all I need to know is if there's a place where we can put the kangaroo for the night?" Pudge requested.

"You mean, *we're* going to take it?" Bull was dumbfounded when he heard what he thought to be an outrageous idea.

"If you want to get back at them, we're going to have to," Pudge insisted.

"I guess I could put it in my garage. My mom's car is in the shop, so she won't be going out there in the morning for anything."

"Perfect. My plan is that we move the kangaroo over to your house. In the morning, Josh and Patrick will be looking for the kangaroo. You have a couple of options here on what you can do with this."

"Like what?" Bull sounded skeptical.

"Well, for one thing, you can tell Patrick and Josh that you have the kangaroo and that if they don't do what you want them to do, you'll either hurt the kangaroo or call the zoo and tell on them. "

"What do I want them to do?" Bull asked Pudge.

"I don't know. You could hold the kangaroo for ransom. Josh has a lot of money. You could get money!"

"I don't need any money. My dad is loaded."

"Okay, then," Pudge continued, "you could get them to do something for you. Think about what you would like them to do for you."

"I'd like Patrick to quit being a dip and I'd like Josh to go home."

"Well, there you go. You could threaten to expose what they did to the rest of the school if Josh didn't promise to go home early."

"What do you think would happen if I did tell everyone at school what they did?"

"If you told everyone that the kangaroo was really from the zoo, you would ruin Josh's wonderful reputation. People wouldn't think he was so perfect if he did something like this, and Patrick, no doubt, would get kicked off the team for participating in another scam."

"Okay, so what's my other option?"

"The other thing that you could do is to say nothing. Let Josh and Patrick sweat it out for awhile. They'll be going crazy when they get up and find that the kangaroo is gone. The zoo will report the kangaroo missing and in the meantime, we can sneak the kangaroo back into Patrick's basement, call the police and tip them off. Now, the consequences... Jethro will probably lose his job and Josh and Patrick will get kicked off the team."

"Can I sleep on it and make my decision in the morning?" Bull asked, scratching his head slowly.

"You're the boss," Pudge reminded him as they made their way toward the cellar door in hot pursuit of kidnapping a kangaroo.

Chapter Ten

It was still dark outside when the alarm went off the next morning.

"No, not yet," Patrick begged, slamming the alarm with the rolled up magazine as usual. But then he remembered that this was no ordinary morning. There was a kangaroo in the basement! He self ejected from the top bunk and sprung into action, grasping Josh's shoulder firmly to wake him, as well. "Get your pants on! Let's go!"

Josh obeyed his command and trailed after him methodically, although he was still half asleep. They tiptoed down the stairs, traipsing through the living room and kitchen until they reached the basement door. Patrick turned on the basement light and proceeded to creep meticulously down each creaky wooden stair until he reached the bottom.

Anxious to see how their furry friend had fared through the night, Patrick cast a glance toward the corner where they had left the kangaroo. With a horrendous gasp, Patrick froze in his tracks upon discovering that the steel cage and its innocent occupant had disappeared.

"What's the matter?" Josh asked, having heard Patrick's gasp from midway down the basement stairs.

"It's gone! The kangaroo is gone, the cage, everything is gone!" Patrick was panic stricken! "Where could it have gone? What are we going to do?"

Josh just shook his head in disbelief, coming to life when he heard Patrick's pleas for answers. "Someone had to have taken it. But who would have done such a thing? Maybe someone did catch wind of this and decided to play a practical joke on you!"

" I bet I know exactly who did it. There could only be one person stupid enough to do something like this!"

"Bull?" Josh took a lucky guess.

"It had to be him, but I wonder what he's going to do with it. Peabrain isn't smart enough to come up with an original idea of his own. We've got to get over to his house and see if we can figure out what's going on!"

Without further hesitation, the boys dressed and vanished from the house, Patrick leading the way to Bull's house just two blocks away. Bull's mother was just coming out of the front door when the twosome arrived in the driveway.

"Good morning, boys," she chirped with a suspicious pleasantness in her tone. "Can I help you with something?"

"Oh, no, Ms. Bull. We were just excited about the first game and all today and we thought we'd stop by and see if Bull was up .... so that we could go over some plays with him." Patrick was pleased that he had been able to come up with such an excellent excuse in spite of his skyrocketing anxiety level.

"He doesn't usually get up for about another hour," she informed them, examining their faces for clues that might reveal their ulterior motives.

"That's okay. We'll just wait for him out here, if it's okay with you?" Patrick asked timidly in an effort to appeal to her sense of congeniality.

"Well, I suppose it would be okay," she responded warily as the two innocents smiled boyishly and plopped themselves down on her front porch steps.

"Can I open your garage for you?" Patrick asked abruptly, thinking that perhaps the kangaroo would be stashed there.

An odd look came over Ms. Bull's face as she declined, explaining that she would be taking the bus to work today as her car was being repaired.

"Oh, so your garage is empty then?" Patrick asked, shaking his head up and down as though he had uncovered an important element in his quest for the kangaroo.

She nodded in agreement, but became even more suspicious of the boys' motives than she had been before. "I have to go now," she clamored uneasily as she strode down the sidewalk, glancing back from time to time at the boys until she was around the corner and out of sight.

The detached garage was located in the backyard with a long driveway leading to it.   Josh and Patrick beat

96

feet to the garage. Patrick grabbed the garage door handle in an attempt to pull it up, but it was locked securely. Josh found a side door which he tried to open, but it, too, was locked. They continued to snoop, finding a curtained window through which to look, but to no avail since the curtain was drawn tightly. It would be impossible to find out what contents were contained within the four walls of the garage without breaking and entering.

"We've got to do something!" Patrick scowled in frustration, jiggling and fidgeting with the doorknob on the side door in the hope that it would magically open.

"Maybe we should wake him up and weasel our way into the garage somehow. Maybe the keys are hanging somewhere real obvious and one of us could act like he wants to go over some plays while the other one gets the keys and opens the garage."

"He'd never let us in the house. He'd know we were up to something," Patrick repudiated Josh's idea. "I've known Bull since kindergarten and this is only the second time I've been at his house."

"When was the first time?" Josh asked, realizing that the intensity of the boys' feud might be deeper than he had imagined it to be.

"In kindergarten. He had a birthday party. I peed on his mother's petunias and she sent me home. I've never been back since. That's probably why his mom kept looking back at us on her way down the street. She was probably afraid that I'd wee wee in her flower bed again."

In spite of the nervous knot in his stomach, Josh couldn't help but laugh.

"Maybe I can get this door unlocked," Patrick continued, taking out his pocket knife and poking one of the attachments into the keyhole.

"Wait!" Josh tried to stop him. "Peeing on the petunias is one thing, but breaking into someone's garage is something else!"

"So, don't you think that that's exactly what Bull did at my house?" Patrick took another desperate stab at the keyhole.

"It doesn't matter. If you do it and you get caught, you'll be the one who gets in trouble," Josh said, trying to convince his friend of the impending consequences to his actions.

"I don't care. Don't you get it? There's more at stake here than me getting into trouble. There's you getting busted for not being who you are supposed to be when you can't come up with a stupid kangaroo. They'll probably send you back to California and put you into a juvenile detention center. And there's Jethro who will get fired if anyone has any clue that he is involved when the kangaroo comes up missing. We have to get it back! We just have to! And the first step to getting it back is finding out if it's in this garage!" He cringed as he thrust the pocket knife appendage forcefully into the hole again.

"That's not going to work. Stop now before you break the lock. Why don't we just ask Bull if he took our kangaroo? We could level with him; we could tell him that my dad couldn't send one right away and that we just borrowed this one to keep the kids at school happy until we could get one from my dad. Maybe we could just let him in on this and he wouldn't make a big deal out of it."

"You don't know Bull very well. He'd do anything to get you and me into trouble. Remember, he's the one who despised the idea of changing the team's name to the Kangaroos. The last thing that he is going to do is to go along with us on this. Besides, I wouldn't give Bull the satisfaction of knowing what we're doing!" Patrick again stubbornly dismissed Josh's suggestion.

Josh attempted to reason with his friend once again."Let's just go back to your house, eat breakfast, calm down and call Jethro to let him know there may be possible complications to our plan. Then maybe we'll be able to figure something out on the way to school."

But by the time Josh and Patrick arrived at school, they were no closer to solving the mystery of the missing kangaroo than they had been two hours earlier. Both boys waited anxiously for Bull's arrival, not noticing or associating Pudge's absence with Bull's absence.

Halfway through Mrs. Grouse's boring lecture on bryophytes, the lesson was interrupted, marking the first of a series of interruptions that would transpire throughout the class that morning. It was Bull, sheepishly entering the classroom and handing the middle aged teacher the pink, unexcused tardy slip that was necessary for his admittance to class at such a late hour. She did not allow the disruption to break her stride as she continued on, directing the students to take notes from the overhead projector where she had written volumes of useless information on the subject.

Josh and Patrick searched Bull's face for clues as to his involvement in the case of the missing kangaroo, but his expression was as vague and as lifeless as it usually was. About ten minutes later, the monotony of the lecture was again interrupted, this time by Pudge's arrival. He, too, looked subdued, but his eyes shifted suspiciously when he glanced in Patrick's direction.

Five minutes hadn't passed when, again, another interruption occurred. A bold, deliberate knock broke the silence in the room, where the only sound now being heard was the scritch scratch from the students' pens and pencils as they frantically copied down the notes from the overhead before they were erased.

Mrs. Grouse threw her hands in the air and walked towards the door, relinquishing an exasperated sigh. It was Mr. Webber, but he wasn't alone. Accompanying the coach were two uniformed officers of the law.

"We're sorry to interrupt your class, Mrs. Grouse," Mr. Webber apologized, "but we need to see two of your students."

Josh held his breath. Patrick's heart was racing as he thought about what had probably transpired since they'd gotten to school. Bull had probably called the police and told them about Jethro bringing the kangaroo to Josh and Patrick. Jethro had probably been arrested, and Josh and Patrick would be next.

"Bull and Pudge, would you please join us in the hallway ?" Mr. Webber directed.

Josh released the breath that he had been holding in and Patrick gulped so loudly that students in the front row heard it.

Pudge and Bull were taken into the hallway and then removed from the school premises in a squad car as the entire class watched in disbelief through the window.

Josh looked over at Patrick whose eyes were as big as saucers and whose ruddy face had turned to albino stone.

"What's going on?" Mrs. Grouse asked Mr. Webber as the car disappeared from the students' view.

There was complete silence in the room as the students strained to hear the explanation for the sudden removal of their classmates.

"Well, as odd as it may seem," he began, lowering his voice and turning away from the students, "one of Bull's neighbors was out walking her dog this morning and she noticed two boys outside struggling with something that appeared to be on a leash, and get this, wearing clothes."

"What?" Mrs. Grouse giggled, glancing briefly at the students who were as tuned in as they could possibly be.

"Her dog started going crazy, so she couldn't get any closer to see what it was, but when the boys saw her they raced back to Bull's garage and put it away. She thought it seemed suspicious, so she called the police. They got a search warrant and found a kangaroo in the garage. When they contacted the zoo, sure enough, one was missing."

"Well, isn't that something? What in the world were they doing with a kangaroo?" Mrs. Grouse wondered.

"We'll soon find out," Mr. Webber stated positively.

This was getting worse and worse. As soon as Bull told the police what really happened, Josh, Patrick, and Jethro would be dead meat. Now there was nothing they could do, but wait.

Class was almost over and Mrs. Grouse had just threatened to remove the current overhead projector page from view and begin enlightening the class on the characteristics of liverworts when there was another knock on the door.

Josh and Patrick heard a man's voice and could see more navy blue apparel on the visitor in the doorway. Again, fear gripped the two boys.

"Ooooh!" Mrs. Grouse exclaimed after she had engaged in thirty seconds of conversation with the handsome, young man.

Neither Josh or Patrick could tell if her exclamation was one of joy or one of horror. It would be several more minutes before they would find out. She closed the door and called for Josh to come up to the front of the classroom.

She put her hand on his shoulder and then began, "Josh, Josh, Josh... As you all know, Josh promised us that he would look into the possibility of getting a kangaroo sent to us from his father's kangaroo farm in Australia. Well, this may come as a surprise to all of you. This day certainly has been full of surprises, hasn't it, Josh? I know it came as a surprise to me..." She opened the door and announced brazenly, "Our kangaroo has arrived!"

In walked a lanky Federal Express man, wheeling a large steel cage, not unlike the one that had housed the zoo's kangaroo, only a little bit smaller.

"Everyone, say hello to Smitty, our new mascot!" Mrs. Grouse rejoiced in a boisterous howl.

Both Patrick and Josh let out huge sighs of relief as they eyed the sandy colored marsupial who was asleep in her cage.

"There's a letter here from Josh's father which says: 'Dear Josh and classmates, I hope you will enjoy Smitty, a ten month old female kangaroo who would love to be your school mascot. There's a book enclosed which will tell you what she eats and how to care for her. Enjoy! Yours truly, JC Montgomery II' Isn't that wonderful? We'll have to take a few days off from our current studies to learn all we can about kangaroos!" Mrs. Grouse beamed.

When class was dismissed, instantaneous rumors began circulating in the halls as to why Pudge and Bull had been taken away in a squad car. Since no one had been able to hear what Mr. Webber had been saying, the rumors soon became more and more controversial and disturbing. Some people were saying that Bull and Pudge had planted a bomb somewhere in the school, whereas others had heard that one of them was packing a pistol. The rumors spread so rapidly and grew to such astronomical proportions, that the principal was forced to take action during second period to dispel any and all rumors. What method did he use to dispel the fears that were multiplying? Quite simply, he told them the truth.

101

The teachers were instructed to turn on the television sets in their classrooms where the principal, Mr. Younkers, and the disciplinary advisor, Mr. Webber would enlighten the students as to why two students were taken away by two law enforcement agents earlier that day.

Without ever mentioning the names of the two suspects in custody, Mr. Younkers began, "It has come to my attention that there are rumors going around pertaining to the removal of two students from the school grounds this morning. Normally, it is not customary for school administrators to discuss such events with students, but in this day and age, I find it necessary to communicate with you, not to give you the details of the situation, but rather to dispel the rumors which some of you feel inclined to dispense. I am here to tell you that the two youths have simply been taken into custody for questioning. The incident did not, at any time, constitute any threat to any students, faculty or administrators in any way. I'd like to turn this over to Mr. Webber who met with the officers prior to the students being removed from the grounds. Mr. Webber.."

Patrick and Josh were shocked at the formality of the speaker and the amount of attention being given to this matter. They listened intently as Mr. Webber took his turn speaking, hoping that he would elaborate on what actually *did* happen, not just dispel rumors about what *didn't* happen.

Fortunately, Mr. Webber did go into greater detail about what had happened. "I'm sure that some of you are still feeling as though you are in the dark here about what's going on. All I can tell you is that two boys were seen handling some kind of an animal this morning outside of one of the boy's homes. It was reported to the police and the police did find a kangaroo in the boy's garage. Reportedly, there was a kangaroo missing from the zoo, so the boys were taken downtown to tell the investigators what they know about this particular kangaroo."

A dull rumbling of laughter echoed through the school. "Speaking of kangaroos, we have just received word that our official kangaroo has arrived from Australia.I understand that her name is Smitty and I, also,

102

understand that the student council will be holding a special election today to vote on changing the name of the team from the Rockets to the Kangaroos. Voting will take place during lunch, so be sure to pick up a ballot to cast your vote. Remember a two thirds majority is needed to make such a change, so your vote is very important. Thanks students and teachers for your time. We now return you to your regularly scheduled classes." Mr. Webber smiled warmly into the camera as his image vanished from the classroom screens.

When the longest day of the school year finally ended for Josh and Patrick, the two boys moped all the way to the locker room to prepare for their first basketball game. Mentally, they were drained and neither the snappy tunes being played by the school band or the peppy cheers being sung by the cheerleaders could bring either one of them back to life.

"You two have been awfully quiet about what happened today," Jennifer stated gleefully as the three friends met on the gym floor. "I figured you, Patrick, would be having a field day with what happened to Bull."

"We all do stupid things, sometimes. He just got caught," Patrick responded, still clinging to his depression.

"Are you fired up for your first official basketball game, Josh?" Jennifer asked, turning her attention away from her downhearted cousin.

"I'm pretty psyched," he answered, "although I haven't had much time to think about it with all that's been happening today."

"You know what I heard?" Jennifer said, realizing that she was contributing to the gossip pool, but at the same time finding it impossible to keep from diving in. "I heard that the kangaroo they found was seen wearing a hat and a T shirt, oh, and sunglasses. Can you believe that? It was like they were trying to make it look like a person or something. Isn't that funny?"

Patrick retorted abrasively, "It's not like you to gossip, Jen. It doesn't look good on you. Give it a rest."

Having been put in her place, Jennifer rescinded the remark, embarrassed by her cousin's derogatory comment. "You're right, Patrick, that wasn't very nice of me. Can we just go out there and play some basketball?"

She knew her cousin too well to think that his solemn mood was due to his sympathy for Bull. What was making Patrick so touchy and irritable? It just didn't make sense, given the usual amount of animosity Patrick exhibited towards Bull. She could only hope that he would lose some of this intense animosity towards her and everybody else once he started playing the game. Sports always made Patrick lighten up, unlike some people, like Bull, who would grow more intense and competitive on the basketball court or the football field. Patrick always seemed to do the opposite - the greater the challenge, the bigger his smile.

With the physically mature Evansville Eagles warming up on the court and with the absence of Bull, Coach Webber realized that he had a little juggling to do with the lineup. Josh was selected to play center, while Jennifer and Patrick aspired to their positions as forwards. Two athletically challenged teammates were chosen as guards. The first quarter was shaky with the Eagles taking an early 15 to 5 lead.

"We've got to start taking some shots," Coach encouraged the players at the end of the quarter. "Don't be afraid to shoot. That's one of our strong points at this stage in the game. They're stealing the balls right out of our hands before we even get a shot off. I've seen you all shoot; you've got the talent. Don't be afraid to use it! Think about the plays we practiced and concentrate on staying in control of the ball. Get those rebounds and come back and score some points. You can do it! Okay, break!"

The war waged on throughout the rest of the second quarter and then throughout the entire second half with the home team fighting aggressively to redeem themselves. With or without Bull, these challengers were giving them a run for their money.

With three seconds left and the Kangaroos down by two, Patrick lunged to a point just outside the three point perimeter and fired a final shot. In slow motion, the ball perused the air, finally detonating the rim with intensity as it whooshed through. The buzzer sounded. The final score: Kangaroos 45 - Eagles 44.

Jennifer's theory regarding Patrick's disposition proved to be true. Physical activity had allowed him to forget the adversity in his mind and to feel and act more like himself again.

Josh and Patrick made a pact to just wait this thing out and not let it get to them. They decided that it was senseless to worry about it. They would deal with it, if and when, the subject reared its ugly head again.

Holding true to the pact turned out to be easier said than done. Although the two boys had laid low over the weekend and hadn't heard much about Bull and Pudge's situation, rumors were again spreading like wildfire on Monday morning when the boys arrived at school.

Some people were saying that the two boys had been sent away to the state's juvenile detention center. Others said that they were home, but that they'd both been suspended from Westbrook. People were also theorizing about why they had done it. Most said that Bull was so jealous of Josh that he was trying to be the first one to produce a kangaroo to become the school's mascot. Others had conspiracy theories about how the kidnapping had come about, linking insiders at the zoo to the pair of alleged kangaroo thieves. These were the most threatening pieces of information that Josh and Patrick were hearing. They might eventually link Jethro to the crime since he had previously been employed by the Westbrook Middle School. But so far, the boys hadn't heard anything from Jethro.

Things certainly had not turned out the way Patrick had planned. The only plan that was going on without a hitch was the plan being made by the science club and the pep club to construct a comfortable habitat of adequate size for Smitty, the new mascot. Josh, Patrick, and Jennifer, too, were on hand after practice on Monday afternoon to help put on the finishing touches. Playing hard and working hard seemed to alleviate some of the guilt induced stress that the boys had been experiencing throughout the day when the rumors had been flying.

They became so relaxed that afternoon while building Smitty's new home, that they heartily accepted an invitation from Coach to have dinner at his house the following night.

Chapter Eleven

"We're going now, Mom," Patrick yelled to his mother as he and Josh pulled on their jackets and made their way toward the front door en route to Coach's for dinner.

"Where are you guys going?" Amos nagged, forming a human blockade with his body against the front door.

"It's none of your business," Patrick snapped back rudely.

"Can I come?" Amos pleaded, looking to Josh for mercy and permission to tag along. "I never get to go anywhere."

"Sorry, mate, it's not up to me. But I promise that Patrick and I will take you somewhere this Saturday. Okay, sport?" Josh said, rubbing Amos's red spiked head of hair.

"Where? To the arcade? Will you take me to the arcade?" Amos was effervescent again at the thought of actually being escorted to the arcade by his older friend.

"As long as it's okay with your mom," Josh said.

"Mom, will you tell this little rugrat to move? He's blocking the door. We're going to be late," Patrick bellowed belligerently.

"Come on, Amos. Let the boys go. Patrick, don't stay out too late. You have school tomorrow, you know," Patrick's mother reminded him sternly, coming down the stairs to see them off.

"Mom, we're going to Coach's house. It's not like he's going to keep us over there all night smoking cigarettes and drinking beers, you know?" Sarcasm dripped from Patrick's tongue.

"Okay, wise guy, just get going. Call us if it gets too late and you two need a ride," Mrs. Baker offered.

"Sure thing, Mom," Patrick said and took the opportunity to physically remove Amos from the doorway by picking him up by the belt loop on the back of his pants and dropping him on the hardwood floor.

"How far away does Coach live?" Josh asked once they had headed out into the dark night.

106

"I'm not sure, probably about a quarter of a mile away," Patrick guessed. "We have to go by your girlfriend's house to get there," he teased.

"What girlfriend?" Josh played dumb.

"Jennifer, da," Patrick said, feeling that he was stating the obvious here.

"I'd hardly call her my girlfriend. The only time I ever see her is on the basketball court."

"Well, we'll have to do something about that," Patrick stated decisively. "I can tell that she likes you. She's probably just waiting for you to make the first move."

Josh didn't respond to Patrick's comment. He simply kept walking with his head down to avoid the brisk wind that seemed to slap him in the face each time he looked up and to watch for uneven slants in the sidewalks.

When they reached the streetlight which stood in front of Jennifer's house, Patrick darted, leaving Josh standing alone on the sidewalk. He then proceeded to run up the front porch steps, ring the doorbell, and dive into the bushes lining the front of the house.

The front porch light went on and Josh suddenly became painfully aware that he had been deserted by his best friend and was now standing solo in front of Jennifer's house.

But it didn't seem to surprise or phase Jennifer's mother as she opened the door and yelled into the bushes. "How are the bushes tonight, Patrick?"

"Oh, pretty good, pretty good, Aunt Jill," came a tiny voice from the shrubbery.

"Good, good," she replied. "Hi Josh! How are you tonight?"

"Fine, thanks," Josh responded politely and then waited for his friend to join him again.

"I wonder how she always knows it's me," Patrick contemplated once he was out of the bushes and back on track to Coach's house again.

"Gee, I wonder!" Josh mused.

As they rounded the next corner, Josh could see a stately, but rather quaint colonial home perched on a small knoll. A white picket fence outlined the well trimmed lawn which seemed to have fared well, in spite of recent rains and frigid temperatures. Both boys opted to hop the fence rather than to use the gate. Tall pearl columns graced the entranceway, welcoming them as they made their way through the maze of mature pines, oaks, and willows which blanketed the yard.

"This is an awesome house; it looks so big!" Josh exclaimed, eyeing the intricate details of the doors and windows as they stood on the porch.

"It's very empty inside," Patrick responded in a serious tone, ringing the doorbell at the same time.

"What do you mean?" Josh asked, but was prevented from finding out what was behind Patrick's comment, as Coach promptly opened the door to greet his young guests.

Once inside, Josh was impressed by the grandeur of the spiral staircase that rose majestically to the second floor. "I like your house," he said, fixing his eyes upon the crystal chandelier in the foyer. He was disappointed, however, when he turned his attention to the adjacent living room and its modest furnishings, thinking that they lacked the opulence that a house such as this mandated.

"Thank you. We have hopes of turning it into a bed and breakfast someday, but as you can see, we have a long way to go," Coach said, pointing to a dilapidated wooden floorboard which was protruding from the floor in dire need of repair. "We bought it for a good price as a fixer upper, but it takes time and money to actually complete such a big project. I've just about finished the outside, but the inside seems to be taking me longer than I'd expected."

"How long have you lived here?" Josh asked.

"We've been in here about four years now. Wow, the time has gone by quickly," Coach recollected, as his wife joined him in the foyer. "This is my wife, Tara." He directed the introduction at Josh since Patrick already knew her. "And this is Josh, the exchange student from Australia who I've been telling you about," Coach beamed. "I told Tara about how it's only your first year playing and already you're one of the best players."

"Thanks Coach," Josh accepted the compliment with humility.

"It's nice to meet you, Josh. I *have* heard a lot about you," Tara admitted, her clear blue eyes crinkling up at the corners when she smiled. She looked to be in her late twenties, but those smile lines around her eyes hinted at perhaps just a year or two more.

"What about me?" Patrick interrupted in an attempt to regain his ordinary status as the center of attention. "Did you catch my awesome three pointer at the last game?"

"No, but I heard that you almost found yourself a permanent position on the bench by pulling some kind of pickled frog prank on Mrs. Grouse."

"Oh, yeah, that," Patrick concurred sheepishly.

"How about I take your coats and you boys join us in the living room? There's something I want to talk to you about," Coach insisted.

"May I use your bathroom first?" Josh asked nervously as he feared the worst in what Coach might want to talk about with them.

"Sure, follow me," Coach directed, leading Josh up the stairs and down a dark hallway as he felt along the wall for the lightswitch. "Sorry, the one downstairs is out of commission. Here you go. Oops!" he said as he switched on the light and discovered something hanging on the bathroom doorknob. "It's Tara's over the shoulder boulder holder," he announced, confiscating his wife's undergarment and stuffing it into his pocket. "Sorry about that," he apologized when he noticed that Josh's eyes were open so wide that they looked like they might actually pop out of his head.

"Oh, that's okay. I've seen a bra before," he asserted, regaining his composure. "It wasn't the bra that surprised me, it was what you called it. You called it an over the shoulder boulder holder. Three Stooges, right?" Josh asked, recollecting that he had never heard anyone besides his father and the Stooges use that expression.

"That's right! Not too many people know where that's from. Do you have the Stooges in Australia?"

"I used to watch them with my dad a long time ago, but I haven't seen them in a long time."

"I know, they're hardly ever on anymore. Once in awhile, I'll catch them when I can't sleep and I'm flicking through the channels during the middle of the night. And once in a great while, someone will host a Stooge Fest. I'll tell you what, if I hear about one after the season is over, I'll have you and Patrick over for it, okay?" Coach invited, failing to realize that Josh would be long gone even before the regular season ended.

"Well, that would be great, but I'm not going to be here after the season is over," Josh replied.

"Well, that's one of the things I want to talk about with you tonight," Coach confided with a hopeful look in his eyes. "I'll see you downstairs."

When Josh returned to the living room, Patrick and the two adults terminated the conversation in which they'd been engaged and acknowledged Josh's presence.

"Come in, Josh, sit down." Tara was motioning him over to take a seat next to her when suddenly she noticed something white sticking out of her husband's pants' pocket. "What's that in your pocket?" she asked, pulling firmly on a strap that caused the bra to spring out into the open. As the identity of the item was revealed, Tara became mortified, her cheeks turning a crimson shade, noticeable even though the only light in the room came from the fire in the fireplace. She retrieved the item swiftly and tucked it down between two couch cushions, hoping that no one had seen it.

"I'm sorry, honey," Coach said endearingly, "it was hanging on the bathroom door."

Patrick, determined not to let the opportunity for a good one liner pass him by, responded eagerly saying, "It's okay, Mrs. Webber. I've seen one of my mom's before. It looks just the same, only maybe hers is a little bigger."

Josh's eyes widened, as did Coach's and Tara's as they digested what had just spewed out of Patrick's mouth. Immediately, Patrick realized that he had gone too far.

"Did I say that out loud?" Patrick tried to cover himself with another one liner. "I didn't mean to say that out loud, really I didn't," he sputtered unconvincingly.

"Right," Tara responded with cynicism. "You just wait, buddy, I'm going to get you for this," she laughed, punching Patrick in the arm.

Josh and Coach were now basking in the verbal lashing that Tara was giving Patrick.

"I'm sorry, okay?" Patrick begged for mercy. "Don't hit me anymore, that's my bad arm."

"Since when is that your bad arm?" Coach asked, snickering in anticipation of Patrick's next response.

"Since your wife punched me!" Patrick charged indignantly. "Why does everybody always have to punch me?" Patrick whined meekly, rubbing his wound in an effort to gain sympathy and to squelch the onslaught of negativity that was coming his way.

"Okay, Patrick, I forgive you," she said sympathetically, putting her arm around him.

Just then a buzzer sounded in the kitchen, signaling that the chicken broccoli casserole was ready to come out of the oven.

After they were all seated, Josh returned to a previous topic, thinking it wise to leave the living room conversation back in the living room where it belonged.

"You mentioned that you'd like to turn this place into a bed and breakfast. If you did that, you wouldn't quit teaching and coaching, would you?"

"No, no, I love what I do. The bed and breakfast was sort of an idea we got when some other plans we'd made didn't work out," Coach replied as he passed a plateful of biscuits in Josh's direction.

"What other plans did you have?" Josh found himself asking, not knowing if he, too was crossing the line between appropriate and inappropriate questioning.

Coach looked in Tara's direction to seek approval as to whether or not she wanted to disclose this pertinent bit of information to this young man. He searched her face for the look that would tell him if he should go on, but she seemed to be preoccupied with stabbing an unruly piece of lettuce with her fork. And so he continued.

Or so he tried, but before he could utter another word, Patrick seemingly purposely dropped his fork onto the floor between where he and the coach were sitting.

Without hesitation, Coach retrieved the lost fork and replaced it with another from the hutch expeditiously.

Patrick knew the story behind the house and was anxious not to go there. In fact, he would do whatever he could to avoid hearing the tragic tale that lingered within the walls of that house. He knew how the Webbers had bought it with the sole intention of sharing it with a houseful of baby Webbers and how their dreams had been snuffed out like flames in a fire one cold November afternoon. Now all that was left of their dreams were ashes, scattered haphazardly in their minds. But unfortunately, he couldn't come up with anything clever, or even belligerent to say in time to stop Coach from continuing on.

"We bought this house," Coach began solemnly, "so that we could have a big enough house to have lots of children. We'd been living here for a couple of months when Tara became pregnant with twins - a boy and a girl. She was only about a week away from her due date when we were involved in an automobile accident."

Tara rose from her place at the table, still expressionless, as her husband elaborated on the unfortunate events that had left her barren and childless.

Seeing that she was distressed, he stopped and addressed her with compassion. "I'm sorry, honey, we don't have to talk about this."

"No, it's okay. I'm just going to get some napkins. I forgot to put them out. Really, I'm fine," she assured him.

Now, Josh, too, was feeling uncomfortable with the conversation that he'd been responsible for initiating, yet he was intrigued by the adversity that they had experienced. Somehow, knowing that they, too, had suffered a significant loss in their lives made him feel connected to them.

"It's okay," Josh said, thinking about how hard it was for him to talk to people, not about his parents, but about how his parents had died. "You don't have to tell me about it."

"It's funny," Tara said when she came back into the dining room, "after all this time, it still hurts. It was three years ago on November 9th that we lost them."

Josh looked over at Patrick to see if he was paying attention, but Patrick was cutting a piece of chicken with his knife, seeming oblivious to the world around him. How could he not remember that Josh had told him that his parents had died on that very same date during that very same year? Obviously, it wasn't something that had struck a chord with him.

The room became hauntingly silent for a moment, the most recent conversation imposing its awkwardness on the foursome. Josh was surprised when he heard his own voice break the silence.

"Have you thought about trying to get pregnant again?" This sounded like something that should have come out of Patrick's mouth, but even Patrick choked on his milk when he heard Josh voice the very personal question. "I mean, you could have another baby, couldn't you?"

Tara seemed comfortable and was even able to smile over Josh's concern for her and her husband. "You know, Josh, at first, I couldn't even bear the thought of being pregnant again, fearing that I might lose another baby. I was afraid of getting emotionally attached again."

Josh knew exactly how she felt. He felt the same way for a long time after his parents had died and when they'd been forced to leave their grandmother. He was almost glad when he and Sarah were shipped around every few months, so that they didn't get too attached to anyone.

"And then, when I thought I was ready to go through it again, I found out that something wasn't right after the accident, and that I couldn't have children. That's when we decided to turn this dinosaur," she said referring to the house, "into a bed and breakfast. At least, that way, we'll eventually have the pitter patter of little feet running down the hallways, even if the little feet don't belong to us." A manufactured optimism echoed in her voice as she attempted to camouflage the still, real pain that resided deep inside of her.

Josh wasn't sure what had gotten into him now. Maybe Patrick was really rubbing off on him. He didn't know. All he did know was that he was about to ask Tara yet another personal question. "Well, have you ever thought about adopting?"

"Actually, we have," Coach interjected. "As a matter of fact, we're on a waiting list, but sometimes it can take years to get a baby."

"Yeah, and nobody wants older children," Josh added dejectedly.

"Oh, I don't know. I'd be open to something like that," Coach reflected. "But Josh, we didn't invite you over here to talk about us, we invited you over to talk about you," he said changing the subject completely. "Where did you learn to jump like that?"

Patrick was feeling like his old self again and couldn't wait to get back into the limelight, dominating any shallow conversation with his wit and sarcasm.

"He learned it from the Aborigines, you know the little guys in Australia. They have to jump really high to play basketball. And I guess you could say that they've perfected the technique. Isn't that right, mate?" Patrick prompted.

"Absolutely, mate," Josh concurred, joining Patrick in his merriment.

"I heard that the kangaroo that your dad sent was a big hit at the game on Friday night," Tara commented.

"Oh, it was!" Patrick again answered for Josh. "I can't believe you weren't there for our first game, Tara?"

"I'm sorry. I had to work, but I promise I'll come to the next one. So, what were Bull and Pudge trying to do by stealing that kangaroo from the zoo? Were they trying to show you two up or something?"

Josh shrugged and glanced at Patrick, who was again, at a loss for words.

"Do you know that they even tried to blame it all on you two guys, saying that you had stolen it from the zoo and that they had gotten it from your basement? Can you imagine them saying that?" Coach exclaimed.

Patrick and Josh both shook their heads in disbelief.

"What are they going to do to them?" Patrick asked.

"Well, if they're lucky, the authorities will treat this like a school prank. If so, they may get off with just a brief suspension, or a fine, and some community service. Otherwise, they could be charged with a felony."

Patrick choked on a forkful of something and then released a huge gulp before responding to this new glut of information from Coach.

114

"I hope they go easy on them," Patrick said, thinking about how his own goose would have been cooked if he had gotten caught instead of Bull.

"That takes a big man to say that, Patrick. I'm proud of you, especially since they tried to blame you two for the entire incident."

"Did anyone believe their story?"Josh interjected.

"Of course not. It just didn't make any sense. Why would you steal a kangaroo from the zoo when your father was sending you one? Those boys could learn a thing or two from you and Patrick about honesty and integrity. And this might be the lesson they need. There's only one thing that the boys said that the police haven't been able to check out yet?"

"What's that?" Patrick asked nervously.

"Do you remember that janitor that we used to have? Jethro, I think his name was."

"Yeah," Patrick answered, averting Josh's gaze from across the table.

"Pudge said that it was Jethro who delivered the kangaroo, but unfortunately Jethro left for a two week vacation a couple of days after the incident occurred and the police never had a chance to question him."

"Phew," Patrick exhaled reflexively. "Will Bull be able to play basketball on the team again this season?"

"Well, that's hard to say. I won't have him back on my team until he completes his sentence. However, I heard a rumor that he might move over to Redmont."

"Redmont?" Patrick's voice cracked in surprise. "They're our biggest competitors."

"Yes, his father lives over there and is pretty good friends with the middle school coach. From what I've heard, he could have a starting spot in the lineup over there right away." Coach paused for a moment and addressed Josh directly. "Redmont is our biggest rival. Over the past five years, we've gone up against them for the league championship. We've only beaten them once in all of those years. We're due. And with a couple of upstanding, hardworking boys like yourselves on the team, we should be able to win this year, with or without Bull on the team."

The two boys were gluttons of guilt, as well as chicken casserole, by the time they finished eating their dinners and Tara began to clear their plates.

"How about a tour of the house before dessert?" she suggested. "I made blueberry cheesecake. You'll need to get a little exercise to make room for it."

They all stood up and stretched as Coach led the way up the wide, winding staircase in the foyer.

"We still have a lot of work to do," Coach explained, going into explicit detail as to what needed to be done as they walked from room to room to room. Josh was interested in how the transformation would take place, while Patrick mostly looked for opportunities to crack jokes about whatever he could.

When they came to the last door, Tara opened it hesitantly. "This would have been the nursery," she said.

Tucked into the corner of the large, but vacant room were two baby bassinets and two cribs, covered partially with sheets. Other baby paraphernalia, such as colorful mobiles, stuffed animals, and a rocking chair, littered the room, but were barely recognizable under a thick layer of dust. The room haunted Josh. It wouldn't have surprised him if eerie music mysteriously began to play or if a miniature clown was to have suddenly popped up out of a creepy jack in the box.

But those images disappeared and the reality of what this room had meant to the Webbers was reawakened in Josh's mind when Tara spoke again.

"I'm not sure what to do with this room. I know it's probably unhealthy, but sometimes I come in here and sit and rock and think about what could have been. I just don't want to forget my babies, even though I didn't have a chance to get to know them."

"You should have a yard sale and get rid of all this junk. You could make a lot of money." The obnoxious suggestion came from Patrick.

"Or you could keep it until you're ready to let it go and then donate it to a children's charity, a crisis pregnancy center or something," Josh suggested tenderly, while he elbowed Patrick in the ribs to prevent him from spewing out yet another insensitive remark.

"Sometimes I think it would be a lot easier just to sell everything, including the house, and just start over - maybe build a little log cabin in the woods or something. But then I think to myself, who would buy this place the way it is?" Coach concurred.

"Oh, I would," Josh exclaimed. "It would be awesome to work on it, but then, a log cabin doesn't sound too bad either."

"When do you go back to Australia, Josh?" Coach asked.

"I'm scheduled to go back on December 23rd, two days before Christmas."

"Do you remember earlier when I mentioned that I wanted to talk to you about something?" Coach asked, but didn't wait for an answer. "Well, maybe now is the time. Would you consider either staying here for Christmas and then staying through the end of the basketball season or going home for Christmas and then coming back for the remainder of the season?"

"How long would that be?"

"The regular season ends in mid January and then if we win the league championship, we would go on to the regional playoffs which would last until around the first week of February."

"Whoa, that's a long time," Josh said under his breath, considering the extensive amount of additional time that he would have to be away from Sarah. On the other hand, what did he have to lose? If he could let Sarah know that he was okay and tell her to hang in there just a little bit longer, this fantasy dream world in which he was living wouldn't have to end in less than a month. Of course, if the kangaroo kidnapping caper was ever uncovered, leaving Westbrook sooner rather than later, might be a welcome option.

"I know it probably seems like a long time for you to be away from your family, but if you decided you wanted to go home for the holidays and then come back here, Tara and I would be happy to have you stay with us. Or, if you want to just stay here for the holidays with us, you're welcome to do that, too. Whatever works for you."

Josh was beginning to wonder why Coach wanted to do this. Was he doing this just so the team would have a better chance of winning the league championship? If so, Josh would have to be sure that he didn't let himself become too attached to Coach and his wife. He knew that it would be difficult not to become emotionally involved since Coach was the first male role model that Josh had been able to relate to since his father had died. After all, the man watched the Stooges, loved basketball, and was into building, three interests which Josh and his own father had shared in the past.

"Thanks, Coach," Josh answered after much contemplation. "I'd like to think about it for awhile. Could I let you know later?"

Coach assured him that he could, and the foursome headed down the stairs and into the living room where they devoured Tara's homemade blueberry cheesecake.

The night air was frigid and the sky was clear as the two boys stepped outside, ending their leisurely, yet somewhat awkward evening with the Webbers. Their pace on the way home was quicker than it had been on the walk over as the biting, below freezing temperatures beckoned them to seek warmth and shelter.

"Do you feel guilty, Josh?" Patrick asked, his breath visible in the darkness.

"About what?" Josh asked, increasing his gait to a steady jog. "You mean because Coach said that Bull could learn something from us about honesty and integrity?"

"Exactly. And I was just thinking that if I feel this guilty," Patrick huffed and puffed, "you must really feel bad. I mean all I did was lie about this one little thing with the kangaroo. But you, your whole life is a gigantic lie right now. I never thought about what it must be like for you until tonight. You must feel like a total fake, a cheat and a fraud."

"Well, to tell you the truth, I've never really looked at it that way until now. I feel worse about the kangaroo thing than I do about impersonating JC because no one is getting hurt by that. I guess I just feel bad because Bull and Pudge are taking the heat for something that we were partially responsible for. Even though Bull has never been nice to me, I'm not sure he's getting what he deserves. And all the rest of this, I'm just doing so that

118

Sarah and I have a better chance of being able to stay together."

"Well, the way I've been trying to look at what happened with the kangaroo from the zoo is that it wouldn't have become such a big deal if Bull hadn't butt in and stolen it. It would have gone back to the zoo that morning and none of this would have happened. So, in a way, he is getting what he deserves," Patrick tried to rationalize to ease his own conscience. "So, what did you think of dinner?"

"The food was good. The conversation got a little weird at times, I thought, but there was a bright side to it," Josh sparked.

"Are you kidding, Josh? When was this? Between the time I insulted Tara's bra size or when I told her she should get rid of the baby junk in her house?"

Josh chuckled. "Well, okay, so maybe *you* didn't think there were any bright sides to the night, but I did. I lost my mom and dad on the exact same day that they lost their twins. Isn't that weird?"

"And that's a bright side?" Patrick questioned cynically.

"Well, it sort of made me feel connected to them," Josh admitted.

"So, how did that make you feel *connected*?"

Josh thought that he heard a trace of sarcasm in Patrick's voice when he said the word *connected*. He felt as though Patrick would only be patronizing him if he were to continue discussing this with him.

"Never mind," Josh replied bluntly. "It's not important. Besides, if you can't see how this would make make me feel connected to them, I guess you're just not deep enough to understand what I've been going through for the past three years. Let's just drop it."

"Fine, let's do that!" Patrick answered in a hostile tone and then picked up his pace to beat Josh home.

Neither boy was quite sure why the other had reacted with such vengeance, but neither one of them said another word until long after they were back to Patrick's house and laying in their separate bunk beds.

It was Patrick who finally broke the silence. In a quiet voice, he asked, "What's it like to lose your parents?"

119

"Well," Josh began, after pondering the question for a moment, "have you ever fallen asleep and had a bad dream and even though you're asleep, you have this sickening feeling in your stomach and you keep wanting it to go away, but it won't?"

"Yeah, I guess," Patrick answered cautiously. "And then something happens, like the alarm goes off and you wake up and for a minute you still have that sinking feeling, but then as soon as you're awake, you realize it was a dream and it goes away."

"Yeah, that's it exactly. Only when you lose your parents, it's the exact opposite. You have that sick feeling in your stomach after you wake up and pretty much all the time."

"All the time?"

"All the time, for awhile, anyway. Sarah and I were living with my grandma for a long time and I can't remember a day when I didn't feel that way."

"Whoa," Patrick exclaimed faintly.

"But do you know what's even worse than that?"

"What?" Patrick wanted to know.

"Sometimes when I fall asleep, I dream that my mom and dad are alive. And it's really weird because a lot of times when I'm awake, it's hard for me to remember what they were like, like how they looked or how they talked or what they would say. But when I see them in my dreams, they are exactly like they were in real life. They look exactly like they did and when they talk they not only sound the same, they say the same kinds of things they would say in that same situation, if they were alive. One time, in a dream, my dad and I were building the log cabin that he and I were supposed to build and I knew he had died, but somehow he was alive again, or it was a mistake and he didn't really die. Sometimes I dream that my mom and I are shooting hoops at our old house in the driveway and that I'm little again. The sick feeling goes away while I'm asleep, but then when I wake up it comes back. That's why I said it's the exact opposite of having a bad dream and having that sick feeling go away, because instead of going away when you wake up, it comes back."

"It's kind of good though because at least you get to see them," Patrick replied sheepishly, not knowing what else to say.

"This is going to sound stupid, but when I was younger and they used to show up in my dreams, I figured it was really them and that was God's way of letting me spend time with them. But then when I got older, I started to think that my brain had just stored up all these memories of them and that's why when I saw them in my dreams they were exactly like they were when they were alive."

Patrick shrugged. "It's hard to say."

"The other thing that I remember, you know about having that sick feeling in my stomach all the time, was when I'd be watching TV and all of a sudden I'd laugh at something that someone would say or do, and I'd realize that I was laughing, like it was such a big deal to be doing that. At the beginning, when it first started to happen, I felt bad for laughing, like if I was laughing, it meant that I was starting to forget about my parents. I thought I was supposed to be sad for the rest of my life. Then my grandma told me that it was okay to be happy, that my mom and dad would want me to be happy. She said that they were happy being with Jesus. I couldn't understand how they could be happy with Him without us around, but then what did I know?"

Patrick kind of laughed, and Josh continued with his story, oblivious as to whether or not Patrick really wanted to hear it.

"Things were okay for awhile until my grandma burned down her trailer."

"How did she do that?" Patrick asked, lowering his upper body down from the top bunk, so that he was hanging upside down in Josh's face when Josh recounted this tale. "Was it an accident or did she mean to do it?"

"Well, I guess you could say it was an accident. She was getting a little senile and she started thinking that there were little green men in UFOs flying all around. We lived on a mountain in California in the middle of nowhere. We saw a lot of shooting stars up there and she started freaking out. For some reason, she thought that the red glow from the burners on the stove would scare them away, so almost every night she would turn on the stove when we were getting ready for bed. She thought that the aliens were afraid of lights, especially red and green ones."

"Why didn't she just get a big neon beer sign and stick it in the window?" Patrick asked, trying to make a joke.

"Very funny," Josh said dryly. "Besides I heard that they like beer."

"So, what happened?"

"The first night that she did it, we... I mean, Sarah, was very freaked out about it, not just about the burners being on, but also because she was afraid that maybe there really were little green men out there. I told her to go in and tell Grandma that she was scared and to ask her if she could sleep in Grandma's bed. Then I would go and turn off the burners."

"Did it work? Obviously not, or you wouldn't be telling me this story about the trailer burning down," Patrick answered his own question.

"Actually, it did work that night, but it went on for days. She got more and more paranoid. She'd stand out on the front steps in the middle of the night and yell, 'Get the heck out of here you little green men!' Or she would get up in the middle of the night and sit in the living room in pitch darkness, looking out the window through a pair of binoculars and cursing at imaginary sightings of aliens. It was so weird to hear her cuss. I never heard a single cuss word ever come out of her mouth before, so in some ways, it was kind of funny when she did it."

"That's pretty freaky," Patrick stated, his interest still sparked. "So, when did the trailer finally go up in smoke?"

"Well, it was kind of weird. We thought she was getting better. For about a week, she didn't mention the UFOs or the little green men. She wasn't turning the burners on anymore at night either. I got pretty lax and figured everything was going to be all right. Then one night, I woke up and smelled smoke coming from the kitchen. By the time I got Sarah and my grandma outside, the trailer was toast."

"Was everybody okay?"

"Yeah, we all got out okay, but we didn't have much left. Sarah must have had a feeling that something like this was going to happen cause she grabbed a photo album that she had stashed under her bed. And I grabbed my basketball, of all things. It's a good thing that Sarah grabbed those pictures. Otherwise, we wouldn't have any pictures of us when we were little or of my parents left at all. There was one good thing that came out of the trailer burning down though."

"What was that?"

"It must have scared away all the little green men cause we never did see them again."

"Very funny!" Patrick yelled and threw his pillow down from the top bunk. Did you just make that whole story up?"

"No, I'm sorry to say, every word of it is true."

"At least you can laugh about it," Patrick said. "Hey, I'm sorry about the way I acted before. I was just feeling sorry for myself because you said I wasn't deep."

"Really? I'm sorry. I didn't really mean anything by it. Sometimes I feel like I'm just so different than other people because I think about everything so much. I don't think I would be like this if my mom and dad were still alive. I think I'd be more like you. I'd like to be more like you," Josh admitted.

"So, where do you think your parents are?" Patrick asked.

"In Heaven," Josh replied matter of factly.

"Well, where do you think that is?"

"I don't know, just with God somewhere."

"How do you know?"

"Cause my grandma told me that that's where they were," Josh answered, wishing that Patrick would discontinue this line of questioning.

"Josh, correct me if I'm wrong, but isn't this the same grandmother who thought that there were little green men outside of her trailer and so she burnt it down?" Patrick teased.

"Yes." Josh couldn't help but smile at this bit of irony. "But she told me this a long time before she burnt the trailer down or even started seeing little green men, okay?"

"Okay."

"So, do you know anything else about why Coach and Tara can't have kids?" Josh decided to change the subject.

"Well, my mom said that when Tara got pregnant with the twins, she had been taking fraternity drugs."

"Fraternity drugs? You mean she was doing illegal drugs?" Josh lowered his voice to a whisper.

"No, no, fraternity drugs - they help women get pregnant," Patrick assured him.

"No, not fraternity drugs, you doof, you must mean fertility drugs. A fraternity is something guys belong to in college. Fertility drugs are what you take to get pregnant," Josh admonished him.

"I *know* what a fraternity is," Patrick defended himself. "I just got the words mixed up. What I was trying to say was that it was hard for her to get pregnant in the first place. After the accident, she was probably even more messed up."

In spite of the hour, Patrick now seemed to be in a talkative mood himself, after having been stifled for so long during the boys' silent treatment episode and then again when Josh had shared his story. "Do you believe in reincarnation? You know where you come back as someone or something else after you die?"

"I *know* what reincarnation is." Now Josh was sitting on the other side of the defense post.

"Well, do you believe in it?"

"No," Josh answered.

"Why not?" Patrick badgered him.

"I just don't," Josh stated firmly.

"Did you know that there are people in other countries who *do* believe in it?"

Josh glanced up at Patrick from his bunk and noticed his eyes widening and a little stream of drool starting to seep out of the corner of his mouth, the way it often did when he was getting ready to tell someone something that he thought was really exciting. He had had that same look and the saliva thing going on that first night when he had told Josh about his pickled frog project.

Josh kept his eye on the little stream of drool as Patrick continued. "There are people who walk around all skinny and scrawny, virtually starving to death and they won't even think about making the hundreds of cows in the streets into nice little, juicy burgers. And the cows, they're walking around all skinny and scrawny, too. And do you know why? The people think that the animals, even the bugs, might be some of their long lost relatives and they don't want to eat them. Can you believe that?"

Josh was actually becoming quite drowsy now, as he had used up most of his mental energy when he'd divulged his emotional recollections to Patrick. "Uh huh," he managed to mumble from below, opening one eye from time to time to check on the drool situation.

"You know, if that was me, if I was a bug or a sick looking cow, I wouldn't take it. I'd check into the nearest roach motel or I'd find my way to the nearest meat packing plant. And do you know why I'd do that?" Patrick waited for another weak acknowledgement from his friend before he continued. " So that I could come back as something better! Think about it! If you were a cow and you knew if someone ate you, you'd get to come back as something better, wouldn't you want someone to eat you? If these people would apply a little more logic to their belief systems, they might not be going hungry." Patrick seemed quite impressed with his own brand of logic, and as Josh drifted off to sleep, he could have sworn he heard Patrick mutter, "And this guy didn't think I was deep!"

Chapter Twelve

That night he had "the dream" again. Only this dream was not the kind of dream he had described to Patrick earlier, where he went to sleep, spent time with his parents, and then woke up to the gut wrenching reality of their absence. No, this was even worse. It was a sheet thrashing, wake up in a cold sweat kind of dream.

The first time that he'd had the dream was about six weeks after his parents had died, when he and Sarah were first living with their grandmother. In the dream he was looking up at Boulder on the Shoulder when all of a sudden a gigantic hand came up from behind it. The hand was so mammoth that it made the boulder resemble a garden pea, the kind he used to flick off the side of his plate, aiming for his sister's milk or mashed potatoes or anything else he could ruin on her plate. The index finger on this monstrous hand was rounding back to meet the thumb to initiate the same type of flick that Jeff had so often capitulated. With one quick flick, that finger sent the boulder hurling down the mountainside right into the path of Jeff's parents' car.

Only, oddly enough, it wasn't the car that they had actually been driving that day. Instead, the car in the dream was one of Jeff's shiny red remote control cars, and Jeff, who found himself watching from a short distance away, was holding the car's remote control. He jerked the lever back and forth, into reverse and then forward again, desperately trying to get the car out of the path of the blasted rock that was now hurling down the mountain in slow motion. But no matter what Jeff did to the lever, he couldn't move the car out of the path or stop the rock from plummeting down.

What was happening was beyond his control. There was nothing that he could do, even in the dream, to save his parents' lives. Instead, he watched in horror, hearing his mother scream, as the reality of the accident unfolded before his very eyes. The boulder bounded down the mountainside, now raging full speed, hitting the car, flipping it over, and sending it plunging into the rushing river below.

He had awakened in a cold sweat and had flown into his grandmother's bed where she had held him closely and they had cried together for the first time ever.

When Jeff had told her that he was afraid to go back to sleep because he was afraid he'd have that dream again, she had made a suggestion. "If you do have the dream again, try to picture that same hand being held out to your mom and dad and lifting them up into Heaven."

About eight weeks later, Jeff did have the dream again. The dream changed a little this time, as it would each time he'd have it in the future. This time, the boulder was a giant basketball bouncing down the cliff and demolishing the remote control car as both items plunged into the water below. Jeff had again been at the controls for the remote control car and unable to prevent the accident. But this time, the giant hand had lifted his parents into the sky toward Heaven where they disappeared into a cloud.

That was the last time he'd had the dream until long after he and Sarah had moved in with the Johnsons, more than a year later. In this dream, the basketball had been transformed into a giant pea and the goliath fingers were taking aim to send it hurling down the hill. The remote control car with Jeff in control remained, but this time after the crash, not only did he see his mom and dad being taken up to Heaven in the palm of the giant hand, he also saw his grandmother resting there, waving happily as she made her way towards Heaven, as well. She nudged her son and his wife and instructed them to look downward, where they, too, smiled and waved goodbye to Jeff and Sarah who were left standing on a hillside across from where Boulder on the Shoulder had been.

The next day Mrs. Johnson had received a call from the nursing home where the children's grandmother had been living since the trailer had burnt down, informing her that Jeff and Sarah's grandmother had passed away during the night.

When Mrs. Johnson had come in to break the news to Jeff and Sarah, Jeff had not been the least bit surprised. "I had a feeling that she died," Jeff had informed Mrs. Johnson. "I was just telling Sarah about the dream I had

127

last night. She was in the sky with our mom and dad. She smiled at us and waved goodbye."

"You saw them in the sky?" Mrs. Johnson had been surprised by Jeff's remark.

"Yes, in my dream," he had repeated. "I've had the dream before. Grandma knew about it. It used to be really scary cause I'd relive the whole accident." He had gone on to tell Mrs. Johnson the gory details of the dream and how his grandmother had told him to picture his mom and dad being lifted up to Heaven by the giant hand. "She was with them last night in the dream and she seemed really happy. It was like she was her old self again, too. That's why I wasn't very surprised when you told me that she had died. I sort of already knew."

"Tell me more about this dream, Jeff, about the giant hand," Mrs. Johnson had coaxed. "Whose hand do you think it is?"

Jeff had shrugged, not wanting to say.

"Do you think it could have been God's hand?" Mrs. Johnson had questioned.

"Maybe. I think it might be God's hand, but I don't want to say that because I don't want Him to get mad at me."

"Why do you think He would get mad at you?"

"He might think that I'm blaming Him for what happened to my mom and dad."

"Oh, I see," Mrs. Johnson had concurred, not being quite sure of what to say next, so she had asked another question. "Why do you think that the car in your dream is your remote control car and not your parents' real car?"

"I don't know," Jeff had answered blankly.

"Well, in the dream, you were holding the remote, and you couldn't get the car to move, right?"

"Right. In my dream, I tried to move the car, but I couldn't. It was all my fault. I couldn't save them, even though I knew the boulder was going to fall," he had whimpered dejectedly.

"In the dream, you felt like it was all your fault. Do you feel like it was all your fault in real life, as well?"

"Well, sometimes I do," Jeff had admitted.

"Why? You and Sarah were at home. How could it have possibly been your fault?"

"The reason that my mom and dad were at that exact spot when the boulder came down was because I kept them from leaving when they wanted to."

"What do you mean?" Mrs. Johnson had asked, brushing the hair out of his face as he hung his head low.

"My mom and dad were all excited about showing us the lot they were thinking about buying. They wanted me to come along, but I kept saying, ' I want to stay home, I want to stay home.' We went back and forth about it for about ten minutes and then Sarah asked if she could stay home, too. When they finally said that both of us could stay home, Mom started telling me not to be mean to Sarah or lock her in the neighbor's dog cage like I'd done once before and to remember to do this and not to do that. If I would have just hopped in the car when they first said they were going, they wouldn't have been in that exact spot when the boulder fell."

"Oh, Jeff," Mrs. Johnson had sympathized, "I had no idea that you were carrying this around with you. You mustn't blame yourself. It wasn't your fault; it was beyond your control. It was beyond anyone's control."

"I guess that kind of bugs me, too, that I can't control what happens to me or to anyone else."

"I can see why you feel like that, Jeff. You've been moved around from place to place ever since your parents died. Other people are always making decisions for you. And you know, there are things that you can't control, but there are even more things that you will be able to control in the future. I know it doesn't seem like it now, but when you're a little older, you will have control over many things in your life. I just want to tell you this now, because I see how much all of this is bothering you. I want to give you something to keep you going until that day when you do have more control over your life. I don't want to see you mess up your life because of how you are feeling right now. Even though, you may feel desperate about your situation today, you still need to think carefully about the choices you make. One bad choice can affect you for the rest of your life."

Jeff had not been exactly sure what Mrs. Johnson had been referring to, perhaps to drugs or to any number of other diversions out there to take one's mind off of one's problems. As for Jeff, he didn't really consider himself a candidate for this lecture. He had been one of the lucky ones, able to learn from the mistakes he had seen other people make. He had seen those mistakes in the faces of other foster kids during his travels throughout the state of California. Countless nameless faces, some even younger than Sarah, had eyes that were void of clarity and perception and bodies that were lifeless and limp, having been robbed of their childhoods by their own self inflicted addictions.

They were visions that he would have liked to erase from his memory, as well as from Sarah's, but as long as the images remained, he knew that no temptation to deviate in their footsteps would ever cross his mind.

"I've seen a lot of messed up people," he had assured Mrs. Johnson. "I don't even want to remember it, let alone go there myself."

The advice to weigh his decisions before he acted upon them would stay with Jeff for the rest of his life, but ironically, it was this advice and the concept that someday he would be able to have control over his life that catapulted him into making the decision to leave the Johnsons on the eve of his fourteenth birthday.

Other questions that concerned Jeff had surfaced that morning after his grandmother had died. "There's other stuff I just don't get," Josh had continued when he had recognized that her attentive gaze was still upon him. "Like why does horrible stuff have to happen? And when it does, was it supposed to happen? Did God know ahead of time that it was going to happen or does it just happen? Like when a drunk driver goes out and kills someone, does it happen because God wants it to or just because some guy broke the law and was driving drunk?"

"I wish I had the answers for you," Mrs. Johnson had answered, "but unfortunately I don't think anyone really knows for sure. All I know for sure is that you never really know what's ahead. All you can do is to live each day to the fullest and try not to let the little things get you down. Treat the people you love, everyday, the way you would treat them if you knew it was your last day with them. Because you never know, it could be."

"I feel like Sarah and I learned that the hard way," Jeff had added.

Sarah had been listening intently and silently, thus far, throughout the entire conversation. When she had finally spoken, it had been her sweet voice of innocence and her childlike wisdom that had astonished both Jeff and Mrs. Johnson.

"Grandma used to read me Bible stories," she had begun. "There was a guy like you, Jeff, in one of them. His name was Joseph and he used to have weird dreams like you do. A bunch of bad things happened to him. His brothers sold him as a slave, then he was put in jail, but he got out and the king put him in charge of all his stuff. All the while he was going through rough times, God hadn't forgotten about him. Even though bad things happened to him, God still made good things come out of it. The way I see it, if you have Jesus in your heart, you don't have to worry about what happens to you because He's going to be with you to help you get through it. And if He takes you home, then He takes you home. We all have to go sometime."

After that, Jeff and Mrs. Johnson had become quiet. It was obvious that Sarah's simple faith and understanding were the elements that had sustained her thus far and had given her wisdom beyond her years.

That was the last time he'd had the dream, the night that his grandmother had died. But now, he was having the dream again.

He tossed and turned and burned profusely in the bottom bunk as he watched the giant finger flick the pea sized boulder down the steep terrain and onto his parents' car. The remote control car no longer existed and he could see that his mom, dad, and grandmother were being airlifted up to Heaven, stopping just outside of a golden gate. Now their bodies had become translucent and they wore flowing robes of the purest white Jeff had ever seen.

Then the strangest thing, beyond Jeff's wildest imaginings, transpired. At that very moment, Coach Webber and his wife appeared at the golden gate. This frightened Jeff immensely. Was this some kind of premonition of things to come? Would this vision foretell their destinies as it had foretold his grandmother's passing? Even in his sleep, it scared him. But then he noticed that their bodies were normal, not translucent like his parents' or grandmother's, and that they were wearing normal clothes. In fact, Coach was wearing the worn out pair of sweats with the hole in the knee that he always wore for practice.

Next to them were the tiny white bassinets from the nursery, only they hauntingly resembled tiny, white coffins with open lids. Jeff tried to purge this morbid image from his mind, shaking his head to blur the pictures that had become unwelcome intruders in his head.

When he looked back again, he saw Coach and his wife bending over the tiny bassinets that were now lidless. Each one picked up a baby. The infant that Mr. Webber was holding was wrapped loosely in a blue blanket, while Mrs. Webber held a baby wrapped in pink. Jeff could see the smiling babies wiggling and cooing as the Webbers kissed them one last time and handed them over to Jeff's mom and dad.

"Whoa!" Jeff sprang up in his bed, cracking his head on one of the wooden slats above. It took a few minutes for him to catch his breath and for his heart to stop racing. He wished that Mrs. Johnson or Sarah were there to help him through this one. He shivered in the darkness and prayed to God to take away his fears.

Chapter Thirteen

Perhaps there had been some ingredient in one of the sidedishes or in the turkey itself that had triggered the chemical reaction that occurred in Josh, Patrick, and Jennifer soon after they had eaten Thanksgiving dinner that day. Whatever it was, it hadn't sent anyone to the hospital, but rather, it had sent all three into mindless fits of giddiness that lasted throughout the entire evening. No one could even remember when the frivolity had begun, but they knew that it was sometime after the adults and the younger children in the Baker and Watson families had retired to Patrick's living room to watch TV, and the threesome had ended up at the kitchen table alone, eating pumpkin pie smothered with whipped cream.

Patrick had taken it upon himself to ignite an explosive conversation by simply asking Jennifer to give him one good reason why she had ever liked Bull.

"He was one of the few guys who was taller than me," Jennifer answered casually, hoping that Patrick would drop the subject if she threw him a bone.

"ANNNT!" Patrick buzzed, suggesting that the answer was unacceptable. "I need another reason. That wasn't good enough. Besides the only reason he's taller than you is because this is his third time going through the eighth grade."

"Oh, it is not," Jennifer defended Bull. "It's only his second time through. And why are you all of a sudden getting on his case again when you were being so sympathetic towards him when he got busted with the kangaroo?"

"Well, he didn't get in as much trouble as I thought he would. He'll probably only have to do some community service and Coach said he might be moving to Redmont so that he can play basketball for them. So, did you think he was cute?" Patrick continued with his obnoxious line of questioning.

"Why? Did you think he was?" Jennifer threw the question back at Patrick.

"How should I know?" Patrick said defensively. "I'm a guy - how should I know if another guy is good looking?"

" How come guys always act like they don't know if other guys are good looking or not? Girls aren't like that. We'll tell you right out whether or not we think another girl is cute."

"Okay, I'll tell you who I think is cute." Patrick agreed to break with male tradition. "I'm definitely a hunk and Josh here, he's okay, too. Now, back to the reasons you went out with Bull. We could do a top ten list - reason number 10 - you liked going out with someone whose shoe size was higher than his IQ."

Josh decided that he didn't like where this conversation was going, so he came to Jennifer's rescue by changing the subject. "Hey, you guys, there's something I've been wanting to ask you. Does Bull have a first name? I mean I've never heard anyone call him anything but Bull or Mr. Bull, including Mrs. Grouse and Coach Webber."

Patrick switched gears in anticipation of this newest twist in the conversation, abandoning the top ten list to Jennifer and Josh's relief. "Yeah, but you don't want to know what it is. Trust me."

"Yes I do. Is it really weird or something?" Josh persisted.

"I'm not going to tell him what it is. You can tell him if you want to, Jennifer, but I think we should make him guess."

"Yes, I rather like that idea, too," Jennifer agreed. "Let's make him guess."

"Well, you guys have to give me some clues, okay?" Josh insisted.

"Let's start by making him guess the names of some of the other members of his family!" Patrick suggested jovially.

"Do we have to?" Josh asked.

"How bout ... yes," Jennifer answered.

"Here is your first clue. He has an older brother who is a real pushover. You can tell him anything and he'll believe it. Do you want to try to guess his name?" Patrick asked whimsically. "Think about it. He'll believe anything you tell him."

"I don't know - Fred?" Josh blurted out.

"Josh, I'm very disappointed in you," Patrick flattened his friend's ego. "It was Gulla."

"Gulla? What kind of a name is Gulla?" Josh wondered until he put the first and last names together. "Gulla Bull, Gulla Bull, oh gullible!" He chuckled, finally catching on and flicking a spoonful of whipped cream onto Patrick's nose."Oh, I see where this is going!"

"Oh, no, wait. Gullible, that's not Bull's brother's name; that would be *you* !" Patrick laughed hysterically at his own joke, wiping the whipped cream off of his nose and disgustingly licking it off of his finger. "You know if Coach's wife would have married Bull instead of marrying Coach, you know what her name would be?"

Jennifer and Josh took a moment to put the two names together.

"Tara Bull. Terrible!" Jennifer shouted, thrilled with her deduction.

"Okay, okay, I have another one," Patrick sputtered in anticipation. "Remember when we saw Bull's mom leaving the house the other morning? She's divorced, you know, and not dating anyone. Do you know what *her* name is?"

Josh and Jennifer both shook their heads negatively.

"Availa. Her name's Availa. Get it? Available!" Patrick roared at his own wit. "And, and..." Patrick's saliva pool was beginning to fill up again and creep toward the corner of his mouth, "Bull has an uncle who lives in Africa and he likes to eat people."

"Let me guess," Josh interrupted euphorically. "His name is Canna! Canna Bull! Cannibal!"

Now all three were in hysterics. Jennifer was doubled over, with tears of comic relief streaming down her cheeks. Patrick continued to rip off puns, as well as occasional unannounced turkey farts.

"His dad is a tough guy, like a Hefty bag. Any guesses on what his name is?" Patrick toyed with them. "Dura, his name is Dura! Durable! Come on, you guys, don't give up so easily. You can do this! And his wonderful little sister, her name would be... oops! I let a stinkie!"

"Her name is Oops I Let A Stinkie?" Josh teased. "That's a funny name."

"Is her name Adora Bull?" Jennifer guessed.

"Yes, you are correct!" Patrick congratulated his cousin in his game show host voice. "I think I might have burned a hole right through these pants and right through the bottom of this chair."

Jennifer frowned disdainfully and backed away.

"So, what is *Bull's* first name?" Josh asked, also distancing himself from Patrick.

"Are you sure you want to go there now? I mean there are a lot more relatives that you can guess first. There's his grandma, Lika, his grandpa the tax consultant, Deducta, and his bratty little cousin, Incorriga."

"As much fun as that sounds, let's just skip those and get down to what *Bull's* first name is."

"Okay, be that way. Here's your clue. You remember Bull's uncle Canna? Well, this guy's always trying to take a bite out of Bull." Immediately after Patrick gave this clue, he began singing the final Jeopardy tune as he waited for Josh's coveted answer.

"Tasty Bull, Delecta Bull?" Josh blurted, grasping for straws. "I don't know."

"ANNNT!" Patrick initiated his obnoxious buzzer sound again. "No, but I like that Delecta Bull, I wish I'd thought of that. The correct answer is ... Jennifer, would you do the honors?"

"Eddy Bull!" Jennifer announced zealously.

"Ding! Ding! Ding!" That is correct!" Patrick blared, moving almost instantaneously on to a new adventure."Hey, I know what we can do!" Patrick sounded rejuvenated now that a clever, new idea had filled his head. "We can play CLUELESS!"

"Don't you mean CLUE?" Jennifer asked.

"No, no. It's a new game. My mom bought it. I think she was going to give it to you for Christmas, Jennifer, but she won't mind if we play it now. It's like CLUE, but it's based on a mall and you have to figure out which chick buys what outfit at what store and for how much."

"It sounds like fun," Josh said in a cynical tone.

"Good, I'll go get it!" Patrick scurried up the stairs to his parents' room to retrieve the game, ignoring the sarcasm in Josh's response.

Josh and Jennifer were alone in the kitchen for a brief moment, awkwardly awaiting Patrick's return when Jennifer's mother, father, and little sister entered and informed her that it was time to go.

"You know what tomorrow is, don't you Jennifer?" her mother quipped when Jennifer showed reluctance to leave. "It's the biggest shopping day of the year. We have to get up early to get to the mall in time for all of the early bird specials."

"That's one thing I've never been able to understand. Why would you want to go to the mall on the day that is known to be the busiest shopping day of the year? It seems ludicrous!" Jennifer's dad chuckled, handing Jennifer her jacket.

"That's when all the best sales are!" Jennifer, Mrs. Watson, and Mrs. Baker all admonished him in unison.

"You've trained her well," Mr. Baker joined in, referring to Jennifer's thorough understanding of North American women's shopping rituals.

It was clear to see that in these two households, as much as turkey, dressing, sweet potatoes and pumpkin pie were part of the Thanksgiving holiday tradition, shopping on the day after Thanksgiving, was an even more treasured family rite.

"Why don't you and Patrick come, too?" Mrs. Watson invited Josh. "We'll pick you up at 6:45, it'll be fun!"

"Where are we going?" Patrick asked, bounding down the staircase while carrying the CLUELESS game under his arm. "Are you guys going home right now?" he lamented.

"We're going Christmas shopping tomorrow morning," Jennifer informed him, suddenly noticing that a dollop of whipped cream remained beneath his nose. "You've got a little something right there," she pointed to the same spot on her face to show him where it was.

He touched the spot, not noticing that his finger now was tainted with the white foam. "Did I get it?" he asked.

Amos took advantage of the opportunity to get even with him by jumping into the conversation. "You've got a little something over here, too," He said pointing to his left cheek and then drawing a line down with his finger.

Patrick followed suit, not realizing that by doing so, he had spread the foamy cream down his entire cheek.

Patrick's mother got into the action, as well."Honey, honey, there's a little more right there on your chin."

Patrick smeared the remainder of the sticky goo on to his chin. By now everyone in the room was giggling. Patrick had inadvertently spread the whipped cream from his nose, down his cheek, and onto his chin. He glanced into the foyer mirror and wailed, "Hey, you guys, that is *not* funny. That's not funny at all!" He smiled at the white streak, for the first time realizing how it felt to be the recipient of a silly practical joke.

Early the next morning, the overzealous sisters rounded up the troops and headed for the nearest mall twenty two miles away. The troops, in this case, only turned out to be a party of three, Jennifer, Josh and Patrick, who were anxious to leave their small town for some action in the suburban shopping mall. Amos and Jennifer's little sister had opted to stay home with their fathers, having been promised a trip to visit Santa Claus first thing on Saturday.

The parking lot was filling up quickly. Mrs. Baker eyed an empty space close to one of the entrances and instantaneously switched on her blinker to stake her claim. But before she had a chance to initiate a left turn into the space, a woman driving an oversized SUV and kibitzing on her cell phone, came straight toward them and stole the parking space right out from under them.

"Did you see that? She pretended that she didn't even see us!" Patrick's mother exploded.

"What an inconsiderate woman!" Mrs. Watson exclaimed.

"Nobody does that to my aunt!" Patrick announced boldly, throwing open the minivan's sliding door and jumping out impulsively.

The preoccupied female had already exited her vehicle, but had left the motor running, as if to insinuate that she would only be a minute if they just wanted to wait. That's when Patrick decided to take matters into his own hands.

"What are you going to do?" Patrick's mother rolled down her window and asked apprehensively.

"I'm going to teach her a lesson," he said, opening the door to the humming sport utility vehicle. With a sudden click, click, slam, slam, he was back in the minivan. "I hope she carries a spare set of keys," Patrick stated proudly.

"Patrick, I can't believe that you did that!" his mother scolded, doing her best to conceal a grin that wanted to spread across her face. "There were plenty of other parking spaces where we could have parked."

"Hey, what else could I do? You mess with my family, you mess with me!" he explained frankly.

Mrs. Watson hit the gas and headed for the opposite side of the mall. "I don't want to be here when she gets back!" she stated in a panic, speeding through the half empty lot.

Once inside, Josh, Jennifer, and Patrick explored the mall for hours, trying on clothes, checking out the latest, greatest CDs, and daring Patrick to get his belly button pierced at the earring shop.

When they grew tired of all that the mall had to offer, they dined on tacos a la food court and headed across the street to a giant toy store.

"Now this is more like it!" Patrick exclaimed as they walked through the tinsel town playhouse which was adorned with sparkling lights and tacky, oversized toys, presents, and ornaments.

As they made their way towards the first aisle, Patrick spotted a giant sign that read, "Donate A New Toy To A Needy Foster Child!" Immediately upon seeing it, Patrick began pulling toys off the shelf in front of him and loading them into the designated box below.

"Hey, Nerdbrain," Jennifer enlightened her cousin, "you're supposed to *buy* the toys before you donate them."

"Well, I can't afford to do that, Jennifer," he explained to his cousin as if what he was saying was common sense.

"What are you guys doing?" Josh asked, joining the two at the display.

"Nerdbrain is donating toys to foster kids without buying them first."

"I still don't see what's wrong with that," Patrick said in his own defense. "Do you?" he asked Josh.

"Well, nothing other than it is STEALING!" Josh answered vociferously, accentuating the last word so that it might sink in to Patrick's brain.

A manager of the store looked over when he heard Josh speaking so loudly, and Patrick proceeded to unload from the box all of the the items that he had illegally donated to it.

"Well, *I* can buy some," Josh reasoned aloud, realizing that he'd only used his gold card a few times for small increments of cash so far. "I have a very special place in my heart for foster kids."

"Yeah, especially for a certain little girl," Patrick whispered, nudging Josh in the ribs with his elbow. Josh shushed him so that Jennifer wouldn't get suspicious.

For the next twenty minutes, they terrorized the store on a whirlwind shopping spree, hoping that their efforts, now, would spread holiday cheer to the neediest of children, later. Patrick surfed the shopping cart, balancing in a squatting position as the wheels wobbled and rattled beneath him. Remote control cars, CLUELESS games, checkerboards, baseball gloves, hand held video games, fashion dolls, and everything else imaginable and within reach of Patrick's grasp, flew into the cart as Jennifer and Josh rolled him up and down each aisle.

"We'd better get something for our own brothers and sisters," Jennifer suggested, taking a breather.

"That's a good idea," Josh replied, thinking of what a great way that would be to surprise Sarah. He picked out a Tiny Tinkles baby doll and a Baywatch fashion doll complete with plastic lifesaving devices and a waverunner.

Just as the manager of the store was becoming suspicious of the three amigos again, Patrick hopped out of the cart and separated from Jennifer and Josh, as they headed into the check out lane.

Jennifer was holding a moose puppet for Amos and a Baywatch fashion doll ensemble for her little sister, identical to the one that Josh had picked out for Sarah.

"Go ahead and put them in the cart. I'll pay for them if you want," Josh offered generously.

"Oh, that's okay," Jennifer insisted. "I'll get these. You're already getting so much."

"I'll let you get these," Patrick said, resurfacing from beneath another load of merchandise, mostly sporting goods this time. "They're for Amos."

"These are for Amos?" Jennifer questioned, holding up a pair of inline skates that looked to be closer to Patrick's foot size than to that of his brother's.

"He'll grow into them. Okay, okay, they're for me," he finally confessed, glancing dejectedly toward Josh.

"That's okay. You can have them. I've been living at your house for the past few weeks, it's the least I can do. Grab some for Amos if you think he'd like some. Jennifer," he asked sensitively, "is there anything that you'd like?"

Jennifer declined sweetly and when the shopping spree was over, the damage rang up to the tune of $2027.42.

"Whoa!" the threesome exclaimed in unison when the total was revealed.

"Are you sure you want to spend this much on toys?" Jennifer asked.

"It's only money," Josh replied casually. "Besides it's for a good cause. Who else is going to look out for foster kids. They deserve to have a decent Christmas, too."

The clerk examined Josh suspiciously as he handed her the gold card. She called for the manager's approval, although the transaction had already received proper authorization before he arrived at the register. Josh held his breath as the overstressed, underpaid toy store manager shook his head at the employee who had called him over needlessly.

"There's no problem with this transaction," the manager informed her curtly. "Do you need any help out with these items?" he asked Josh, regaining his composure.

"Well, actually, most of this stuff is going to your box for foster kids over there," Josh said, pointing to the empty box.

"Are you serious?" The manager was astounded by the youth's generosity.

Josh assured him that he was, indeed, quite serious, as the clerk bagged the remaining items and the threesome darted across the crowded parking lot and back across the street toward the mall.

"That was invigorating!" Patrick proclaimed. "There's nothing like a good cruise through a toy store to put one in the holiday spirit!"

They joined Patrick in his festive mode as they made their way toward the designated meeting place inside the mall where both Mrs. Watson and Mrs. Baker were waiting patiently with achy feet, droopy eyelids, and cotton mouths, their voracious appetites for shopping having been satisfied.

All five marathon shoppers were exhausted on the ride home, yet they found contentment as they watched the sky fill with billowy clouds and begin to change from hues of blues and golds to hues of pinks and oranges.

"Look, there's an old man in a bathtub!" Patrick announced exuberantly as he pointed toward the clouds.

"Where?" everyone asked simultaneously, Josh and Jennifer being the only ones to realize instantaneously that he was referring to formations in the clouds.

"Right there, straight in front of you!" he directed them. "See, that's his head where that big blob is."

142

"Do you see it, Mom?" Jennifer asked her mother.

"Yes, I do. And I see the beautiful colors that God is painting in the sky for the sunset tonight. He is quite an artist, isn't He? she exclaimed in wonderment.

"He *is* an artist," Patrick answered his aunt, "but I see Him as being as much a sculptor as He is a painter. I know He paints beautiful sunsets everyday, but I think He gets a real kick out of doing cloud sculptures to keep us all entertained in His spare time. I mean, just think of all the things you've seen in the clouds, especially on long rides home? It's like He just puts them up there, waiting for us to notice them."

They continued to canvass the sky for more images, marveling at the cloud sculptures that seemed to divinely appear and disappear before their eyes. Finally darkness coveted the sky, making it impossible for them to see the remaining cloud formations and squelching the flow of their imaginative juices during the rest of the ride home.

Chapter Fourteen

Since Mr. Watson's truck was parked in the Bakers' driveway when Mrs. Watson pulled in to deposit Josh, Patrick, and Mrs. Baker, she decided to join her husband and youngest daughter inside, as well. As it turned out, the men had ordered pizza for the youngsters and had helped themselves to what was left over from Thanksgiving dinner.

Josh, Jennifer, and Patrick opted not to eat dinner and headed up to Patrick's room to unveil their recently acquired treasures. Josh had ended up buying himself a new pair of jeans, leather basketball shoes, and insulated gloves. Patrick was busy lacing up his new Rollerblades and then skating backwards in little circles around his room.

"Josh, let's see those toys you bought for your little sister," Patrick requested with boyish eagerness.

"Don't you mean sisters?" Jennifer corrected Patrick.

"Oh, yeah, sisters," Patrick said, plopping himself down on the chair by his desk and reaching for the plastic bag from the toy store. He pulled the Tiny Tinkles baby doll and the Baywatch doll ensemble from the bag.

"What are you doing?" Jennifer asked her cousin as he opened the box containing the Baywatch doll and removed it from its packaging.

"I want to see if this is an authentic Baywatch doll," he answered peeking down the front of the doll's bathing suit. "Hmmm... just as I thought. These appear to be made of some sort of artificial, synthetic material, just like the ones on Baywatch."

Josh and Jennifer rolled their eyes as Patrick proceeded to open the Tiny Tinkles box, as well.

"And this one," he said, cradling her in his arms like a real baby, "smells like she needs a change." He followed through by removing her plastic diaper, holding it up with two fingers while plugging his nose with two other fingers. "I think she's thirsty," Patrick decided, getting up to fill the plastic bottle with water.

"Don't even think about it!" Josh warned his playful friend. "I can still take back those Rollerblades, you know?"

Patrick complied, putting the dolls back into their places, just as he had been put back into his place.

"You're about one nut short of a fruitcake today," Josh teased, putting the boxes under the bed and out of Patrick's reach.

"Well, well.. you're about one ornament short of a Christmas tree!" was Patrick's rebuttal, realizing as soon as it came out of his mouth that it made no sense.

Jennifer, who had been ignoring the boys' foolish follies, was standing in the corner, quite preoccupied with examining the cross necklace which she had picked up off of Josh's dresser. "Whose is this?" she asked, fondling the silver piece and turning it over to catch a glimpse of the inscription.

"Oh, it's mine," Josh answered nervously.

"Who's Sarah?" she asked with just a tinge of jealousy in her voice and without looking up at him.

"She's my..." Josh started to say, but stopped short. What could he say? If he told her that Sarah was his sister and she, too, had seen his profile sheet as Patrick had, she would know that his sisters' names were supposed to be Lindsey and Katie. "She's a friend," he answered, and then seeing the disheartened expression on her face, wished he hadn't.

Jennifer placed the necklace back on the dresser and excused herself from their company by saying that she wanted to go downstairs and grab some pizza before it was all gone. Josh followed her, but noticed that in spite of the fact that she made the effort to put a slice of Hawaiian pizza on her plate, she never did take a bite out of it. Josh longed to take her aside and find out what was bothering her as she had suddenly turned stone cold towards him. Whatever it was, he knew that it had something to do with the necklace and the fact that he had told her that Sarah was a friend.

Unfortunately for Josh, he never did get a chance to talk to her privately that night, for shortly thereafter, she and her family left for home.

Josh trudged dejectedly up the stairs and back to Patrick's room where Patrick was putting the final touches on one of the presents he had wrapped for Josh's sister.

"I figured if I wrapped these, I wouldn't be tempted to play with them anymore," he told Josh. Then seeing Josh's own disheartened expression, he asked, "Trouble in paradise?"

"Yeah, I didn't know whether or not Jennifer knew JC's sisters' names, so when she asked me who Sarah was, I said she was a friend and she got all upset and now she won't talk to me. She probably thinks that Sarah is my girlfriend or something."

"Yeah, she probably does. And by the way, she didn't."

"She didn't what?" Josh asked, plopping down on his bed and stretching out his arms and legs.

"She didn't know what your sisters' names were. You could have told her that Sarah was your sister. As far as I know, she never saw the profile sheet and nobody ever told her what their names were."

"Now you tell me," Josh said sullenly.

"Oh, she'll get over it. Take it from me. I know women. She'll forget about it by tomorrow," Patrick assured him confidently.

"How did you get to be such an expert on women? I haven't seen any girls knocking down your door to get to you?" Josh pointed out.

"I'm in the process of just getting over a tough break up from a long term relationship."

"Oh really? With who?" Josh quizzed him, doubtful of his sincerity. "And how long did you two go out?"

"You don't know her. She's a cheerleader from Redmont. We went out for one whole day. I met her at one of the football games this fall and I took her out to the Taco Palace afterwards. I choked on a nacho and barfed all over the table. Maybe I'll call her up and see if she wants to go to a movie. You could call Jennifer and see if she wants to go. Your treat."

"My treat? Thanks a lot. Okay, but you have to call her for me. Don't act like we're going out or anything, just see if she wants to go," Josh emphasized.

"Okay, but first, I could really go for a nice hot fudge sundae, smothered with thick, bubbling fudge, topped with nuts, whipped cream, and a maraschino cherry. How about you?"

" Yeah, that sounds good," Josh said, falling into Patrick's trap.

"Okay, then, why don't you go and make one for each of us and I'll make the phone calls while you're gone?"

"I should have seen that coming," Josh acknowledged with a shake of his head, but yielded to the request anyway, heading down to the kitchen expeditiously.

It took Josh a long time to make the sundaes. By the time he was finished and brought the desserts upstairs, Patrick was hanging up from his last phone call with Jennifer.

"We're all set," Patrick confirmed. "Ashley was waiting for me to call. It's been pure torture for her."

Josh laughed. "Well, I'm sure it has. What did Jennifer say?"

"Don't worry about a thing, Josh. I took care of everything. Jennifer's not the least bit worried about who Sarah is anymore."

"That's good," Josh conceded, "I really don't want anything to come between us since I only have a little bit of time left here."

"Have you given any thought to what Coach said about you staying longer?" Patrick asked.

"No, I haven't figured out what I'm going to do. I guess I should call my uncle and see what's up there. If he'd be willing to take us right away, I think that would be the right thing to do and end this charade."

"How much money do you have left to give him?"

"There's a little more than $7000 left on the credit card, but I'm only going to offer him $5000. I'll keep the other $2000 for Sarah and me in case we ever need it."

"When are you going to call him?"

"I don't know. Maybe in a week or two. I'm just not ready yet. If the human resource people are looking for me and contacted him, which is probably the case, he might ask me too many questions and try to track me down. I don't want to have to leave here any earlier than I had planned, you know?"

"Yeah, I know, man. I want you to stay, too," Patrick replied. "Hey, what do you think?" He handed the presents with the lopsided wrap job back to Josh. "I even found a cardboard box for you. All you have to do is address it and I'll have my mom mail it on Monday morning. I'll just tell her that you're sending it to a friend of the family."

"Thanks, Patrick," Josh said, putting the presents back into the toy store bag and then sticking it into the box. He addressed the box to Sarah Farnsworth C/O Jane and Harold Johnson and completed the California address in large block letters below. He had forgotten what JC had said to him about sending mail from the local post office since it would be an easy way for the authorities to track him down.

Everything was going smoothly the next morning when Josh and Patrick were readying themselves for their so called dates at the movies. Josh was wearing his new jeans and Patrick even treated himself to a luxurious bath in sweet smelling bath oils until close to noon.

While Patrick was bathing, Josh decided to take the time to write Sarah a brief, but loving note to put in with the gifts. That was when Amos burst through the door and announced that he was ready for Josh to fulfill his promise by taking him to the arcade.

"Whoops!" Josh said when he realized the date to take Amos to the arcade was today. "I'm sorry, buddy," he apologized, "Patrick and I made plans to go to the movies today. Can you take a raincheck? I thought you were going to see Santa Claus today with your dad."

"We're back already! I told him that we had to get back because you were going to take me to the arcade,"

Amos attacked him blatantly. "What's a raincheck?"

"It means that I could take you another time. Like maybe tomorrow?"

"Yeah, right, and when tomorrow comes, you'll say you have to do something else," Amos continued to blast him. "If you aren't going to take me to the arcade, then can you take me to the movies with you?"

"I can't Amos. It's rated PG-13. Your mom doesn't let you see those, does she?"

"Sometimes she does. I'll close my eyes on the bad parts," Amos promised.

"Take a hike!" Patrick commanded belligerently, as he made his way into the bedroom, clad only in a towel wrapped around his waist. "You're not going with us. Now get out of here!" Patrick shoved his little brother out into the hallway and slammed the door.

"We'll go another time," Josh yelled through the closed door.

"Yeah, right!" Amos replied angrily. "I'll never get to go!" He stomped deliberately all the way down the hallway to his room where he slammed his door, as well.

"I wish you hadn't done that," Josh said to Patrick.

"Why not?" Patrick answered with a defensive question. "He's a little twerp!"

"I guess I just don't need the little twerp to be upset with me. Remember what he did with the fax I got when he wasn't even mad at me ?"

"Ah, don't worry about him. I'll kick his butt if he tries anything again. It's your fault for promising him that you'd take him to the arcade. Just don't make promises to the little loser. I never do."

Josh was amazed at how rotten Patrick treated his little brother, but then he reflected back to how he had treated Sarah before they had become orphans. Locking her up in the neighbor's doghouse might have been considered somewhat deviant, even to Patrick. He laughed at the thought of it.

Patrick's mother had volunteered to drive the three teens to the theater which was located in town. Jennifer was her usual congenial and receptive self when the boys and Mrs. Baker arrived at her house. Patrick stayed in the front seat, so that she and Josh were forced to share the back seat of the compact car.

Patrick met Ashley in front of the old brick theater, intentionally having left his wallet at home on the dresser, so that Josh ended up paying for everyone.

Josh was nervous sitting next to Jennifer in the dark theater, so nervous that not once could he bring himself to fake a stretch and put his arm around her or to even touch her hand in an effort to hold it.

Patrick, on the other hand, wasted no time in taking advantage of the situation, this being his second official date with the sassy brunette. He grabbed her hand immediately.

"So, did you hear the news?" Ashley chattered, as the foursome waited for the previews to start. "Bull is moving to Redmont and he's going to start for us!"

Josh wasn't sure in what context the news she had shared with them had been made. Was she excited that Bull was joining their team and trying to rub it in their faces or was she simply passing on the news? Patrick wasn't sure, but out of reflex, he squeezed her hand so tightly that she cringed in pain.

"You have really strong hands," she remarked through clenched teeth.

"Thanks, I, ah, work out!" Patrick boasted, not even realizing how tightly he had squeezed her hand. "And, yeah, we heard." Patrick announced belligerently, hoping that there would be no reason to bring up the subject of Bull again.

"Well, I thought you would want to know since I heard that your team really needs him," the naive girl contended.

"Yeah, right, we really need him," Patrick laughed, although deep down he was perturbed that someone had the audacity to say that Bull was an integral part of the team - that Jennifer, Josh, Patrick, and the other players couldn't pull off a winning season without him.

The movie began and ended much too soon, as far as Patrick and Josh were concerned. Patrick had only stolen one kiss from the perky Redmont cheerleader and Josh hadn't even glanced in Jennifer's direction throughout the entire flick. It was dismal and sleeting heavily when the four left the moviehouse and since Ashley's mother was already waiting to pick her up outside, the double date ended, not with a bang, but with a whimper from Patrick.

"How was the movie? And how is Ashley?" Mrs. Baker asked the three amigos when she picked them up in front of the theater.

"It was okay," Patrick answered. "I realize now that she's not the brightest lightbulb in the world," he said referring to his date. "I think I'm going to have to dump her."

Josh and Jennifer laughed, relieved to know that Patrick wasn't going to let himself get hung up on this bubblehead.

"So, she wasn't your soul mate?" Mrs. Baker asked, glancing at Josh and Jennifer in the rearview mirror.

"Nope, I guess I'll just have to keep my eyes open. I know she's got to be out there somewhere," Patrick shook his head despondently.

Again, Patrick's mother, cousin, and best friend laughed, although Josh had blushed when Mrs. Baker had used the term soul mate. For some reason, he'd been wondering for the longest time, if perhaps he'd found his, in Jennifer.

Jennifer opted to go home when given the option of visiting with the boys for the evening, saying that she was going to a girlfriend's house to spend the night.

The rest of the weekend was just as uneventful as rainy, dreary, chilly afternoons in late November in Ohio can be. The boys were anxious to get back to school on Monday in order to get their minds back on basketball and off of girls. And since no adult had been willing to transport Josh and Amos the twenty two miles back to the mall where the arcade was located, Josh's promise to Amos remained unfulfilled.

Although Josh had not been able to keep his promise to Amos, Patrick's mother did keep her promise to Josh, getting his package out first thing on Monday morning.

After standing in line for twenty minutes at the post office, the observant postal worker noticed that there was something missing from the box.

"We need a return address on here, maam," he requested politely.

"Oh, yes. Josh must have forgotten to put that on," Mrs. Baker apologized.

151

Hastily she wrote Josh Montgomery and her return address in the left hand corner of the box, and handed it to the man behind the counter. The package was on its way.

Chapter Fifteen

About once a month, the lady from the human resource office paid a visit to the Johnsons' house. She looked to be in her mid fifties, although she could have been older. Her hair, dyed jet black to camouflage the gray, was wound tightly in a tiny bun which stuck to the back of her head. She always wore a long, black suit which accentuated her bony physique and she always smelled like French onion soup.

Even though Mrs. Johnson ran a respectable, loving foster home, she became anxious when Ms. Oger paid her an unexpected visit. Ms. Oger always carried a little black notebook with her and would take notes on the conversations that transpired, looking up from her horn rimmed glasses that were set halfway down her nose. You could never tell what her motives were or what she was writing down. She had ways of manipulating conversations to make Mrs. Johnson or the children say things that could be used against them. For example, once Mrs. Johnson had mentioned that she had taken the children to a drive-in movie in another county. Ms. Oger had jotted down some notes and then informed her that she had broken two rules. First, she had taken the children across county lines without permission, and secondly, she had broken curfew. From then on, Mrs. Johnson was very careful about how she answered Ms. Oger's questions.

Sarah could hear the black, thick soled shoes clomping up the wooden porch steps. But something sounded different this time, as if there were more footsteps than just Ms. Oger's. Sarah peeked through the living room blind in time to see a middle aged man dressed in a navy blue suit accompanying her.

Mrs. Johnson heard them coming, too, scurrying toward the door nervously as she swept her hand through her hair and adjusted her loose fitting sweatshirt and jeans. "I wish she would give me just a little time to prepare for her visits," she complained, but she knew that the surprise visits were all a part of keeping the foster parents on their toes.

"There's a man with her," Sarah announced. "Should I go into the other room?"

"I thought she sounded unusually noisy coming up the steps today. No, just sit here next to me. I have a feeling that the man with her is here because of Jeff. He may want to ask you some questions."

"What should I say?" Sarah asked nervously.

"Just tell him the truth. After all, we've been looking all over for him, too."

"I hope nothing happened to him," Sarah said suddenly, realizing that the man's presence could mean that they were coming to bring bad news.

"Let's just open the door and see," Mrs. Johnson said calmly, holding her precious Sarah's hand.

"Mrs. Johnson," Ms. Oger responded with chilling formality when Mrs. Johnson opened the door, "This is Mr. Pinkman from Social Services. He's doing an investigation on Jeff's disappearance. He would like to talk to Sarah alone."

"He may speak with Sarah, but I see no reason why he should need to speak to her alone. How do you do, Mr. Pinkman?" Mrs. Johnson acknowledged him, suddenly remembering her manners.

Ms. Oger ignored Mrs. Johnson's greeting, not allowing Mr. Pinkman to return the salutation, before she spouted out rudely, "We have our reasons why he should speak to her alone."

"It's simply a formality, Mrs. Johnson," Mr. Pinkman spoke up, trying to ease the mounting tension that Ms. Oger seemed to be inflicting upon all parties. "We just need to ask both of you a few questions, and we feel the children are more likely to speak openly if not in the presence of their caregivers."

"I don't understand what difference that makes. Sarah is perfectly comfortable talking in my presence."

Mr. Pinkman took Mrs. Johnson aside and started to whisper. "It's my job, Mrs. Johnson, to investigate the disappearance of foster children. Part of the procedure involves making a determination of whether or not the disappearance of the youth was due to the treatment he was receiving as a foster child in your home. Do you understand what I'm saying?"

"Oh, so you're investigating *me* ?" Mrs. Johnson was emphatically indignant at the allegations.

"We have to cover all of the bases, maam. It's just routine. I'm sure you run a decent foster care home here. My job is simply to determine why he might have left, locate the boy, and return him to his proper home," Mr. Pinkman tried to assure her.

"His proper home? And where might that be?" Mrs. Johnson probed. "The state's plan was to move him to a new foster care facility on his fourteenth birthday. As of right now, he has no proper home!"

"I'm sure the state has secured a suitable home for him, although it is my understanding that since he ran away, he may have to serve some time in a juvenile detention facility before he is permitted to live in a foster home again."

"You people are incredible," Mrs. Johnson couldn't help from saying. "First, you tell the boy that he'll have to be moved away from his little sister and from the only secure environment he's had in years, and then you punish him for going out there and trying to fix things himself."

"So, do you think he ran away because he was going to be moved?"

"Do you think?" Mrs. Johnson answered with such blatant sarcasm that Sarah almost laughed. "Of course, that's why he ran away. Why else would he go?"

"That's what we're here to find out! If you would kindly leave the room, Mrs. Johnson, we'll let you know when we're finished discussing the issue with Sarah." Ms. Oger viciously attacked Mrs. Johnson with her cruel words.

"Fine," Mrs. Johnson retaliated cynically, "Sarah, you call me if you need me. I'll just be in the kitchen."

Mr. Pinkman began his investigation by appealing to Sarah's sense of concern for her brother. "Now, Sarah, I'll bet you miss your big brother a lot, don't you?"

Sarah nodded without looking up as she stared steadily at her folded hands.

"And I'll bet you'd like to have him back here with you as soon as possible, wouldn't you?"

"Yes, but you said that he wouldn't be coming back here with me," she said, challenging his previous statement.

"Well, you're right, I did say that, but let's just say that if we could get him back home with you, you'd want that, wouldn't you?" Mr. Pinkman fumbled.

Sarah nodded again and continued staring at her intertwined fingers, noticing that the pretty pink nail polish Mrs. Johnson had put on her fingernails was beginning to chip off.

"You know, if he told you where he was going, we might be able to find him and bring him back. Did he mention where he might go?" Mr. Pinkman prompted.

"Yes..." Sarah hesitated, but then remembered that Mrs. Johnson had told her to tell the truth. "To Uncle Frank's."

"Hmmm," Mr. Pinkman said, pondering his next question while reflecting on the fact that Uncle Frank had already been contacted and threatened with incarceration if he failed to notify the California authorities upon Jeff's arrival. "Do you know why he left? Was he unhappy about having to move to a new foster home? Or was it something else, something that would have upset him here? Did he have a fight with Mr. or Mrs. Johnson? Did one of them yell at him or hit him?"

"No, nobody yelled at him or hit him!" Sarah felt herself becoming angry at the accusations being hurled at the Johnsons, but she had learned to control her emotions in situations like these a long time ago. "He liked it here. It was the first thing - having to go to a new foster home. He didn't want us to be separated, so he was going to see if Uncle Frank would take us both in."

"Did he have any friends that he might have stopped to see along the way?" Ms. Oger demanded.

Sarah shrugged her shoulders and called for Mrs. Johnson to come back into the room, fearing that she'd said too much already and that she'd betrayed her brother's trust.

Just then the doorbell sounded. Mrs. Johnson opened the door to see Mr. Grant, the mailman, holding a box.

"Good afternoon, Jane. This was too big to fit in your mailbox," the friendly mailman explained as he handed her the box.

Mrs. Johnson thanked him quietly, and quickly disposed of the package in the front closet when she noticed that it was addressed to Sarah.

Having witnessed Mrs. Johnson's rapid concealment of the package, Ms. Oger made a diversionary request. "Would you be so kind as to get me a glass of water, Mrs. Johnson? I'm feeling quite parched."

Suspicious of Ms. Oger's sudden change in tone from that of sour to sweet, Mrs. Johnson hurriedly made her way into the kitchen and grabbed a glass from the cupboard. But before she had a chance to fill the glass, she heard Ms. Oger cackle with uncustomary glee, "Well, what have we here? A box for Sarah! I wonder who *that* could be from?"

Abandoning her task in the kitchen, Mrs. Johnson flew back into the living room where Mr. Pinkman and Ms. Oger were in their glory, slicing the edges of the box open with a pocket knife.

"Who *that* is from is none of your business!" Mrs. Johnson protested as the two vultures devoured the outer contents of their cardboard prey.

"Oh, I'm afraid it *is* our business," Ms. Oger contested vindictively. "While Jeff is missing, we have the right to confiscate any and all materials that come into this house. Your effort to conceal evidence could be used against you."

"You've got to be kidding!" Mrs. Johnson exclaimed obstinately. " Besides, you don't even know who it's from!"

"It's from a Josh Montgomery in Ohio," Mr. Pinkman stated. "Does Jeff know a Josh Montgomery in Ohio?" The question was directed at Sarah.

"I don't know," she answered, becoming irritated with the strange man's nagging questions.

"I may have to take the contents as evidence," he informed Ms. Oger, as Mrs. Johnson and Sarah looked on.

"I see no reason for that," Mrs. Johnson objected. "Take what you need, but leave the child her gifts."

"Well, if I am to do that, then I will need to have her open them now, so that I can examine them," Mr. Pinkman instructed.

"You sure know how to take the fun out of getting presents," Sarah mumbled condescendingly under her breath.

As she lifted the first present from the large cardboard container and then from the plastic shopping bag, the handwritten note that Jeff had written fell back down into the bag. Sarah let it go, hoping that no one else had noticed it, but unfortunately, Mr. Pinkman had a keen eye for details and recognized it right off.

Without giving her a chance to unwrap the first gift, he reached down into the bag to retrieve the flimsy piece of paper. What he came up with was even more substantial than he could ever have imagined. Along with the heartwarming note that Jeff had written to his sister, was the toy store receipt totaling $2027.42.

Mr. Pinkman took his time examining the receipt, as well as the personal note and was about to stick both items into his coat pocket when Mrs. Johnson objected.

"May we see what you've got there, please?" Mrs. Johnson asked assertively.

Reluctantly relinquishing the two items to Mrs. Johnson, Mr. Pinkman waited impatiently while Mrs. Johnson helped Sarah to decipher Jeff's handwriting.

"It says: Dear Sarah, I haven't forgotten about you. Hope to see you soon. Love, Jeff," Mrs. Johnson read, folding the note and then glancing at the toy store receipt briefly before surrendering both papers to Mr. Pinkman.

Sarah then proceeded to open up both gifts, pleased that her brother had taken the time to remember her while at the same time, feeling disheartened by the scrutinizing eyes that inspected each box and its contents, as they hungered to find more revealing evidence that would lead to the discovery of his whereabouts.

When the interrogation was over, Mr. Pinkman and Ms. Oger confiscated the original cardboard box, the receipt, and the note from Jeff.

"We'll need to get a handwriting analysis done for the handwriting on this note to see if it matches the signature on the credit card slip," Mr. Pinkman informed Ms. Oger. "We could be dealing with more than just a runaway here."

"Darn them!" Mrs. Johnson thundered when the two finally left moments later.

"What did they mean when they said that they might be dealing with more than just a runaway?" Sarah asked Mrs. Johnson.

"I'm not sure, but I think they want to find out if Jeff might have signed that credit card receipt."

"Why?"

"The name on the card was Josh Montgomery. I think they want to make sure that Jeff didn't use someone else's credit card."

"I don't think he would do that. That would be like stealing, wouldn't it?" Sarah looked up at Mrs. Johnson with a look of confusion on her face.

"Perhaps this Josh Montgomery, whoever he is, left his receipt in the bag, or maybe he bought the toys for Jeff to give to you."

"Well, what are we going to do now?" Sarah asked.

"I'll tell you what we're going to do. The name on the box and on the credit card slip was Josh Montgomery. I wasn't able to catch the name of the town, but I did see that the box came from Ohio. We'll go to the library and get the phone numbers for every single Josh or J Montgomery in the state of Ohio. Then we'll call every one of them until we find the one who knows something about Jeff," Mrs. Johnson promised, grabbing her jacket and summoning Harry, and his little sister, Jamie, from the backyard into the house to prepare them all for a journey to town.

Unfortunately, Mrs. Johnson's efforts to contact every J Montgomery in Ohio were in vain since no J or Josh Montgomery listed in the directory had ever heard of Jeff Farnsworth.

Chapter Sixteen

The three weeks following Thanksgiving flew by quickly. Josh, Jennifer, and Patrick were busy going to basketball practices four days a week and playing in games on Friday afternoons. Josh was so busy, he had little time to do anything but eat, sleep, do homework and play ball, let alone prepare for the inevitable time, less than one week away, when he was scheduled to leave. But in spite of his busy lifestyle, he did make time to send messages to the real Josh's father in Australia, messages proclaiming the triumphs and challenges that he was experiencing in America.

Josh was happy to be busy. It wasn't just because being busy allowed him to escape the dismal reality that lurked just outside of his assumed identity, but it was also because he was able to focus on more than just the inner thoughts that had plagued him for years. He was working hard, pushing himself to the max physically and mentally. The muscles in his legs were strong and taut and his mind was sharp. He was part of something again, a team and a school, and in an odd sort of way, he was part of a family - a multifaceted family network which included Sarah and himself, the Bakers, the Johnsons, and even his fictitious family, the Montgomerys.

Although Josh hadn't communicated with JC's mother, other than saying, "tell Mom I love her," when he emailed his father, Josh had grown quite close to Mr. Montgomery. He pretended that he was writing to his own father, sharing the moments of his life, the way that he wished he could with his real mom and dad.

It was early Friday morning, December 17th when Josh woke up early. The sun had not yet risen, but he was wide awake and unable to go back to sleep. He wasn't sure if he was anxious about the game which they would play later that afternoon or anxious because time was running out. He decided to get up, get dressed, and go for a jog. In the fresh, brisk December air, he could do the thing that he had been avoiding of late - think.

He ran down the street, then down to the next block and around the corner to where Jennifer lived. He stopped momentarily beneath the streetlight, but seeing that there were no lights on in the house, continued on to the schoolyard. He was huffing and puffing when he noticed the metal ladder leading up to the roof above the classrooms, and then another one leading up to the roof above the gym. He decided to make the ascent to the top and watch the sun rise over the sleepy town. High above the housetops, the town resembled a miniature Christmas town, the lights in the town center still twinkling in the moments before dawn.

His mind methodically reviewed the concerns that had disturbed his slumber. This would be the fourth game of the season for the Kangaroos. He remembered last Friday's game. His jump was high, his perception keen, as he, Jennifer, and Patrick had played like a well oiled machine, single minded in their pursuit to reign victoriously. The adrenaline had run like water through Josh's veins and he looked upon himself and his friends as being unstoppable.

The crowd had chanted,"Kangaroo, Kangaroo!" as he swished shot after shot through the hoop. In the end, he was named the player of the week, having scored 27 of the 52 points that had clinched the victory.

He was both excited and nervous about the game that they would play tonight, but he knew that wasn't the real reason that he had awakened so early. He knew that it was time for him to face reality. In only six days, he would be boarding a plane to who knew where. If he didn't call his uncle soon, he would never know if the possibility of going there existed or not. He had procrastinated long enough, not wanting to leave this ideal fantasy life behind. And, as of yet, he hadn't ruled out the option that Coach had given him to stay through the Christmas holiday and into January, or possibly even into February. But now, as the clock ticked away, he knew that it was time to explore one of his options further. He made up his mind, that tonight, no matter what, after the game, he would call his uncle.

"Hey, what are you doing up there?" Josh heard a girl's voice yell from across the field. It was Jennifer, clad in jeans, a snugly down jacket, and mittens.

He waved her up to join him on top of the world. "What are you doing out so early?" he asked, holding his hand out to her as she stepped over the last rung.

"I just woke up early and when I looked out my window, I thought I saw you jogging down the street, so I followed you. What are you doing up here?"

"I couldn't sleep. I just came up here to think and to watch the sunrise," Josh answered, pulling the sleeves of his jacket down to cover the exposed parts of his wrists.

"What are you thinking about?" Jennifer inquired, noticing that her breath had vaporized in the frigid air.

"Lots of things, the game tonight, but leaving here mostly."

"Have you thought about staying here until the end of basketball season?" she asked with a hopeful smile on her face. "It won't be the same here without you. Actually, it will be the same, the same as it was before you came - boring."

"I'd like to stay, you have no idea how much I'd like to stay, but I have responsibilities that I have to take care of," Josh admitted.

"You're only fourteen. How could you have responsibilities? My parents are always telling me that I should enjoy myself now cause I'll have plenty of time to be responsible later."

"Really? They tell you that?" Josh wondered.

"Yeah, I have to clean my room and do my homework and stuff, but they want me to enjoy being young."

"I wish I had parents who would tell me things like that," Josh replied wistfully. "And I wish I could justify staying here. You and Patrick are the best buds I've ever had."

"I feel the same way," Jennifer admitted shyly. Then feeling embarrassed by her confession, she changed the subject. "It's beautiful up here with all the Christmas lights on in town and on the houses and trees down below."

"I can see your house from here," Josh noted, pointing toward the modest, but tastefully decorated home.

"Look at Coach's house!" Jennifer pointed toward the splendid mansion which was adorned with tiny white twinkling lights outlining the perimeters of the house. "It's gorgeous!" Jennifer said, dazzled by its brilliance.

"Did you know Coach and his wife when they lost their babies?" Josh asked, suddenly remembering the dusty room upstairs with the infant furniture tucked into the corner.

"Oh, yeah. It was really sad . Everyone was so excited about Tara having twins and then one night about a week before the twins were due, they were hit by a drunk driver. I think he might have run a redlight or something. He hit Tara's side of the car. She lost the babies and was in the hospital for about a month, I think."

"That's too bad. How were the Webbers after it happened? Were they really shook up?" Josh asked.

"They were really sad, but I think they're pretty strong in their faith, and that helped them to get through it."

"That still must have been tough, though. They went through all that stuff to try to have kids and then in a moment, their babies were gone. Patrick told me about the fertility drugs, only he called them fraternity drugs."

Jennifer laughed. "That's funny. I mean the part about Patrick calling them fraternity drugs, not the part about the babies," she responded, her tone sobering when she realized her reaction might be misinterpreted. "That part was really sad."

"So, Jennifer, do you believe in God?" Josh inquired, hoping to break the ice into unchartered conversational waters.

"Do I believe He exists or do I believe *in* Him?"

"Well, either one, you tell me," Josh reciprocated.

"Well, then I guess I'd have to say that I believe in Him in both ways. I believe He exists and I believe *in* Him," she answered.

"Do you think that you'd believe in Him if something terrible happened to someone in your family?" Josh asked.

"Do you mean like if one of them died or something?"

"Yeah."

"Well, it's hard to say because I've never been through anything like that, but it's kind of like if you already believe, then how can you just stop believing? I mean you can stop following Him or praying, but then what good does that do? Then you don't have any hope. I would hope that I'd just make the choice to keep following Him even though I might not understand why it happened," Jennifer elaborated.

"It's really hard though," Josh stated, almost forgetting to stay in the character of Josh Montgomery, the boy whose life was full of riches and blessings and whose only sorrow stemmed from a self inflicted alienation from his father. The impersonating Josh longed to tell Jennifer his story and how he had been plagued everyday of his life since the accident, wondering why God had allowed it and if he, Jeff, had played a part in causing it to happen. But he knew he couldn't, not just yet. So, he went on. "Like do you think God knows what's going to happen?"

"Yeah, I think He does know what's going to happen," Jennifer answered thoughtfully.

"So, with that drunk driver that hit the Webbers' car, did He know ahead of time that that was going to happen? And if so, was it part of His plan or was it just an accident? And if it was just an accident, and He knew it was going to happen, why didn't He just stop it? Does He just let circumstances dictate what happens or does He control what happens?" Josh knew that he was babbling, but these were the kinds of thoughts that had repeated themselves over and over in his head for the past three years. And for the first time, he felt that he'd found someone with whom he could share these thoughts, someone who might possibly be on the same wavelength. He swallowed hard and waited patiently for Jennifer's response.

"It's hard to say. I was brought up believing that God knows everything that is going to happen," Jennifer began, "but it's hard for me to believe that it was His will for that guy to be drunk and for that accident to happen. I see that more as somebody being irresponsible and going out, getting drunk and getting behind the wheel. I don't really see it as being God's will. Like I don't believe that if the drunk driver hadn't hit them, something else would have happened to take the twins' lives. I don't believe that it had to be that way. I don't believe that God necessarily wanted them to die."

"But then, why did He let it happen? That's what I don't get. When I was growing up, I believed that God loved us and was watching over us. And most of the time, it seems like He does. My grandma said that He was totally in control and that nothing happened without His okay. That made me think that nothing bad would ever happen. So, then when something horrible did happen, I just didn't get it. Does He sometimes just let nature take its course or is it really part of His plan that it happens?" Josh stammered, steam evaporating from his lips as the words left his mouth, while his body shuddered from a brisk breeze which seemed to wisp through him like a chilling apparition.

"I was brought up that way, too, so it is hard to understand when He doesn't stop bad things from happening," Jennifer agreed. She could feel her fingers and toes numbing as the temperature plummeted a few more degrees while it waited for the sun to rise. But she didn't seem to mind the biting cold; she could tell that having this conversation was important to Josh, so she simply waited patiently for the next facet to present itself.

"Another thing that my grandma used to tell me was that everything happens for a reason. Do you believe that?" Josh asked.

"That's funny that you should say that because my grandma is always telling me things like that, too. Only I guess, I don't know if I believe that everything happens for a reason as much as I believe that God can make good things come out of bad things that happen."

"I went to a double funeral one time." Josh was referring to his parents' funeral. "Someone stood up and said, 'God had a plan for these two people's lives. He had a reason for taking them from this earth to be with Him.' It made me so mad. I wanted to stand up and say, 'How do you know? How do you know that this was God's plan for their lives? Maybe what happened was just an accident!'"

"I know. It bugs me, too, when people say things like that cause no one really knows except for God."

"Yeah, I know. So, how do you think good can come out of bad stuff that happens?"

"Like in Littleton, Colorado, at Columbine High School, where those students and their teacher were shot and killed, I don't believe that God wanted that stuff to happen, but He allowed it to happen and then He brought some good out of it. It brought people together and it brought people to God. Our church was packed the Sunday after it happened. I don't know if people wanted to come together to mourn or if they were trying to make sense out of what happened or if it just made them want to turn to God for answers and reassurance. But for whatever reasons, they were there." Now Jennifer, too, seemed to forget the frigid temperatures as she reflected upon the heartwrenching tragedy that had gripped the nation. "It's just too bad that it takes a tragedy to bring people together and to God. We should be coming to Him and to each other daily instead of just when there's a tragedy."

"I hear you," Josh agreed, but then elaborated on another aspect of the Littleton tragedy. "I know what you're saying about God being able to bring some good out of things like this, but for those people who lost family members, their lives will never be the same. Everyone else has gone on with their lives and Littleton is just a sad memory. But for them, the fact that there is an empty place at the dinner table everyday, is a constant reminder that they've lost far more than we have gained. All the factors that people put into the equation for what may have caused it - the accessibility to weapons, violence in the media, or even the antagonistic intolerance that people display towards others - may have made people more aware for awhile, but in the long run, nothing is really going to change very much."

166

"I disagree. What happened opened up a lot of people's eyes. Those people who died will always live on in the hearts of almost all Americans," Jennifer debated, downhearted because of what Josh had said.

"I know, that's true, they will. I'm just saying that in spite of what good has come out of it, and some has, the people who lost loved ones are still left to bear the pain."

"I know. We just have to hope that those people can hang in there and have faith that they will someday be reunited with their loved ones. I think that when something like this happens, it forces us to realize that life is short and that there are no guarantees. It makes some people realize that they should live life to the fullest and appreciate the people in their lives, and it makes others see what I like to call the big picture," Jennifer stated emphatically.

"And what is the big picture?" Josh lightened as he saw his own seriousness mirrored in Jennifer's words of wisdom.

"The big picture is that life is short and maybe this life isn't all there is. And if it isn't all there is, then maybe we should be thinking more about God and who He is and what comes next instead of worrying about making a lot of money and achieving or acquiring a lot of things here on earth. After all, He's the one who we're going to have to answer to when it's all over. I think what's important is to to get to know Him, do what we enjoy, and to be kind to other people because we never really know when it could all end."

Josh felt an uncontrollable grin creeping across his face and he couldn't stop himself from releasing the satirical thought that had just crossed his mind. "Oh, that's just what poor people say," he teased, shrinking back while he waited for Jennifer's reaction.

"Very funny!" Jennifer shot him an unappreciative grin. "I'm freezing to death out here, trying to be all serious and you're making fun of me!"

"I'm sorry. I'm only kidding. You're right. You've got a really good way of looking at things, but it's not easy for me to make sense out of things like you do."

"What do you mean? What things don't make sense to you?"

"Well, like a week or two after the shootings in Littleton, I was watching the news and there were a bunch of tornadoes that swept through Oklahoma, killing a bunch of people."

"And..." she prompted him to continue.

"And it just seemed weird to me," Josh answered.

"What seemed weird to you?" she prompted him again.

"Well, life is supposed to be precious, right?" he said, lifting his eyebrows.

"Right," Jennifer answered, still unsure about where he was going with this.

"Well, if life is precious, why did God cause those tornadoes to come through and kill all of those people? Everyone was upset about what happened at Littleton, but yet God took twice as many lives a couple of weeks later in Oklahoma and hardly anybody said anything."

Jennifer responded to Josh's concerns with a question of her own. "Well, did God send those tornadoes or did they just occur naturally and those people just happen to be in their paths?"

"It sounds as though we're back to square one with our original question," Josh asserted, "so, let's just say that whether He sent the tornadoes or whether it was just nature taking its course, He allowed it to happen. My question is: why didn't people around the country react to those people dying in the same way that they reacted to the people in Littleton dying?"

Again Jennifer seemed to have her theology stashed away neatly in her pocket, responding this time to Josh's concerns as though, she, too, had pondered similar questions. "The people in Oklahoma who it affected probably did react in the same way. But for the rest of us, for one thing, it wasn't covered by the media near as much as Littleton was, and maybe it's just easier to accept when people die in natural disasters because there's no one to blame. When one human being is responsible for taking the life of another human being, it is hard to take. When God allows nature to take its course and there is no one to blame, it's easier to accept. I think that sometimes we belittle God and make Him out to be less than who He really is, too."

"What do you mean?" Josh asked.

"Well, when I was six years old, I invited Jesus into my heart to be my Lord and Savior. But I guess because I thought of Jesus as being my friend, more than as Him being God, I started to think of Him as just being my buddy. I mean, I felt like I could talk to Him anytime, and I still do, but I guess I started taking talking to Him for granted, like it was no big deal. Do you see what I'm getting at?"

"I'm not really sure, but go on," Josh said encouragingly, catching another grin that was trying to erupt on his lips and terminating it quickly. He didn't want Jennifer to see him smiling for fear she would think that he was patronizing her again. When in fact, he couldn't help but smile for he had never witnessed anyone so passionately and eloquently defend their faith.

"He's the Creator, you know, He made everything and everyone. He made the sun and the moon and all of the stars. He made all of the animals. He made the tiny little grains of sand and the petals on flowers and the tiny little mites that we can't even see. He made all of the creatures in the ocean. He gave us minds, so that we could figure out the intricate system of numbers that He also created. I mean, think about it, when you do a math problem, you're taking part in solving a puzzle that God designed. I think sometimes we think we know it all and we don't acknowledge who *He* really is." She realized that she was starting to sound like the preacher at church, so she cut her speech short. "I guess what I'm saying is that whether we live a long life or die young is totally up to Him because after all, He is God."

"Yeah, you're totally right, but that still doesn't explain whether or not He's controlling everything or if He lets circumstances control what happens or why He lets horrible things happen if He loves us. Like freak accidents, what do you think about those?"

"What do you mean by freak accidents?" Jennifer asked, looking at her watch to see if it was time for them to head home to start getting ready for school. It wasn't.

"I mean the kinds of things that happen when there is no one to blame, like when the tornadoes whipped through and killed a bunch of people, or like being in the wrong place at the wrong time like someone getting hit by a stray boulder coming off of a mountain and getting thrown into the river. Do you think those kinds of things are acts of God that were meant to be?"

"I guess they could be. Maybe it was just their time," Jennifer suggested.

Now we're getting somewhere, Josh thought. "But couldn't circumstances have altered where the people were and prevented the accidents from happening?"

"Well, maybe, but not if God had already decided that it was time to take them home," Jennifer implied.

"So, do you think that it could actually work both ways? Some things He makes happen and they are meant to be, like freak accidents, and then other things He just allows to happen, where there are people who are responsible, and then He just finds ways to find good in them?"

"Maybe," Jennifer answered, still trying to decipher exactly what Josh had said and then pondering the implications of such a scenario. "It seems like that sometimes. It also seems like the more I think about it, the less I know for sure."

"Yeah, I know." He looked down, seeming exasperated again. "Then how much control do we have over our lives? If everything is all planned out, then the choices we make are all just a part of what is meant to be and we really aren't making those choices at all. On the other hand, if nothing is planned out, we have to be on the look out at all times because we're the only ones responsible for what happens to us. It's like when I was flying here, I started thinking how weird it was to be cruising at 30,000 feet in the air in some flimsy piece of scrap metal. I thought about how little faith I had in that plane being up there. Then I thought about the odds of it crashing. Hundreds of planes fly everyday and there are hardly ever any crashes. So, that made me feel better, but then I realized that I have absolutely no control over what happens to me as long as I'm on this plane. When I get like this, I try to pray, but I can't stop thinking that God doesn't always take care of people. And I know what you said about God being God and that should be enough for me to accept whatever happens, but it's still hard for me to understand why He lets horrible things happen and why He takes loved ones away and makes life so painful." Josh could feel his throat tightening, his voice cracking, and his tear ducts swelling with moisture, so he hardened his heart to squelch the emotion which would have otherwise poured out. "There were times when my little sister and I were in some scary situations," he continued, almost forgetting who he was supposed to be. "I wish I could tell you more about it, but I can't right now. All I can tell you is that when she was scared, I would tell her to pray *that* everything would be all right. I never told her to pray *and* everything would be all right. Do you see the difference? I was afraid that if I told her to pray and things got worse, she would lose her faith in God."

"That's so sad, Josh. But God did take care of you, didn't He? I mean you're here right now and your sister is okay, too, right?" She waited for a nod from Josh before she went on. "I don't know what you've been through, but I know I can count the times when it seems like God has reached down and taken care of me. One time my mom and I were driving down a two lane highway on our way to my grandma's house. To get to her house, we had to make a left hand turn onto a dirt road. This particular time when my mom slowed down, put her turn signal on and was about to turn, something told her to check the sideview mirror. Just as she did, a pickup truck came screaming by us on the left going about 80 miles per hour, right where we would have been turning. Afterwards, she said she'd made that turn at least a thousand times before and had never had any inclination to check her mirror before. But that day, something made her check."

"I know - things like that happen all the time. And I have to admit that God has taken care of me. I'm here in Westbrook and I'm happier than I've been since I was a little kid. But I can't help but wonder when it comes to being responsible, if I'm just supposed to trust God or if I have to be on the look out all the time for myself?"

"I know cause we all have choices about what we do and where we go, but do those really matter? Like when someone gets killed in an accident or because of someone else's actions, did God know all along - like from the time that person was a little kid - that on such and such a day, all of these particular events would fall into place and this would happen? Or does He just let people's actions and where they happen to be totally dictate their fates? It seems as though, most of the time, the choices we make lead to the circumstances we find ourselves in, and ultimately determine our destinies. And if we have free wills to do whatever we want, it almost seems like we do determine our own fates and even the fates of others."

Even though Jennifer had said a mouthful, Josh knew exactly what she meant. "Exactly. And sometimes I feel like I'm sitting on two sides of the fence with this one. If God has it all planned out and you're only going to die when He says it's your time, then you really don't have to worry about what you do. I've heard about people falling off of mountains or getting into horrible accidents and living. But then I've heard about other people like this family who took a wrong turn in LA and ended up on a dead end street and some gang members took their little girl and murdered her right there in front of them. When I hear things like that, I think where was God? I'd better be responsible for every move I make because I am the only one watching out for me. Nobody else is going to keep me from making the wrong move or from going down the wrong street. I have to look before I leap, think before I act. And those are the times that I feel the most alone, when I think it's only me, and I can't depend on God or anyone else."

"So then, do you pray?" Jennifer asked, sounding doubtful.

"Well, yeah, I pray," Josh answered, picking up on the hint of doubt in Jennifer's voice. "I pray because I believe that God does have the power to take care of us. And I think that sometimes, maybe prayer helps Him decide what to do. Maybe not always, but I pray anyway."

172

"So, then you believe that He has the power to take care of us, but sometimes He just lets people and circumstances dictate what happens?" Jennifer quizzed.

"Yeah, that's pretty much it. And I just want to know why. Is it part of His plan that these things happen or does He operate on more of a cause and effect system, you know, for every action, there is an equal and opposite reaction?" he answered, not being quite sure he had mastered the quote. "Another thing that I don't get is why God seems to watch over some people and lets horrible things happen to other people. Have you ever watched the news after a terrible earthquake somewhere and they interview a survivor and the person is all thankful and they tell their story and everyone is all touched by it? Do you know what I think about when I watch scenes like that? I think, that's great, but what about the 400 other people who were crushed to death in the building behind you? What are their stories? And it also seems like some people go through life and nothing bad ever happens to them and other people go through life with one bad thing after another happening."

When Josh finished his speech, Jennifer let out a "I've been holding this in for a long time" sigh and sucked up a sniffle through her delicate nose. She stared down at her mittens and watched an unannounced tear form a droplet on one of them. She even felt a little guilty for she knew she was, indeed, one of the lucky ones. She had been blessed with a life void of tragedy or trauma, having been raised in a small town with supportive parents and sisters who loved her. Her heart went out to her friend, for she knew that in the midst of what seemed to be a fairy tale life, he was still fighting some sort of burdensome dragon. She said the first thing that came to her mind once she had composed herself. "Kind of like the Kennedys."

"Yeah, just like the Kennedys. They seem to have it all, but then one tragedy after another happens to them. Jennifer, I don't want to freak you out or anything. I know you must think that I'm obsessed with all of these weird thoughts, but I want to tell you one more thing that

173

I've noticed. For about three years, I've been paying close attention to news shows and newspaper articles that have to do with freak accidents or horrible things that happen to people. There was one where a bunch of kids on a school bus were coming back from a Christian rock concert, and a drunk driver, who was driving down the wrong side of the highway, collided with them head on. The front of the bus burst into flames and there were stories of kids coming down the aisle of the bus on fire and dying right before their friends' eyes. Then, there was this pastor and his wife who had nine kids. Three of them had already left the nest, but six of them were still little. And basically, the mom had devoted her life to raising her children. She homeschooled them and taught them how to play the piano - they were her whole life. One day the family was taking a road trip. They were on the highway and the truck up ahead of them had some big metal part hanging off of it. Other truck drivers saw it and tried to motion the trucker to pull over and even talk to him over the CB radio, but the driver didn't understand English, so he just kept going. Well, pretty soon the piece fell off and there was nothing the dad could do, but to run over it. The parents lived, but the metal caused the gas tank underneath the minivan to explode and all six children were killed. It supposedly uncovered some political scandal that involved truckers in this particular state and people were trying to put the blame on some government dude who was allowing non English speaking people to get their trucking licenses. But the bottom line was, God had allowed it to happen. And in Littleton, when they showed all those kids who had been shot and killed, did you notice anything? It doesn't seem to me that a lot of people go to church anymore, but guess what? Most of those kids who were killed did. Do you see a pattern here?"

"Are you saying that more bad things happen to people who believe in God than to other people ?"

"I don't know. Sometimes it just seems that way to me," Josh added sheepishly, wondering if he had gone too far in revealing his most profound observations.

Jennifer didn't respond directly to Josh's theory, but started with a story of her own, shivering as a gust of wind blasted their icy perch. "There was this guy in our town about five or six years ago. His name was Rick. He was the youth group leader at our church when my older sister was a freshman in high school. He was about twenty four, I guess. He had a girlfriend. They were the cutest couple. He was about 6'4" with dark wavy hair and big, gorgeous blue eyes. I still remember those eyes. She was really little, about 5'2" and they looked so cute together. Anyway, about a month after they announced their engagement, he started getting really bad stomach pains. It turned out to be cancer. For the next year or something, he went through chemo. He lost all of his hair. I remember seeing him at their wedding, after not having seen him in awhile. Without any hair, he looked like an old man. Every Sunday at church, everyone would pray for God to heal him, but God never did. Rick just got weaker and weaker and scrawnier and scrawnier. Even after his hair grew back, you could see that he was getting worse. His eyes and his cheeks had that hollowed out look, like a Holocaust victim. But no matter how bad he looked on the outside, he was still the same on the inside. He would still come up to you wearing this great big smile and put his arm around you and make *you* feel good about the whole situation. I guess that's why I was never scared of him, no matter how scary he looked. He was still the same guy when he was weak and sick as he was when he was handsome and strong." Jennifer gazed into space as she reminisced.

"So, what happened?" Josh prompted, feeling numbness in his toes when he tried to wiggle them in his shoes.

"Oh, well, no one in the church would ever bring up the fact that maybe Rick was going to die, as if it would have been sacrilegious or it would have shown a lack of faith or that it would have just been in poor taste to do so. Until one day, when, who else, but Patrick, walked right up to this 6'4" skeleton of a man and had the nerve to say, 'What if God doesn't heal you? What if you die?' Well, everyone, including me, who was standing nearby, wanted to stick a sock in his mouth and get him the heck

175

out of there. But not Rick. Rick wasn't affected by it in the least. In fact, it seemed like he was happy that someone had been honest enough to bring up the alternative to his being healed. He squatted right down, so that he was eye level with Patrick, put his hand on Patrick's shoulder and said, 'Patrick, I'm glad you asked me that. You know, all of us will have to die sometime. It's not something any of us likes to think about. But with this cancer, it's something that I've had to think about lately. Because as you know, there is a real chance that I might die. And sometimes when I think about it, I get real sad cause I'll have to leave Abi,' that was his wife's name, 'and all of my little buddies like you.' Then Patrick asked him if he was scared. And he said, 'I'm sad, but I'm not really scared. See, I've known Jesus ever since I was a little guy like you. And whatever He wants for me is okay with me. I trust Him. I know He'll be there for me - whatever happens. All of us are going to have to face this sooner or later. I may just have to face it a little sooner.' When he finished, there was dead silence. We all just stood there in awe. Never before and never since then have any of us witnessed such pure faith. After that, we knew that if he was okay with dying that we could be okay with it, too."

"Did he die?" Josh asked somberly.

"Yes, he did, about six months later," Jennifer answered, staring aimlessly at the hole near the baby toe of her left basketball shoe so that Josh wouldn't notice the emotion welling up in her eyes.

"I wish I had that kind of faith, that kind of trust. My little sister is like that. She just figures that we all have to die, so all we should be concerned about is where we're going afterwards. It just doesn't come easy for me. I see all the pain that people have to go through while they're alive and I just don't get it. I don't see why life is so easy for some people and has to be so hard for other people. It just doesn't seem ..." his shaky voice cracked and faded out before he finished his thought.

"It just doesn't seem what?" Jennifer prompted.

"I don't really want to say."

"Why not?" Jennifer asked innocently.

"My grandma had this thing about not doubting God or questioning anything that we don't understand about Him. I'm afraid if I say it, it'll just make God mad," Josh confessed, feeling idiotic for having revealed such intimate thoughts and fears to the one he wanted to impress the most.

"Well, I'm sure God already knows what you were thinking. I'm the only one in the dark here," Jennifer pointed out.

"You're probably right," Josh concurred. "What I was going to say is that sometimes it just doesn't seem fair. Like the good people seem to be the ones who have to go through some of the worst stuff. And the people who don't even believe in God end up having it easy their whole lives."

"It seems that way, but they're still going to have to face God someday. And maybe He takes the ones home who He knows are ready to go. Their hearts and minds aren't totally focused on the things of this world. It's like Rick said, 'we all have to face it sooner or later.' Maybe He uses those situations to bring more people to Him."

"But what about the people who are left behind? Like the mother and father of the six children who died when the gas tank exploded? Or the two kids I heard about whose parents were crushed by a gigantic boulder?" Josh eyed her curiously, wondering if he was divulging too much of the truth that he'd been forced to conceal.

But her expression showed no signs of having unveiled any startling revelations as she went on to explain, "Hopefully, those who are left behind will be strong enough to endure by the grace of God until they are reunited with their loved ones someday. And God did bring some good out of Rick's death. Twenty seven people accepted the Lord that day."

"Yeah, but think about how many more people he might have led to the Lord if he had lived to be 100?" Josh was playing the devil's advocate again.

"You know, for someone whose grandmother told him not to question God, you sure do question Him a lot."

177

"Yeah, I know, I can't help it," he apologized.

"I guess what I'm trying to say is that we have to let God be God and to realize that whether it's God's plan or if it's circumstances that decide our destinies, there are no guarantees. None of us knows when his or her time will come. Most people actually do live relatively long lives. But my point is, if you spend some time getting to know God now, then maybe leaving this earth won't seem so scary when the time comes,"Jennifer clarified.

"Yeah, maybe, but that seems so cut and dry, so absent of human emotion that accompanies every heart-wrenching tragedy," Josh objected. "You can't just put your feelings aside when you lose someone you love, even though you know they're in Heaven. It still hurts really badly and you miss them."

"You're absolutely right," Jennifer admitted, "but you also have to figure out some way to deal with the pain and go on with your life."

Josh nodded in agreement. "You're right, too. I guess it's just really hard to do sometimes. There's something else that I've noticed. It's kind of strange, but I've heard of it happening a lot," Josh continued.

"What's that?"Jennifer asked, still enthralled with Josh's depth of emotion and character.

"I've noticed that sometimes when someone in a family dies, a little while later, someone else from that same family or a close friend dies, too. Have you ever noticed that?"

"To tell you the truth, I have," Jennifer confirmed.

"What do you make of that?" Josh asked.

"Well, my mom and I were talking about that when John Kennedy, Jr. was killed in the plane crash. We were watching all these shows on TV about the Kennedy curse. You know what my mom said that made me feel better? She said that maybe when someone dies, they start to miss their loved ones here on earth and maybe they ask God if they can have someone they love come up to be with them in Heaven. I mean they have already realized that life on earth isn't all there is, so it probably doesn't seem like such a big deal to them to ask for someone else to come up. Like you said before, it's hardest on those who are left behind."

178

"Sometimes it's just hard to think of any kind of afterlife as being as good as this life. You know, when you think of Heaven, you think of being in a place where you just hang around and sit on clouds and play the harp all day. It doesn't seem like it could be as great as life is here where you can snowboard and play basketball."

"I know. I think that's why we try to have it all while we're here because we can't imagine it really being better there."

"So, then why not just go on to the next life right now if it is so much better?" Josh asked.

"I don't think God wants us to do that. I think He wants us to make the most of our lives here and to depend on Him for strength when times are tough."

"Maybe so, but I just don't see why people have to get old or get sick or even die at all?"

"If no one ever died, no one would ever take time to even think about God," Jennifer answered reflectively.

"I like the way you put things into perspective, even though I don't always agree with you," Josh admitted candidly.

"Another thing that my mom and I talked about when JFK Jr. died was that it seemed like God was trying to tell the world to stop believing in fairy tales and to believe in Him, instead. They aren't reality - He is reality. I know that sounds harsh, but when Princess Diana was killed, it kind of ended the fairy tale life that she supposedly had. She'd had a fairy tale wedding, shattered by a divorce and then death itself. And with the Kennedys, my mom told me that President Kennedy and his wife had a fairy tale life, that they themselves called Camelot. That fairy tale life ended when the president was killed. My mom grew up watching John Kennedy, Jr. grow up, too. Everyone had so much hope in him to fulfill the legacy that his father began, maybe not becoming president, but following in his father's footsteps and being someone who the American people could look to for hope and inspiration. That hope disappeared on the day that his plane went down. The legacy ended and he didn't even have a son to carry on the family legacy. There are no fairy tales; there are no princes and princesses in real life. There are just ordinary people like you and me."

179

"Maybe it's better that he didn't have a son. Otherwise people would have done to his son what they did to him. They expected too much from him. Even ordinary people like you and me get caught up in how important we think we are. People are always trying to figure out what they want to be when they grow up or what they should do with their lives. Even Christians try to figure out, 'what is God's will for *my* life?' They put the emphasis on themselves and they think that what they do is indispensable to Him. And then all of a sudden that person dies or something. Then I think, why do people get so carried away with what God wants them to do? He doesn't really need us at all."

"Yeah, but I still think that He wants us to be trying to do what we think He wants us to do, even if we're going to die young. Like with Rick, he went to seminary school for years to become a pastor, but only got to work as a youth leader for a couple of years before he died."

"That's exactly my point. He went through all that, thinking that what he was doing was important to God. And then God took him home instead. So, we're not as important to God's plan as we think we are," Josh argued.

"I don't see it that way. He was doing what he thought God wanted him to be doing *when* God took him home. And that, in itself, is important," Jennifer explained. "You know before when you were saying how it seems like sometimes when someone dies, a little while later a close friend or family member joins them?"

"Yeah." Josh nodded positively.

"I've noticed that other times when someone dies, it seems like the exact opposite happens."

"What do you mean?"

"Well, I knew these people whose daughter died. Shortly after, they got in a really horrible accident, but basically just walked away from it - almost as if she was watching over them."

" Well, I've heard of that, too. And I can't decide if it just adds to the whole idea that none of this makes any sense or if the person who died was watching over them. I mean, why would the daughter be the one to die? She was younger, she had more to live for. Wouldn't it have made more sense for her parents to have died if they were old and for them to have been looking out for her?"

180

"Yeah, I guess so. It's just something that I noticed. I don't really understand it either."

"Something else I wonder about is me being here in Westbrook. Was this God's plan for me from the time I was born, or did He bring me here because of things that happened in my life and this was His way of making something good out of something bad? Or did I just end up here purely by chance?"

"I don't know," Jennifer shrugged, "but I think God must have had something to do with it."

"Yeah, me, too, I guess," Josh confessed, stretching out his legs, "but I'm not 100% sure. There's only one thing that I am 100% sure about right now," he said, changing the subject. "If I don't get up out of this position pretty soon, my cheeks are going to be permanent fixtures on these roofing tiles."

Josh heard a ripping sound when he unweighted his left cheek from the roofing tiles. Then after checking for a rip in his pants, he stood and held out his hand to Jennifer. She, too, rose, her knees cracking from staying in that frozen position for so long.

"Hey, do you want to do something tonight after the game? It's my last Friday night here. My fairy tale life is about to end in a few days and I'd like to take as much memory of you with me as I can," he confessed.

"How can I say no to that?" Jennifer shrugged.

"I hope you can't." He stared hopefully into her deep green eyes. As she moved in closer to face him, he grasped her mittened hands and held them in his. Their slender figures silhouetted the splendid morning sky and they both knew that the moment they'd been patiently awaiting was upon them.

For in spite of their chattering teeth and the taste of salty teardrops now frozen on Jennifer's lips, Josh and Jennifer melted for a brief moment in a delicate kiss, in much the same way that the blazing newborn sun had kissed and melted the earth's frozen horizon just moments before.

Chapter Seventeen

It was close to midnight when Josh and Patrick got home that night, the entire team having celebrated their fourth victory in a row with a night out on the town.

The last thing that Josh was inclined to do when his tired body hit the mattress that night was to get back up and call his uncle. But he had promised himself that, no matter what, he would.

He sifted through his belongings in the duffel bag in search of the piece of paper containing his uncle's phone number. It depressed him to think that he would soon be reclaiming his old life and his true identity. It wasn't that he didn't like Jeff Farnsworth anymore, it was just that as Josh Montgomery, he had been able to leave the sorrow of the past behind and begin a new life. He was afraid that by becoming Jeff again, he would lose the enthusiasm he had for life and become the desperate, contemplative, soul searching individual that he had been before.

He pushed the digits on the touch tone phone and waited for the computerized operator to request his calling card number. He entered the same number that he had the last time he'd attempted to call his uncle from LA, just a month and a half ago. In some ways, it seemed like such a short time ago, but in many ways it felt like an eternity had passed since then.

He didn't worry about waking his uncle up at this late hour. Uncle Frank was more than likely up, finishing off the last brew from a case of beer, it being a Friday night and all.

The phone rang several times while Josh lay in his bed in the dark, awaiting his fate. He could hear Patrick's steady breathing as he had already fallen asleep in the bunk above. He heard a rip thunder through the mattress, reverberating through the mattress springs and down through the wooden frame of the top bunk. Normally, Josh would have laughed at Patrick's uproarious passage of gas, but tonight he was too intent on the phone call to even notice it much.

"Yello," the intoxicated, unemployed uncle mumbled through a mouthful of beef jerky.

"Uncle Frank?" Jeff said.

"Jeff, is that you?" His uncle choked on the beef jerky. "The whole darn world has been looking for you! Where the heck are you?"

Bypassing the question, Jeff got right down to the business at hand. "Have you given any more thought to Sarah and me coming to live with you? You probably heard that they were going to separate us, so I took off."

"Well, Jeff, I wish I could help you, but you're in a lot of trouble, boy. If you come here and I don't turn you in, I could go to jail."

"Is that what they told you?" Jeff questioned in disbelief.

"Yeah, they said that I would be in a lot of trouble, too, if I went along with you. Besides, we've got a baby on the way," Uncle Frank explained, looking over at his second wife whose swollen belly looked as if she'd swallowed a watermelon.

"I might be able to help you out there, Uncle Frank," Jeff remarked. "If you could call them and see if they would allow you to take custody of Sarah and me, I could give you $5000."

"$5000? Jeff, where'd you come up with that kind of mula? Are you selling drugs or something?" His uncle scratched his three day old beard and topped off the question with an unexcused belch.

"No, of course not, I'll tell you about it when I get there," Jeff promised his uncle.

"I'll tell you what, why don't you just send me a cashier's check for the five grand and I'll see what I can do about it?" Uncle Frank suggested tactlessly.

In that instant, Jeff's hopes were shot down. "Okay, I'll do that. Thanks a lot," he murmured sarcastically, desperation rising in the form of a giant lump in his throat, as he hung up the phone.

He spent the next few minutes in a bewildered daze. He would have to come up with another plan. Perhaps he would stay with Coach until the end of basketball season.

And maybe, somehow, during the course of his extended stay, he could muster up the courage to tell Coach the truth. Maybe Coach would sympathize with his situation and help him find a solution. But for right now, Josh decided that he would not rock the boat with details, such as the truth, that might jeopardize the offer to stay with Coach. In the meantime, he would pray for a miracle.

Early the next morning, before either Josh or Patrick was awake, Amos found his way into the forbidden zone known as Patrick's room and began fidgeting with the computer. As the entire family was amply proficient in sending and receiving email, Amos took it upon himself to retrieve the message that was patiently awaiting Josh's attention. He had also taken it upon himself to rifle through Josh's little book of important phone numbers and email addresses a long time ago, and had come upon all of the vital information, including Josh's email address and password, that he needed to access any and all of his messages. He didn't take the time to read the message, but he did recognize Josh's father as being its sender. Amos liked Josh, for the most part, but since Josh still hadn't made good on his promise to take Amos to the arcade, Amos decided to teach the family's guest a valuable lesson in consequences for breaking promises.

Amos deleted the information that had traveled all the way through cyberspace, from Australia to Ohio, to reach its intended destination. He had no idea what disastrous effects this simple act would induce, just as he'd had no clue as to what he'd done when he had stolen the fax which would have let Josh know that a kangaroo was on its way to Westbrook Middle School.

The dirty deed was done before either one of the older boys batted an eyelid towards consciousness on this Saturday morning.

When the boys finally did rise, they spent the day helping the science club prepare its booth for the winter carnival which would be held that night. Patrick was obligated to work three full hours in the science club's mini basketball booth to fulfill his part of the pickle prank agreement.

Smitty would be on hand, as well, to appeal to the crowd's sense of vulnerability to cuteness and to their responsibility to feed and house the school's adorable, new mascot.

Josh looked forward to spending the evening with Jennifer. They had become closer than ever since the day they had shared their thoughts and feelings on the icy rooftop.

Their friendship reminded him of the kind of relationship that his own parents had shared, as best friends first of all. He longed to tell Jennifer the truth about who Sarah really was and all about the events that had changed his life forever. He thought that she would be understanding, but at the same time he feared that she would discount him for his lack of honesty. Plus, he also wondered if what Patrick had said was true. Had she only liked Bull for his money? If so, perhaps that was her attraction to him, as well. He feared that who she liked was Joshua Clayton Montgomery III and all that he was, and that she wouldn't like Jeff Farnsworth, the homeless orphan who was obsessed with questions about life and who was wanted by the state of California for being a juvenile delinquent.

Josh and Jennifer met at the outdoor skating rink, and when they tired of skating, went inside to check out the booths and to warm up with steaming cups of hot chocolate.

Patrick, like Smitty, was stationed in the science club booth. Patrick was putting most of his effort into teaching Smitty how to catch the mini basketballs and shoot them through the miniature hoops. But instead, Smitty, invariably, would drop the balls when Patrick tossed them to her or attempt to eat them or hide them in her pouch. This game went on endlessly, interrupted by an occasional carnival dweller who longed to sink his or her money into the science club's nets.

"What are you giving away here?" Josh asked when he and Jennifer arrived.

"These little aliens," Patrick announced, pulling one of the big eyed, little green men from underneath the table. "Is this what your grandmother was seeing?"

"What?" Jennifer asked, confused by the remark.

Patrick and Josh laughed. "His grandma used to see little green men, didn't she, Josh?"

Josh just smiled and waved a dollar bill in front of Patrick's face. "Let me try this," he demanded.

Josh steadied himself before attempting his first shot through the miniature hoop. Swish went the first shot. Swish went the second shot. One more shot and he'd have an alien to give to Jennifer. He stopped. He popped. Bonk went the last ball off to the side. Since Patrick had turned his attention aside for a minute to see what Smitty had done with the first ball, Jennifer cheered, fooling Patrick into thinking that Josh had indeed sunk the last shot.

"Hey, buddy, way to go!" Patrick exclaimed, turning back to Josh and retrieving an alien from the box below.

"But I didn't make it, Patrick," Josh confessed. "Jennifer was just cheering for me."

"Sure you did. Just take the thing, will you?" Patrick coerced, forcing the stuffed toy into Josh's hand.

"No, Patrick, that wouldn't be right; it wouldn't be legal."

"So what? So, it's an illegal alien, big deal. Hey, get it? An illegal alien." Patrick again was impressed with his stroke of originality and laughed at his own joke.

"I'll just give it back to Mrs. Grouse if you give it to me," Josh stated.

"Okay, then, Mr. Honesty, go ahead and spend all of your money to try to win one fair and square."

So he did. Ten dollars later, when he still hadn't succeeded in sinking three consecutive shots, Jennifer reached into her pocket and pulled out a buck to try her luck. Whoosh, whoosh, whoosh went all three mini basketballs in a row. She handed the alien to Josh.

"Here's a souvenir for you to take home with you," she said.

"Thanks," Josh answered sheepishly. "I guess this is all part of being the deep sensitive guy that I am, not too macho to accept a prize from a girl."

Just then Coach Webber and his wife, Tara, joined Josh, Patrick, and Jennifer at the booth, gravitating towards the curious marsupial as it sniffed each of them inquisitively.

"Can I pet her? Does she bite?" Tara asked, referring to Smitty.

"She won't bite hard," Patrick answered with a deviant grin.

"Hey, whatever happened to Bull and Pudge and that other kangaroo from the zoo?" Tara asked her husband while she petted Smitty on the head.

"Well, remember I told you that Bull moved over to Redmont. He and Pudge kept sticking to their story that the kangaroo was delivered to *these* two guys," Coach said, pointing towards Josh and Patrick, "by our former janitor, Jethro."

"Did they ever get to ask Jethro about it?" Patrick chimed in, having dismissed the issue as dead.

"Yes, they did. When he returned from his vacation, he confessed to having delivered the kangaroo to the corner of Maple and Elm on November 18th at 11:30 pm, but he refused to disclose the names of the two boys to whom he had delivered it. With Pudge and Bull caught red handed and with no other witnesses to prove their allegations against the two of you, the matter was settled out of court. I believe both of the boys received 100 hours of community service and perhaps a small fine."

"And what about Jethro, what happened to him?" Patrick asked anxiously.

"He got fired from the zoo for withholding evidence, but they didn't file any criminal charges against him."

Patrick and Josh found the news about Jethro disheartening, to say the least, as they gave each other bleak stares.

"What's he going to do now? He's got a wife and a kid, you know?" Patrick questioned desperately.

"I haven't heard. I always thought he was a good man when he worked for us at the school district. I'd hire him again if there was an opening," Coach confirmed. "Hey, Josh, have you decided whether you're going to finish out the basketball season with us?"

Josh took a deep breath. He could feel Jennifer and Patrick's eyes upon him. He hadn't told Patrick about the call he'd made to his uncle the night before, the call that had demolished his hopes for the future. "I'm staying," he said timidly.

Jennifer's eyes lit up, as did Patrick's when they heard the news.

"But I'll have to stay with you, Coach, if that's still okay. I'm sure the Bakers are getting tired of me."

"No, they're not," Patrick assured him.

"Well, we'll get together with them and work out the details. Are you sure it's okay with your parents?" Coach asked Josh tentatively.

"They won't even know I'm gone," Josh replied.

"Can you cover for me?" Patrick asked Josh when the Webbers had moved on to another club's booth.

"Sure, what's up?" Josh asked.

"I've got to call Jethro. I feel terrible about what happened. I want to see if there's anything I can do."

Again Patrick's sensitive side was showing as he bolted over the booth's barriers and headed for the phone.

As soon as Jethro answered the phone, Patrick sputtered relentless apologies to him. "I'm so sorry, dude. You should have told them that we were the ones who put you up to it. It wasn't worth you losing your job over."

"It's okay, man, I was getting sick of my job there, anyway. It was a long drive to the zoo from all the way out here in Westbrook. I needed to find something else anyway."

"So, did you find another job, yet?" Patrick asked hopefully.

"Not yet, but I've put in some applications. Don't worry about it. You stuck up for me when I started the trash can fire at the school. By all rights, I should have lost my job then. You saved my butt big time. I owed you one."

"I didn't know I could feel so bummed over someone else's misfortune," Patrick admitted when he returned to the booth where Josh and Jennifer were feeding Smitty handfuls of popcorn.

Jennifer and Josh nodded in agreement, but were having a difficult time sharing Patrick's empathy for Jethro. It wasn't that they weren't concerned about the man's welfare, it was just that the two of them were immersed in the midst of a budding romance that seemed to take precedence over everything else. Even the intense questions and theories that they had postulated during their rooftop conversation seemed inconsequential now as their infatuations with one another intensified.

"Well, I think we're going to take off now," Josh informed Patrick once he had resumed his post.

"Can't you guys wait for me? There are only about twenty minutes left before this thing is over," Patrick requested, but retracted the statement when he saw the pathetic lovestruck looks that Josh and Jennifer were exchanging with each other. "On the other hand, why don't you two just go ahead. Grouchface will probably make me clean up afterwards and take care of Smitty."

"Are you sure?" Jennifer asked halfheartedly.

"I'm sure," Patrick insisted, changing his voice to sound like an old geezer, "you youngsters just run along!"

It was below freezing when Josh and Jennifer made their way up the porch steps leading to Jennifer's home and shared another tender kiss on Jennifer's front porch before saying good night. But neither of them noticed the plummeting temperatures. Both were content just to be together and relieved that Josh had bought more time for them to stay that way.

Chapter Eighteen

It was December 23rd, the last day of school before Christmas break, and also, the day of the Kangaroos' last game of the year.

Josh woke up early, rolled out of bed, and situated himself in the swivel chair at the computer, as this had become his almost daily   routine for the past seven weeks.   He would check his email and respond to it immediately as he hadn't taken the time to do so in the past few days.

His vision was still blurry as he retrieved the mail that was awaiting his attention. He pulled up the screen and was shocked into full consciousness when he read the content of the message.

It read, "I haven't heard from you since I emailed you last weekend.   I hope we're still on for Thursday night. I'm looking forward to seeing you in action. Don't worry about meeting me at the airport. I've arranged for a limo to take me directly to the game. I've never been so proud of you in all my life. Love, Dad."

"Thursday night?" Josh shrieked in a frenzied outburst which awakened Patrick.

"Wassup?" Patrick asked hoarsely, squinting just one eye open to avoid the harshness of the morning light.

"JC's dad is coming!"

"When?" Patrick asked, sitting up in his bed, yawning and scratching his fuzzy yellow head, still seeming relatively unconcerned about the recent development.

"Tonight!" Josh gasped, becoming short of breath as he pointed to the email message that flashed across the screen. "He's coming to our game to see JC play. What should I do?"

"Let me think about it for a minute. This is no big deal.   We'll figure something out," Patrick assured him, trying to downplay the magnitude of the surprise visit. "Well, the first thing you have to do is to call JC and tell him to get his butt up here ASAP.   Then tell him to take a cab to the school and we'll meet him there. It would have been nice if Mr. Montgomery would have given you a little more time to prepare for this!"

"He said he emailed me over the weekend, but I never saw it, did you?"

"No, but I bet I know who did - Amos!" Patrick accused. " I'm going to kill him!"

"You'll have to do that later. There's no time for that now. You have to help me figure out what to do. What if I can't get a hold of JC? And what is he supposed to tell his dad about why he isn't playing in the game?"

"One thing at a time," Patrick said, resuming his composure. "If you can't get a hold of him, we'll, I mean, *I'll* just tell his dad that he didn't get the message in time and left on an earlier flight home. And if we do get a hold of him and he actually comes up here, he can just tell his dad that he hurt his ankle and can't play."

Patrick's confidence had a calming effect on Josh as he fingered through the little black book until he found JC's uncle's phone number in Miami. The phone rang five times and then Josh heard a click. It was an answering machine.

"If you've been hurt in an automobile accident or suffered an injury due to the fault of another, you've called the right place. Leave a message after the siren and I'll get back to you as soon as possible," said a gravelly voice on the other end of the line, followed by a piercing siren.

"Is this a joke?" Josh wondered aloud, feeling unsure about having the right number, but leaving an urgent message anyway. He went into extreme detail about the email message he'd received and urged JC to catch a quick flight up to meet Josh at the school before JC's father arrived. He even provided the injured ankle alibi for JC so that his father would not be suspicious as to why he wasn't playing in the game. When the siren sounded again, Josh knew that his time was up. He hoped that the information he'd left made sense and that JC would get it in time. He decided to email that same message to JC, just in case JC was to check his email before checking the machine. Josh did all he could to cover all of the bases.

191

Getting to school on time prevented Josh and Patrick from waiting around the house for a response from JC. It was quite an ordeal for the two boys when they headed off to school, each one carrying a single piece of JC's luggage in one hand and bending over sideways to roll the largest leather suitcase between them. Each time one of the rollers jammed in a sidewalk crack, the bottom of the suitcase scraped the sidewalk, scratching off patches of leather from its exterior.

"Why are we doing this again?" Josh asked, stopping to rest his arm for a moment.

"We have to bring JC's bags to him so that he can leave right from the school and his dad doesn't have to come back to my house to meet my mom and dad."

"Oh yeah," Josh concurred, recognizing a churning going on within his abdominal walls, much like that of having butterflies in one's stomach, but on a much grander scale. What was seething inside of him seemed more like vampire bats in search of fresh blood.

At lunch when Josh attempted to make the call again, he was greeted by the same absurd ambulance chaser on the machine.

In the gym after school, Josh paced the floor, bouncing the basketball in a methodical, monotonous manner, shooting every once in a while for a change of pace. It reminded Patrick of fathers to be portrayed in old movies as they paced the floor, back and forth, back and forth, in anticipation of the births of their children.

Patrick was downing a juicy burger from the coffee shop, the grease dripping down his chin with nearly every bite he took. Josh was too nervous to even think about eating.

Just then Jennifer entered the gym. "Hi guys. I've been looking all over for you. What are you doing in here so early? The game doesn't start until 6:30, and we don't have to be here for warmups until 6:00. What's up?"

"He's waiting for someone," Patrick mumbled through a mouthful of beef. "Someone very important is coming to town and it's not Santa Claus."

Josh glared at him, his look indicating that he was not happy with Patrick's lack of self control in keeping the information under wraps.

"It's okay," Patrick assured Josh when he caught a glimpse of Josh's expression. "Josh's dad is coming, only he doesn't want anyone to know, so don't tell anybody, okay?"

"Okay, I can do that," Jennifer promised, not even asking why the visit was being kept a secret. "That's really exciting, Josh!"

"Exciting isn't the word for it," Josh answered, palefaced. "A friend of mine from Australia might be coming, too. Right, Patrick?"

"Oh, yeah, that's right. His friend, JC, may be coming, too."

"Well, I was just going to grab a bite to eat at the coffee shop if anyone wants to come with me," Jennifer invited.

"I was alweddy dere," Patrick gurgled, gulping down the last of his burger and stuffing his mouth with fries.

"I'm too nervous to eat. Besides I better wait here in case anybody comes," Josh answered, wishing that he could go with her.

"Do you want me to bring something back for you, Josh?" she asked pleasantly.

"Too nervous," he said, declining her second offer.

"I understand. I get nervous, too, when my parents come to the games. I'll see you guys later," she said, passing five perky cheerleaders on her way out of the gym.

"You should have gone with her," Patrick advised. "It might be the last time you get to see her if things don't work out the way we planned tonight."

"Don't say that, dude," Josh said reluctantly. "I'm depending on you to give me the confidence that we can pull this thing off tonight."

"You're right, man, I'm sorry. We are going to pull this off tonight. And you're going to be here at least until February, if not longer, okay? We've got to think positive."

"Okay, I'll try. I just really don't know how we're going to pull this off."

"Well, just leave it to me. We'll take it one step at a time, buddy, just don't you worry," Patrick tried to assure him.

Again, as fate or luck or divine providence would have it, about an hour later, the young JC Montgomery had just departed from his domestic flight and was walking through the terminal when he noticed his father, JC Montgomery II, also, making his way through the crowded concourse en route to his waiting limousine. JC's father was a handsome man with thick black hair and slightly graying temples. Even standing there in the terminal, clad in casual attire and not surrounded by his usual entourage of body guards and personal assistants, he still caught the attention of passersby simply due to his uncommon good looks. Was he the recipient of stares from women of all ages because they recognized him as the billionaire business tycoon or were they simply admiring his buff physique and youthful appearance? Either way, he attracted attention wherever he went.

"Father," the young JC yelled, sprinting a bit to catch up with him.

"Son!" Mr. Montgomery exclaimed passionately as he turned to embrace his prodigal son. "It's so good to see you."

"You, too, Father," JC answered stiffly, unaccustomed to his father's deliberate show of affection and kind words.

"So, what are you doing here at the airport? Shouldn't you be at school warming up in preparation for your game?"

"I was anxious to see you, Father," he lied. Then remembering his alibi, added, "Besides I sort of sprained my ankle last night at practice."

"That's a bloody shame," his father stated disenchantedly, "but it seemed okay a moment ago when you ran to greet me."

JC bent over to massage his ankle and then hobbled alongside his father, explaining that the brief jaunt had indeed affected his injury.

"Have you seen a physician about it?" Mr. Montgomery inquired, empathizing with his son's plight.

"Yes, he told me to just stay off of it for a couple of days."

"Well, that's probably for the best even though I would have loved to have seen you play. It looks like you've kept your tan since you've been here," JC's father mentioned when he noticed JC's healthy glow.

"Oh, you know me, every once in awhile I hire a cab and sneak over to the nearest tanning salon."

"Well, that's great, son," Mr. Montgomery said reluctantly, feeling that males who frequented tanning salons possessed rather misdirected masculine priorities . "Whatever makes you happy. It looks good on you." He told a little white lie just to keep the peace. "I was really looking forward to seeing you play tonight. But now that you've found your niche in basketball, you can play at home on the academy's team," Mr. Montgomery said, reclaiming a positive outlook on the situation.

"Father," JC asked as he noticed the presence of two men trailing behind them, "are those two men following us?"

Without turning around, Mr. Montgomery concurred, "As a matter of fact, they are."

"Are they your new bodyguards? What happened to Trevor and Luke?"

"They're on Christmas holiday. No, actually these two men are from the United States government. They offered to accompany me here as they're conducting an ongoing investigation. They're searching for a runaway they believe might be in the area. Gentlemen," he summoned the two men, "I'd like you to meet my son, Josh. These are agents Charlie Bryce and Travis Scott."

"Nice to meet you," JC blurted out and then continued nervously, "What does their looking for a runaway have to do with you?"

"It seems that this runaway did more than leave the foster home where he was living in California. The authorities have reason to believe that somehow he acquired one of your credit cards and the address where you've been staying. He made the mistake of leaving the receipt in the bottom of the bag where he bought some toys. When he sent some of the toys to his sister in California, they found the receipt with your name on it. The amount on the slip was over $2000. That's when the feds got involved. This was no longer just the case of a boy running away, it was now a case of credit card fraud, as well. Your mother and I, of course, canceled the card immediately."

"You did what?"

"We canceled the card so that he can't use it anymore. If he tries to use it again, it will be confiscated on the spot," Mr. Montgomery explained while he watched the expression on his son's face sicken. "You didn't by any chance make those purchases and then give those items to a young man, did you?"

"Well, actually, I did. I met this guy and he gave me this sob story about running away from home and just wanting to send his sister a gift for Christmas, so I told him to pick something out and I'd buy it for him."

"Oh, dear," Mr. Montgomery said, scratching his chin and stopping on the concourse to give the two agents time to catch up to them again. "Gentlemen, I believe that we have solved the credit card mystery," he informed them, relating JC's story to them.

"Have you seen the boy since you bought the toys for him?" Agent Bryce, a heavyset balding man, asked JC.

"I can honestly say that I have not," JC replied, eyeing the set of agents suspiciously, thinking that their attire lacked the stereotypical black suits that JC was accustomed to seeing on FBI agents in the movies. "You chaps don't look like federal agents," he added, hoping to change the subject until he could come up with a foolproof alibi that could save his hide and the hide of the runaway in question.

"That's the whole idea," the taller, younger agent chimed in. "We dress this way," he said pointing to the plaid shirt and denim jeans beneath his sheepskin coat, "to blend in with the crowds. If we wore black suits like they do in the movies, the bad guys would see us and get away."

As unprofessional as that sounded, JC believed that it was probably true. In fact, if Josh was to encounter these two men tonight at the game, he would never suspect that they were anything but Kangaroo basketball fans.

"I like your story," the chunkier agent replied, "but it doesn't explain how the Bakers' address ended up on the box, now does it?"

JC glared at the agent, squinting his eyes and shaking his head in reluctant agreement.

"Shall we go?" Mr. Montgomery motioned the two men and JC towards the waiting limo just outside the sliding glass doors.

Once they were all seated inside, Mr. Montgomery directed a question toward the balding agent. "Charlie, what did you say the name of the youth was? And do you have a photograph of the boy?"

"His name," the man said, "is Jeff Farnsworth and here's his picture." He pulled out a photo of Jeff as Mr. Montgomery flicked on an overhead light to take a look.

"Is this the boy to whom you gave the toys, JC?" his father asked.

JC knew that it was indeed a picture of Jeff, but decided he'd better deny it since Jeff would be all too visible at the game. "No, this isn't him," JC stated confidently.

"Are you sure?" Agent Scott, the lanky partner grilled him.

"It couldn't be," JC reconfirmed, "the dude I helped out was black."

The two agents leaned back in their seats, obviously convinced that JC was lying, but not wanting to condemn the lad in front of his wealthy, politically connected father.

"Father, since I can't play in tonight's game and since these two gentlemen have obviously been barking up the wrong tree, what say we skip the game and the four of us all go out for a nice steak and lobster dinner to celebrate my going home?"

JC could see Agent Bryce salivating at the thought of a steak and lobster dinner, but his partner redirected his focus. "Couldn't we do that *after* the game?" Agent Scott

197

advised. "Besides, I don't believe that we have been barking up the wrong tree. In fact, I'd have to say that I believe we are hot on the young man's trail."

"We can dine on steak and lobster anytime," Mr. Montgomery contended. "I'm anxious to see the kangaroo that I sent and the nice apparatus the science club made in which to house it."

He sent a kangaroo? JC thought to himself. What's next?

"I'd also like to meet this Patrick character you've been going on about in your daily email. And your girlfriend, Jennifer, and of course, Patrick's parents who have been nice enough to take care of you for the past month and a half. I'd also like to meet your coach and thank him for helping you to find yourself."

If he only knew, JC was thinking to himself. I didn't find myself, if anything I lost myself in Miami. And what was all that about daily email? I thought I told Jeff to email him every couple of weeks, not everyday. And I have a girlfriend? A lot can happen in seven weeks. I wonder if she's good looking.

When JC came back to reality from his world of wonder, the limo was pulling up to the front door of Westbrook Middle School. The chauffeur did the honors of opening the doors for all of the limo's occupants as they stepped out into the brisk night air.

It was fifteen minutes prior to game time when JC, his father and the federal agents made their triumphal entry into the gymnasium where the teams were warming up amidst record crowds of fans in the stands.

"There they are," Josh whispered to Patrick without even casting a glance in their direction.

"Who are the dudes with them?" Patrick asked, forcing Josh to turn around to look.

"What dudes?" Josh asked, not having noticed the two men accompanying them.

"Those two guys, fatty and skinny?" Patrick replied.

"I don't know. Maybe you can go up there and find out."

"Me? You want me to go up there?" Patrick gasped.

"Who else? I can't go up there. I'm supposed to *be* him."

"Who am I supposed to be?" Patrick asked in a panic.

"You're supposed to be you. JC's dad is probably expecting to meet you. Just go up and introduce yourself. Then tell JC that he's needed in the locker room. I'll meet him in there, so that we can make plans."

"Okay, okay, that sounds easy enough. But what are we going to tell Coach about your sudden disappearance?"

"I'll just tell him that I'm sick and that I don't think I can play tonight. That's not too far from the truth. I might have to take off from here if things start to get weird, so if I don't get to say goodbye, I want to thank you for everything, buddy," Josh stated reluctantly.

"Don't think that way. It's going to be okay. We'll get the real JC and his dad in and out of here without anyone even noticing. Then you can go back to being him for the next couple of months."

"I hope so," Josh replied. "See ya." Josh headed for the locker room.

Being the natural actor that he was, Patrick rose to the occasion, bounding up the bleachers to where JC, his father, and the two unknowns were settling in for the game. He greeted JC genuinely, as though he'd known him for the past seven weeks. "Hey, buddy, we're going to miss you out there tonight. Is this your dad? Hi, I'm Patrick."

Mr. Montgomery stood up and held out his hand to Patrick. "Patrick, it is a distinct pleasure to make your acquaintance. Josh has told me so much about you," he said, referring to his son as Josh since that was how his alleged son had been signing his email.

"Thanks. It's nice to meet you, too." Patrick said, extending his hand to JC's father. "Josh, you're needed in the locker room." Patrick turned his attention toward JC. "Go easy on that ankle," he reminded JC so that he would remember to limp when he walked. "What a great guy! You'd be amazed at how quickly we bonded and how much we have in common."

"Is that so?" Mr. Montgomery smiled approvingly.

JC heeded Patrick's call and headed down the bleachers, following the direction of Patrick's pointing finger towards the locker room. Patrick, too, was about to rejoin his teammates below when someone tapped him on the shoulder. He turned to see who was doing the finger prodding and then squealed in horror as he stood face to face with his own mother and father. Without saying a word, he bolted from the stands down to where his fellow players stood in a huddle with Coach.

"You'll have to excuse our son," Mrs. Baker apologized to the strange, yet familiar looking man with whom her son had been conversing. "He gets a little jumpy before games."

"That's *your* son?" the handsome gentleman asked eloquently. "Then you must be Linda and Dean Baker," he stated, standing once again to make their acquaintances. "I'm JC Montgomery."

"Why, yes, it's wonderful to meet you," Mrs. Baker replied, suddenly recognizing the familiar face from countless magazine covers.

The two men exchanged handshakes and after the introductions were complete, Mr. Montgomery remarked, "You seem surprised to see me here. Didn't the boys tell you that I was coming?"

"Well, no, actually they didn't," Mr. Baker responded, looking at his wife to verify his claim. Mrs. Baker, too, shook her head that she had not heard anything about it.

"Boys will be boys," Mr. Baker commented and then looking around asked, "Where is Josh anyway? And why isn't he starting?"

"You mean the boys didn't tell you that either?" Mr. Montgomery prodded. "He sprained his ankle at practice yesterday. He told me that he saw a doctor. I only assumed that one of you would have transported him there."

"We never heard a thing about it," Mrs. Baker mused. "He looked fine a few minutes ago during warmups."

Now Mr. Montgomery was beginning to have serious doubts about these two adults who had supposedly been responsible for the welfare of his son for the past seven weeks. Not only were they clueless in regard to events which had transpired during the past twenty four hours, they also seemed totally ignorant of the events of the past twenty four minutes. What did they mean, he looked fine during warmups a few moments ago? JC had been in the bleachers with him up until Patrick had called him away and at the airport prior to that.

However, before Mr. Montgomery ever got a chance to question the Bakers about this, an overzealous voice boomed over the loudspeaker.

"Good evening ladies and gentlemen! Welcome to the Kangaroos last game of the year. We thank you for taking time out of your busy holiday schedules to join us tonight as the Westbrook Kangaroos take on the Redmont Wolverines." Cheers of enthusiasm echoed throughout the gymnasium as each side attempted to rally its team to victory with their undaunted cries of support. "I understand that we have a special guest visiting with us tonight. To the students of Westbrook, he is best known for his contribution of Smitty, our kangaroo team mascot. To the rest of the world, he is better known for his contributions to the computer world. Let me introduce to you, the Wizard of Oz, Mr. JC Montgomery II. Please stand up for us, will you please, Mr. Montgomery?" The man's booming voice sounded as if he was announcing a big time wrestling match rather than a middle school basketball game. But Mr. Montgomery obliged the chubby old man by standing up and waving to the crowd. Again shrieks of excitement and applause boomed throughout the gymnasium as the announcer went on to announce the starting lineups for the teams.

"Is Josh okay?" Coach asked Patrick after the team's starters had resumed their positions on the sidelines with the coach just prior to the start of the game.

"No, I think he's really sick. He threw up. I doubt if you'll see him out here tonight."

"Maybe I'd better go check on him," Coach suggested, becoming concerned over his star player's condition.

"No, no, don't do that. He told me to tell you that he's fine. I'll check on him in a little while. The team needs you out here, Coach."

Coach nodded in agreement and watched his revised starting lineup come face to face with the ravenous Wolverines. The starting centers, none other than Bull and Patrick, glared menacingly into each others' eyes as the ref blew the whistle signifying the beginning of the game. The battle began.

The first quarter was filled with random acts of unsportsmanlike conduct on Bull's behalf, consisting of jabbing elbows and even attempts to trip Jennifer and Patrick when Bull was sure that the refs were not watching. He was out for revenge against Patrick, the clown who had allowed him to take the blame for the kangaroo incident, and against Jennifer, who had crossed him by trying to prove herself as an athletic equal. He was anxious to give Josh his share of the revenge package, too, and was disappointed when his biggest rival was a no show.

By halftime, Bull had been charged with two technical fouls, but the intimidation tactics he had instituted had proven successful. By the end of the second quarter, the score was Wolverines 30 - Kangaroos 17.

"Where's your boyfriend? Couldn't he handle the pressure?" Bull asked Jennifer with a disparaging tone after the buzzer sounded ending the first half. She ignored the antagonistic question and followed Patrick towards the boys' locker room.

"Do you think he's okay in there?" Jennifer asked her cousin in reference to Josh.

"He might not even *be* in there anymore," he warned Jennifer. "He might be gone by now."

"What? Why?" she asked desperately.

Before Patrick had a chance to answer her, Coach came bounding hurriedly around the corner. "Patrick, could you do me a favor?" He didn't wait for a response, but continued, "I'd like to introduce myself to Josh's father. Would you go in and see how he's doing for me?"

Patrick obeyed like a well trained canine, leaving Jennifer outside feeling like an abandoned and bewildered outcast.

Once inside the locker room Patrick encountered not the counterfeit Josh, but rather the authentic JC with important news about Patrick's best friend.

"Where is he?" Patrick asked anxiously.

"He took off. Those two guys up there with my father are federal agents. They're here to investigate the fraudulent use of my credit card. It seems that when Jeff mailed a box to his sister, the credit card receipt was in the box and your return address was on the box. So they put two and two together and..."

"And what? Do they know he's supposed to be you or do they just think he stole the credit card?"

"I'm not sure what they think. For right now, they think he just stole my credit card and used your address. I don't think they've figured out the entire scam yet. And they won't have to if we can get my father and the agents out of here before they talk to too many people."

"Well, do you know where he went? Is he coming back?" Patrick persisted, more than just a little worried about his friend's predicament.

"I really can't say. I gave him another $700, so that he'd have some cash to travel with. So, you know about all this?" JC finally asked, having realized that his peer must have known the truth for quite some time.

"I figured out he wasn't you on the first day," Patrick boasted.

"Thanks for not blowing his cover," JC commented.

"No problem. He's a great guy. I'm glad I got to know him. Now, we've got to do something to help him."

Meanwhile, back in the bleachers, Coach was heartily shaking Mr. Montgomery's hand and complimenting him on what a fine and talented son he had. "I want to thank you for letting him stay for awhile longer. He's an absolute asset out there on the court. I just wish he could play tonight. It's too bad he's sick."

"What did you say about him staying longer? He's coming home with me tonight. And he's not sick, he has a sprained ankle! Doesn't anyone know what's going on around here?" Mr. Montgomery cried out in exasperation.

Coach Webber and the Bakers exchanged blank stares until Mr. Baker spoke up. "The boys must be up to something. It seems as though they're trying to keep Josh from playing tonight for some reason. I'm going to find out what's going on."

Just as he stood up and was about to descend the bleachers to the locker room, the chubby agent stopped him.

"Before you go, could you help me out with something here? My name is Charlie Bryce. I'm with the FBI," he stated, flipping open a leather case to expose a shiny silver badge. "I was wondering if you could identify this young man?" he asked, putting away his badge and digging the photograph of Jeff out of his coat pocket again.

"Of course, I know this boy," Mr. Baker stated. "It's Josh Montgomery."

"Yes, that's Josh," Patrick's mother chimed in.

"Let me see," Mr. Montgomery demanded. "That's not Josh," Mr. Montgomery stated emphatically, "*that's* Josh!" He pointed to his son who was now standing in the corner of the gym next to Smitty's habitat, totally oblivious as to what was going in the stands.

"Then, who is *this* ?" Mrs. Baker asked, now totally lost in this sea of confusion.

"His name is Jeff Farnsworth. He's an orphan and a runaway. He sent a package to his sister a few weeks ago. He was dumb enough to put *your* return address on the box. That's how we tracked him down. We have reason to believe that somehow he also got a hold of one of Josh's credit cards and bought over $2000 worth of merchandise at a local toy store, not to mention the other charges and cash advances that were on card."

Mrs. Baker remembered back to the Monday after Thanksgiving when she had stood in the busy line at the post office and hurriedly scratched their return address onto the left hand corner of the box. "*He* wasn't dumb enough to put our return address on it," she defended Josh's character. "*I was* ," she said regretfully. "Do you have any idea why he ran away? He's such a good boy."

"All that I know, maam," said the other agent, "is that the young man was in a foster care facility in California and decided to run away."

"Well, isn't it sort of unusual for the FBI to become involved in the case of a runaway?" Mr. Baker asked Agent Scott.

"Yes, it is. However, because there was suspicion of credit card fraud and since the credit card in question belonged to the son of an international celebrity, the authorities in California thought it best if the case was turned over to the FBI," Agent Scott explained.

"This still isn't making sense," Mr. Montgomery spoke up. "What you're saying is that this chap, Jeff Farnsworth, is the boy who has been living with you for the past month or so, pretending to be my son. However, upon our arrival tonight, your son, Patrick greeted my son as if they were the best of friends. How could that be?"

Mr. and Mrs. Baker looked at each other. "Patrick must be in on it, too," Mrs. Baker admitted, realizing afterwards that she may have just put her son in jeopardy by making this assumption. "But how did the three boys get together to cook up this scam? Do you think they may have met over the internet?"

"That's hard to say. All I know is that sitting around discussing it isn't going to help us get to the bottom of this," Mr. Montgomery decried audaciously. "I'm going down there to talk to my son to find out what *he* knows about this."

Just as Mr. Montgomery finished making this bold statement, a buzzer sounded. Coach Webber turned around to see that it was time for third quarter play to begin. He also noticed that neither Jennifer or Patrick were anywhere to be found. Now, he was missing three of his original starting players. But that wasn't what concerned him the most. He now thought back to conversations he'd had with Josh, how Josh had asked if he and his wife had ever considered adopting children, and how Josh had been ultra sensitive to Tara's sentimental attachment to the nursery. Coach didn't know what he could do to remedy the situation, but he did know that he would do all that he could to help this young man find his way.

Chapter Nineteen

While the adults were waking up to the brutal reality that they'd been duped by a bunch of teenagers, Jennifer and Patrick were frantically searching for their friend.

Patrick wasted no time in getting dressed and heading home to see if Josh had gone back there to pack. Jennifer, too, pulled on her sweatpants and grabbed her down jacket before she headed out the door to explore the school grounds. She plodded around the dark parking lot, her eyes spanning the exterior walls of the building and the rows of frozen vehicles, hesitating to wander too far into the expanse of darkness which existed outside of the spectrum of the parking lot lights.

She could see nothing in the dark sky and her calls out to Josh seemed to evaporate in the air as did her vaporized breath. She was about to give up, feeling compelled to go back inside to fulfill her obligation to the team, figuring that Josh was probably halfway to the next town by now. Then suddenly she noticed the ladder leading up to the roof above the gym.

Slowly and cautiously, she climbed the shaky, frozen ladder, gripping each rung tightly until she scraped her hand on the sharp, cold gravel when she reached the rooftop. "Josh, are you up here?" she whispered softly. "It's me, Jennifer."

She waited for a moment, but heard nothing. Then, as she began her descent, she felt something touch the back of her neck. A shocking chill shot up her spine, immobilizing her where she stood as the fingers on a leather clad hand tightened their grip. She felt a wisp of warm air on the back of her neck, as well, as if someone was breathing on her. She panicked, almost losing her balance, but another hand grabbed her by the arm, steadied her again, and then coerced her into crawling onto the roof. She wailed a faint little "ah" as she felt the leather hand cover her mouth.

"What are you doing here?" a hushed voice whispered to her in the darkness.

The voice sounded hoarse, but familiar to Jennifer. "Josh?" she asked apprehensively as he removed his hand from her mouth. "Is that you?"

"It's me," he admitted. "Sorry about the hand. I didn't know if I should answer you cause I didn't know if anyone else was out there. I didn't want you to make any noise when you figured out I was up here."

"There's no one else out here, at least not yet. I would imagine there will be soon when Patrick and I come up missing, too," she explained.

"How'd you know I was here?" he asked.

"I didn't. I just remembered that this was where I found you once before."

"I'm glad you came up here. I didn't want to leave without saying goodbye."

"What's going on, Josh?"

"It's a long story. All I can tell you is that I'm not who you think I am."

"I know," Jennifer confessed.

"What do you know?" Josh said, turning his back on Jennifer, ashamed to admit what he had done and who he really was.

"I know who you really are," she insisted. "You're Jeff. Jeff Farnsworth."

Josh stopped in his tracks, unable to believe what he was hearing. "How? How did you know?" he asked, realizing the obvious answer the instant the words left his lips.

"Patrick," they both said in unison.

"I should have known," Josh stated.

"It really wasn't his fault. Remember the day we went shopping and that night I found Sarah's necklace on your dresser? Well, when he called me to see if I'd go to the movies with you, I asked him if he knew who Sarah really was. He said he did. I told him that if he didn't tell me, I wouldn't go to the movies with you the next day," she explained.

"That's all it took?" Josh mused.

"Well, he really wanted to go out with that cheerleader from Redmont and I guess he figured that if I didn't go, then you wouldn't go either."

207

"I can't believe he caved under that little of pressure."

"I kind of blackmailed him, too. I told him that I'd tell Coach that he had hidden in one of the lockers in the girls' locker room one day when the volleyball team was in there changing. That was all it took. He told me everything. The only thing that I don't know is who those guys are in there with Mr. Montgomery and the real Josh."

"I didn't know who they were either until JC, the real Josh, came and told me. They're FBI agents, if you can believe that. When I sent that box to my sister, the receipt from JC's credit card was still in the bag. Someone found it and thought that I had stolen his credit card. Mrs. Baker must have put the return address on the box and they were able to track me down. But I don't think they knew that I'd been impersonating JC all this time."

"Do you think they know now?"

"I have no idea what has been going on in there since I left. JC didn't seem to think they were on to that. If I'm lucky, JC and his dad will leave after the game and the two FBI guys will figure that I'm no longer in the area. That is if..."

"That is if what?" Jennifer asked.

"That is if no one talks to Mr. Montgomery or to the agents while they're here."

"Uh, Josh, or should I call you Jeff?" Jennifer asked before she gave him the bad news.

"It doesn't really matter," Josh answered, shrugging his shoulders, "whatever."

"I think I should tell you that I saw the Bakers sitting up there with Mr. Montgomery. JC wasn't with them, so they may not have figured anything out, but they were together and they were talking."

"Oh," Josh uttered and swallowed hard. "Well, in that case, I'm in pretty deep."

"What will they do to you if they find you?"

"They'll probably take me back to California and put me in some kind of juvenile detention center. Not exactly the kind of place where I want to spend Christmas."

"Well, we won't let them find you. We'll stay up here until everyone leaves," Jennifer insisted.

"What's this 'we' stuff? You've got to go back in there and finish the game. Maybe you'll be able to find out more about what's going on for me, too."

"I don't want to leave you. I'm afraid of what's going to happen to you if they find you. You could go to my house and hide. No one's home. The key is under the mat. You could go upstairs and hide in my closet and wait until I get home. I don't think they'll look for you there," she prattled on impetuously, desperate to save her friend.

"Maybe I could," he reflected. "I need to go somewhere to figure out what I'm going to do. And it would be nice to be somewhere other than up here freezing my butt off."

Jennifer's heart lightened. She knew that if he made it safely to her house, she would see him again.

"Could I ask you something before I go?" Josh asked, straining to see into Jennifer's green eyes in spite of the darkness. "If you knew who I was all this time, why didn't you say anything before?"

"I guess I was just playing along with it because you needed me to. Why didn't *you* ever tell *me* who you really were?"

"I wanted to, lots of times, especially the day we were up here on the roof. I wanted to tell you everything, but I was afraid."

"Afraid of what?"

"I was afraid you'd either hate me for being dishonest or not like me because I wasn't rich and popular like you thought I was."

"First of all," Jennifer responded, "you're probably the most honest person I've ever met. That night at the carnival when I tried to trick Patrick into thinking you made all three shots, you wouldn't go along with it. And secondly, *you* were still *you* when you pretended to be Josh. You were still nice and cute and a good basketball player. And last of all, what made you think that I wouldn't like you if you weren't rich?"

Again, after a brief pause, both responded dryly and simultaneously, "Patrick."

"He thought that might have been why you liked Bull - because he was rich."

Jennifer shook her head and rolled her eyes.

209

"So, are you saying that you would have liked me if you knew I was Jeff Farnsworth?"

"I *did* know you were Jeff Farnsworth and I *did* like you," she reminded him.

"Well, then I guess, call me Jeff," he said, answering the question she'd asked earlier, thereby reclaiming his former, but true namesake and identity.

But before Jennifer was able to call him anything, the heavy metal door leading from the back of the gym swung open and then forcefully slammed shut as the two FBI men, not dressed in stereotypical black, darted out.

Glancing around anxiously, the fat one, sporting a powerful, but compact flashlight, began waving it in all directions so that its beams danced off of frozen cars, the skeletons of trees, and the outside walls of the building. That's when he noticed it - the metal ladder leading up to the roof. As soon as he saw it, his bulgy eyes lit up and he bumbled his way towards it, leaving his partner in the dust, or rather, leaving his partner in the crystallized particles which were floating in the frigid air. He hoisted himself up, slipping sporadically on the frosty metal rungs that he hoped would lead him to the prize.

Jeff, formerly known as Josh, and Jennifer were sprawled out on their stomachs on the roof, hoping to camouflage their silhouettes in the darkness as tiny gravel from the coarse tiles gouged their faces with thousands of minuscule imprints. They could see the swirling light from the flashlight as it wavered aimlessly skyward without a steady hand to direct its beam. The intruder had stashed it in his pocket as he trudged all the way up the first ladder to station himself on the first plateau above the classrooms. He stood motionless, only inches away from where Jeff and Jennifer lay. If he were to take another step in their direction or to cast his flashlight's beam their way, Jeff and Jennifer would surely be exposed.

But before the overzealous, overweight man could make another move, his concentration was broken by the sound of footsteps charging towards his partner down below. Huffing and puffing to catch his breath and screeching to a halt upon seeing the man, was Patrick.

"Don't shoot!" Patrick shouted, raising his arms in surrender as the forceful beam of the flashlight landed on his face.

Seeing that the boy was neither a threat or the boy being sought, the lanky agent nearby spoke up. "It's okay, son. No one is going to be shooting anyone. Aren't you the young man who was speaking to JC in the stands?"

"Yes, sir," Patrick responded nervously.

"Do you know where your friend Jeff is?" Agent Scott continued.

Realizing that the agents and other adults must have put two and two together, Patrick replied, "I went back to my house to see if he was there, but he wasn't."

"Were his things gone?" the rounder agent inquired once he'd abandoned his post on the rooftop and joined the two on the ground.

Patrick pondered the question and his answer before he responded, strategizing that perhaps he could help Jeff by leading the agents astray. "I think they were." He hesitated, lowered his head, and then continued in a low voice. "I think I might have seen him running down our street, heading out towards the highway."

"What's that you say? You think you may have seen him heading out towards the highway?" Agent Bryce bellowed.

"I didn't want to say anything," Patrick lied sheepishly, "but I called to him and he looked back and then just kept on going. I didn't want to tell you guys because I don't want anything bad to happen to him. But I know it's not safe for him to be out there alone either. If you catch him, promise me you'll go easy on him. He hasn't done anything wrong."

"Okay, kid, we'll go easy on him," Agent Scott promised. "Thanks for your cooperation."

"You radio the limo driver and tell him to pull up out front. I'll go in and tell Mr. Montgomery that we need to head out!" Agent Bryce barked out the order to his partner as the twosome disappeared through the metal doors, leaving Patrick standing alone in the dark.

211

"Psst! Patrick!" a whisper rustled from above. "Up here!" It was Jeff.

The sudden hiss startled Patrick and he jolted in his skin as if he'd been struck by lightning. "Josh, is that you?" Patrick whispered back, just in case the agents were not yet out of earshot.

"It's me and Jennifer. Is it safe to come down?"

"It will be if you hurry. The feds just went in to get JC and his dad. I told them that I saw you heading for the highway. I figured you were still around here somewhere. Do you know what you're going to do?"

"I was thinking of hiding out over at Jennifer's house until things settle down."

"No offense, dude, but that's a pretty lame idea. Things aren't going to settle down. Besides I'm sure they'll be looking for you over there when they don't find you on the highway. I've got a better idea," Patrick mused, jingling a set of car keys in the air. "We've got wheels."

"Whose are they?" Jennifer asked as she crept cautiously down the icy ladder.

"They're the keys to my mom's car. It's parked right over there."

"What have you got in mind?" Jeff said in a hushed voice as he slithered gracefully down each rung. "You could get in a lot of trouble for driving without a license. Besides, the two of you need to get back in there for the second half. You don't want Bull's team to beat us, do you?"

With raised eyebrows and shrugging shoulders, Jennifer and Patrick glanced in each other's direction for guidance.

Patrick spoke up. "The way I see it, it's not that big of a deal. His team may win this game, but Bull will still always be a loser. Besides, since we're not playing, Bull won't have the satisfaction of having beaten *us*, he'll be up against our second stringers. The victory won't be near as sweet. Anyway, we play them again in January. We'll beat em then. I say, we go for it!"

"Me, too," Jennifer chimed in. "What have we got to lose?"

212

In spite of her youthful optimism, Jennifer was well aware of what she and her two amigos would be risking should they venture out onto the highway in Patrick's mother's car that night. Perhaps everything.

Yet they proceeded, silently and steadfastly toward the ice glazed, late model compact that awaited their arrival. Jeff and Jennifer hopped in the backseat, while Patrick rummaged for an ice scraper in the glove box. When none was to be found, Jeff reached into his coat pocket and retrieved from his wallet, the now invalid credit card that JC had given him.

"Try this," he suggested, not moving from his spot in the backseat where he and Jennifer were huddled close together to try to get warm. "It's not good for anything else now."

Patrick scraped a small portion of the frozen windshield on the driver's side clean and proceeded to hop inside and start the ignition.

"Are you going to be able to see?" Jennifer asked apprehensively, noticing that the passenger side front and side windows were still blanketed with speckled crystals.

"Oh, yeah, I'll just roll down the windows if I need to see out."

Since Jeff and Jennifer weren't willing to give up their cozy spot to remedy the frozen window situation, and with time running out for a getaway, neither one of them said another word about the lack of visibility. Not only was the windshield frozen on the outside, but now it was foggy on the inside, too, with the three of them breathing heavily in anticipation of their next move.

"Where to?" Patrick asked just as he was about to switch on the headlights. No sooner had the words come out of his mouth than he witnessed the limo rounding the corner of the building and pulling out onto the main road away from the school.

The lights inside the cab were on and Patrick swore that he had seen not only JC, Mr. Montgomery, and the two agents, but his mom and dad, as well, driving off into the night.

"There goes the limo. How about we follow them for awhile? I think my mom and dad are in there, too."

"Are you serious?" Jennifer gasped.

"There were six heads in the back. I'm pretty sure two of those heads belonged to my mom and dad."

"No, I mean about following them. Are you serious about that?" Jennifer questioned him.

"Sure. We'll find out where they're going first. Eventually, they'll probably just turn around and come back when they don't find Josh on the highway. By then we should be able to figure out what to do ourselves."

Keeping a fairly safe distance of about 100 yards between his mother's vehicle and the limo, Patrick ventured out behind them. The limo was, indeed, heading for the highway and Patrick followed. The roads were slick. A horn blared as Patrick attempted to ease his way onto the busy highway. He swerved and then skidded to a stop on the right shoulder of the road, the lack of visibility having prevented him from seeing a similar sized compact traveling in the right lane.

"That was close," Patrick admitted, rolling down his window to get a better look before attempting the manuever again. "Any ideas on where you want to go?"

"Well, I was thinking that it might not be a bad idea to head towards the airport," Jeff answered solemnly. "Are we going that way now?"

"We are," Patrick said loudly to be heard over the whirring sound of the defroster.

"I'm thinking that I should go back to California and call the Johnsons to come and get me, so that I can at least spend Christmas with my sister."

"I've got an idea," Patrick piped up again, totally ignoring Jeff's suggestion. "You've got $700. Let's go down south and hit the beaches for a few days. I mean I'm already going to get in trouble for taking my mom's car; we might as well have some fun before this is all over. There's this great beach on the west coast of Florida called Siesta Key. We went there on vacation. The sand is so white and so fine, it's like sugar. Then we can call them and tell them that we're sorry and that we take total responsibility for what we've done. They'll be so relieved to know that we're okay that they might even forgive us. And even if we get grounded, it will have been worth it."

"That would be so much fun!" Jennifer chimed in with uncharacteristic giddiness.

"I don't know what's gotten into you guys, but I can't go along with it. I'm tired of running. Chances are we wouldn't get very far either."

"We could try," Jennifer suggested wholeheartedly.

"Jennifer," Jeff reprimanded her sternly, "it's not going to happen. Now just take me to the airport, Patrick, please."

Jennifer moved away from him in the backseat and faced the window. She knew that her sense of emotion had overrun her otherwise good common sense. Now she was embarrassed by her whimful exuberance, especially since Jeff seemed less than impressed by it.

Jeff, too, was confused, now feeling guilty that he had blown up at her, not even being sure why he had, other than he knew that no good would come of the trivial pursuit that Patrick and Jennifer were proposing.

"Jennifer, I'm sorry," Jeff said, edging towards her again and placing one hand on her shoulder. She shrugged it off, indicating that she wasn't receptive to any attempt at reconciliation. "I know all of this seems exciting to you guys, but it just doesn't for me. I'm already in enough trouble, I don't need to get into any more and neither do you. Sure it would be fun for awhile..." He found himself picturing Jennifer in a bikini on the beach, " but it wouldn't be worth it in the long run. And how long could it last? $700 doesn't go that far anymore."

"I bet it could take us through Christmas break," Patrick mentioned optimistically.

"Yeah, it probably could, but then where would *I* be? You guys would go home to being grounded by your parents, but I'd be sentenced to twice as much time in the state juvenile facility."

"You were more fun when you were Josh," Jennifer mumbled under her breath, just loud enough so that Jeff could hear the hurtful remark.

His heart shattered and crashed to his stomach in thousands of tiny pieces. He closed his eyes and released an excruciatingly painful, yet almost inaudible sigh. He knew it was time to go.

Chapter Twenty

For the next thirty minutes or so, the hum of the engine was the only sound to be heard within the confines of the compact car. The windshield was clear now and the air circulating from the heater made the physical atmosphere warm and cozy. However, the emotional atmosphere remained frigid and unforgiving as neither Jeff nor Jennifer yielded to each other's emotional states. Since Patrick was feeling more and more comfortable behind the wheel, he decided to camouflage the silence by inserting one of his mother's disco tapes into the car's tape player. The funky music did little to stimulate any changes in the occupants' moods.

Now all three occupants could see out in all directions. It was obvious that they were nearing the city of Cincinnati with warehouses appearing on the outskirts, as well as the glimmer of the city lights shining up ahead. Patrick became tense again as traffic intensified. He tightened his grip on the steering wheel, turned down the volume of the music, stared intensely at the overhead road signs which would lead him across the river and to the airport, and did his best to avert his eyes from the blinding glare of oncoming vehicles across the highway.

Realizing that they would be arriving at the airport soon, Jennifer softened, put aside her pride, and appealed to Jeff's sense of forgiveness.

"I'm sorry," she said softly. "I guess I just felt hurt that you didn't want to go to the beach with me, and then I felt like you thought I was being really immature for wanting to do something like that. And so I got defensive and then I felt stupid for getting so defensive. And I said something that I didn't really mean and then I made you feel bad. I'm really sorry. Cause I like you so much and I don't ever want you to think that I don't like you for who you are. I do. I like you a lot. And that's why this hurts so much. Not only that you're leaving, but that we had to get mad at each other right before you were leaving."

"Thank you," Jeff said, hugging her head. "I'm sorry, too." A sense of relief overwhelmed him and he felt the pieces of his heart being grafted back together.

"And you couldn't *be* more wrong," he said after catching a smile that appeared on her face, "about the beach thing. There's nothing I would rather do than go to the beach with you."

"Are you two kids doing okay back there now?" Patrick asked with fatherly concern.

"Yeah, how are you doing up there?" Jeff asked.

"I'm doing all right, but I could use some help reading these road signs. I don't want to miss my turnoff and the traffic is getting pretty thick now that we're getting near the airport."

Cars were beginning to whiz past Patrick now as he slowed to read the upcoming signs. The red and blue flashing lights of a police car bounced off of Patrick's rearview mirror and Patrick, momentarily, felt his heart drop to his stomach, too, until the car screamed past him.

"He must have been after that guy," Patrick sighed, his anxiety intensifying with each minute and each car that passed.

"It's not too much further. I remember those buildings over there when we came to get Jeff in the limo," his cousin reassured him.

"I wish we had commandeered the limo, now, instead of me taking my mom's car," Patrick admitted.

"Hang in there, buddy," Jeff encouraged. "You're doing great. You'll make it."

Patrick did make it to the airport, his white knuckles still clenched as he pulled into a parking space in the airport parking garage.

The threesome clung tightly to each other as they shuffled through the hoardes of hectic holiday travelers who filled the crowded corridors.

The search for signs resumed as they scanned TV screens for flight schedules and eyed ticket counters and departing gates for flights to LA or even San Francisco.

At last they found one. A flight to LA was scheduled to leave from this gate in approximately twenty five minutes. The ticket line and seating area were filled to capacity with weary travelers waiting to make their connections to holiday destinations.

To Jeff's amazement, there was a seat available when he stepped up to the ticket counter.

"That'll be $1357.00," the overdone, middle aged woman requested.

Jeff pulled out the seven crisp $100 bills from his wallet. "Will this do?" he asked hopefully.

"Not unless you have seven more of those in your pocket," the airline employee answered in a stern, unnerving tone.

"Ah, come on, this is all he has and he wants to get home to see his little sister for Christmas, maam," Patrick pleaded.

"I'm sorry, but it is against our rules to let the ticket go for less than face value until every last effort has been made to sell the ticket for full price. The only thing that I can do is to put you on the standby list. If there is room on the plane, I would be able to sell it to you for $649.00."

"Oh, okay, I'll do that. What are my chances of getting on the plane with that sort of thing?" Jeff asked, encouraged by this alternative means of negotiating.

"Well, normally, quite good, but tonight, your chances are somewhere between slim and none." The woman cackled at her own little joke. "Let me take your name anyway, just in case there's a miracle." She sounded quite amused with her own brand of humor.

"Maybe I can help." A voice boomed from behind them, a deep, calm voice that resonated authority.

Jennifer, Jeff, and Patrick turned around and found themselves face to face with JC Montgomery II, JC Montgomery III, the two FBI men, and Patrick's parents.

With the exception of JC Montgomery II and III, none of the others seemed to be in a generous or festive mood. Patrick's parents looked flushed and bewildered, while the two agents appeared to be visibly winded and quite perturbed.

Only JC Montgomery II and his son seemed to be willing to remedy the awkward situation the boys and Jennifer found themselves in.

"Put your money away," Mr. Montgomery directed as he gently mobilized Jeff away from the crowded ticket counter.

"Actually it's your money," Jeff started to say, but was interrupted again by the generous millionaire.

"JC told me everything on the way over here. I have to admit that although I was a bit disappointed in my son's behavior, I was also quite impressed by his quick wittedness in devising such a scheme in such short order. As far as I'm concerned, there are no charges to be filed against you, as my son gave you permission to use his credit card."

"Thank you, sir," Jeff said genuinely.

"Not a problem. I have to tell you how much those emails you sent meant to me during the past seven weeks. I was very proud of you. Of course, I thought you were my own son at the time, but I have to say, in spite of the fact that you weren't, it was amazing watching you change and grow during that time. You went from a cowering, questioning lad, timid about asking his father to send a kangaroo, to a self confident, motivated role model both athletically and academically. I was so proud."

"Thank you, again, sir, and I have to say that I liked hearing from you, too. I don't have a dad and sometimes I felt like I did again, when I wrote and heard from you."

"Okay, let's cut the crap here," Agent Bryce interrupted. "That's all very nice, but unfortunately we have a job to do here. Although there won't be any charges filed by Mr. Montgomery there is still the matter of returning you to the State of California's Juvenile Detention Center ASAP. Cuff him, Agent Scott."

"Hold on there," Mr. Montgomery replied. "I'm sure that won't be necessary. For whom do the two of you work?"

"I thought we made that quite clear to you earlier. I work for the FBI and Mr. Scott here is working with the FBI on behalf of the state of California," Agent Bryce remarked snidely.

"Well, in that case, since I'm not filing any charges, the FBI should no longer be needed, am I right?"

"Agent Scott and I are still involved in a partnership in which I am obligated to uphold my end of the working relationship until the juvenile is brought back to California under both of our custodial care."

"Okay, then, Agent Scott, may I ask who your supervisor is?" Mr. Montgomery requested. "Not your immediate supervisor, but the head of the department for whom you work?"

"That would be the governor of the state of California, sir," Agent Scott testified.

"And who would that be these days?" Mr. Montgomery prompted.

"That would be Byron Long, sir."

"Ah, yes, we used to call him... Well never mind what we used to call him. He was a classmate of mine when I attended USC. He even dated my sister for awhile. We were almost related. Hard to believe, isn't it?"

As Mr. Montgomery gleefully reminisced his college days, the weary and confused eyes of the agents, Patrick's parents, and the four youths were upon him, unsure of where this trip down memory lane was leading.

"Ah, well," he finally said as if he was about to terminate the journey, "shall we give him a jingle to see what he has to say about this young man's predicament? I mean it hardly seems fair that the boy will have to be moved and put into juvenile detention simply because he was trying to find a new home for him and his sister."

Mr. Montgomery pulled out his cell phone.

"Before you do that, may I borrow that?" Mrs. Baker asked tentatively. "I know my sister, Jill, is worried sick about Jennifer. May we call her first to let her know that Jennifer is all right?"

"But of course," Mr. Montgomery offered.

"She's got her cell phone, honey. Give her a ring," Mrs. Baker directed.

Jennifer's mother answered the phone on the first ring. It sounded as if she was still in the stands at the game.

"Mom, it's me. Everything's okay. We're at the airport. I just wanted to let you know that I'm okay. The Bakers are here, too. You can ground me when I get home. I'm sorry. What I did was stupid. I love you."

"I love you, too. I'm glad you're okay," Jennifer's mom related.

"It sounds like you're still at the game. What's the score?"

"It just ended. Your team did really well. They only lost by two. Bull fouled out early. Hold on a second, Coach is coming up here. He wants to know what's going on."

Jennifer went on to explain to her mother, "Well, you guys know that Jeff was impersonating JC Montgomery, right? Well, since Jeff didn't steal the credit card, he's not in trouble for that. But he's still in trouble for running away from home. Mr. Montgomery knows the governor of California, so as soon as we hang up, he's going to call him and see if they can work something out."

Jennifer's mother related the information to Coach Webber and to his wife, who had just joined him.

"Coach says to tell Jeff that he and his little sister can come and stay with them if they need a place to live. He says he'll come down to the airport if he needs to," Jennifer's mother related back to Jennifer. "Make sure you tell them."

"Okay," Jennifer answered in a tone that prompted her mother to believe that Jennifer hadn't heard a word she'd said. "I should be home in a little while. Bye."

Jennifer handed the phone to Mr. Montgomery. In a matter of moments, Mr. Montgomery had contacted enough of the right people to access the governor's private line at home.

After four or five minutes of engaging in witty conversation, Mr. Montgomery explained the reason for his call to the governor, elaborating on Jeff's dilemma. It was hard to decipher what kind of verdict had been reached. The handsome man's forehead was squinched up in a giant wrinkle which made the outcome impossible to predict.

"Okay, uh huh, oh, I see... Well, that is a definite possibility... Possible, but not probable, you say... Oh, yes... hmmm... And all I need to do is... Well, yes, I do... Let me give you the number of my private line."

He went on to give his former classmate the vital information necessary to keep in touch.

"He's going to get back to me within the hour," Mr. Montgomery stated when he terminated the call. "Shall we retreat to the executive lounge and wait? There's a lovely one in this airport. I'll just summon a driver."

As unlikely as it would be for an empty airport courtesy van to appear on the spot at that precise moment, it did.

"Like magic," the younger JC remarked in reference to his father. "Stuff like this happens all the time wherever he goes."

Before long the troop of mismatched acquaintances filed through the doors to a luxury lounge, where tables containing gourmet appetizers and soft drinks were set up for idle consumption, and cushiony, leather couches and chairs were tastefully arranged to accommodate the wealthy, weary travelers.

Looks of disdain from other opulent travelers greeted the hometown folk as they invaded the private domain of the rich and famous, but their snobbery quickly changed to that of acceptance upon the revelation of the troop's leader, non other than JC Montgomery II himself.

Here was a shelter in the storm, a refuge where everyone could recuperate from the stress filled events of the evening and reevaluate the crimes committed and the punishments to be rendered. Patrick hoped that his parents would see the situation in a new light and reconsider what he assumed would be a harsh and terminal punishment in regard to his borrowing his mother's car without permission and without a license.

Several people in the group plopped themselves down on chairs and sofas, while others helped themselves to the snacks. Within minutes, people were talking. Even Mr. Montgomery's seemingly incompatible guests began to talk amongst themselves. Agent Scott related to young Jeff that, he, too, had lost his father at a young age and could understand how Jeff was feeling. They even found themselves mingling with the haves who belonged in the lounge, despite the fact that they, the have nots, didn't.

Mrs. Baker called her sister again to update her on the situation, almost gleefully boasting of where they were patiently waiting for a solution to Jeff's problem.

Patrick took advantage of the joviality of the moment to deliver his "I take full responsibility for my actions" speech.

It did elicit a boisterous laugh from both his parents, but ended with a resounding, "We'll talk about it when we get home," from his father.

Finally, it came. Mr. Montgomery almost did not hear the ringing of the cell phone over the roar of the exuberant merriment.

"Quiet please," he shushed the crowd as Jeff awaited the pronouncement of his fate.

The atmosphere in the room changed from that of celebration to that of deathlike silence. All eyes were focused on JC Montgomery who seemed to hold Jeff's fate in his hands.

No one noticed when the door at the back of the room opened and two more individuals joined the already crowded confines of the lounge.

Mr. Montgomery nodded solemnly as he stated, "I see," and "I'll see what I can do."

After thanking his former classmate and friend, Mr. Montgomery pushed a button on the phone, ending the call and turned his attention towards Jeff.

"My friend," he began, "was able to pull some strings."

Jeff let out a sigh of relief.

"However," Mr. Montgomery continued, "with these strings, come some other mandates. Do you understand what I'm getting at?"

"I'm afraid not," Jeff answered, quite perplexed with where Mr. Montgomery was going again with his thoughts.

But before anyone could venture a guess, Patrick burst out laughing. Jennifer smiled, too, knowing exactly what her cousin was thinking.

"I'm sorry, I'm sorry. It's just that you're talking about strings and there's this joke. You know, a string goes into a bar and they won't serve him because he's a string, so he goes back outside and he ties himself up in a knot and he frays the top of his head so that he'll look different. Then he goes back into the bar and he says, 'Hey bartender, can I get a drink?' And the bartender looks at him and says, 'Aren't you that string that was in here a couple of minutes ago?' And he answers, 'No, I'm a frayed knot.' You were talking about pulling strings, and Jeff said, 'I'm afraid not.' Just like in the joke."

Patrick was talking extremely fast now, as he was painfully aware that all eyes were upon him, and that no one, with the exception of his parents, Jeff, and Jennifer, seemed to have any appreciation for his rare sense of humor. Everyone else just stood there with blank stares upon their faces, as though they weren't familiar with even ever having heard a joke before.

Finally, Mr. Montgomery broke the silence with a rather meek chuckle. "Oh, I get it. A frayed knot. Afraid not. Good one, Patrick. Very good," he sputtered. "Well, shall I go on then? Thanks for breaking the tension, my good man."

The other guests in the lounge relaxed and breathed out even meeker chuckles than Mr. Montgomery had.

"The only obstacle that stands in the way of the governor giving you complete pardon from the incident is the matter of a permanent residence for you and your sister. Your sister would be able to stay with the Johnsons, but again, we're faced with your being fourteen, and therefore, unable to reside there, as well. What we would need to do, would be to establish somewhat of a permanent residence for the two of you, preferably outside of the state of California, so that they could, in a sense, wash their hands of you. Now, I understand that you have an uncle in New York. Is going to live with him a possibility?"

"I don't mean to be negative, sir," Jeff started, "but I don't believe he is financially able to take us in at this time. Also, I believe that he was contacted when I was missing and he was threatened with being put in jail if he offered to help me. He's the kind of person who would be afraid we were trying to trick him or something if we called him now. That's just how he is."

Mr. Montgomery posed another question. "Is there anyone else that you can think of who would be willing to take you in on a permanent basis?"

Almost before the words had left his lips, two voices from the back of the crowded room echoed, "We would!"

Everyone in the room turned around to catch a glimpse of the newcomers. Beaming with warmth and genuine enthusiasm were Coach and his wife, Tara.

"Coach and Mrs. Coach!" Jeff stammered. "You'd do this for me?"

"Of course, we would. I only wish I had known earlier, so that you wouldn't have had to go through all of this," Coach explained.

"Are you sure it's okay? I mean, I don't want to cause you any trouble. I've got a little sister, too," Jeff warned them.

"Well, if she's anything like you, I'm sure she'll be a delight," Tara assured him.

"Thanks," Jeff blushed a little and then realized that there was one more obstacle to overcome. "Coach, uh, Mr. Montgomery, there's just one more thing. How are we going to get my little sister here?"

Without hesitation, Mr. Montgomery provided the solution. "What say we all hop on board my little jet and round her up?"

Patrick, Jeff, and Jennifer exchanged ecstatic looks with each other which transformed into pleading, ecstatic looks by the time they reached Patrick's parents.

"What do you say, Mom? Once in a lifetime opportunity here. You don't want to be shortsighted on this, do you?" Patrick begged.

"Aren't you forgetting about the little matter of you taking my car tonight?" his mother reminded him. "You could have gotten yourselves killed doing a thing like that!"

"But we didn't. Nothing happened. Everything is fine. Here are your keys. You and dad can drive it home."

"You're not kidding, your dad and I will drive it home!" His mother's voice sounded uncompromising.

"So, you're saying that we can go then?" Patrick asked innocently with a twinkle in his eye.

Mr. Baker stepped in to confront his unyielding offspring. "Young man, do you have any idea of what you put us through tonight?"

"No sir, not really, sir. I'm sorry for what I did. I was just trying to do what you've taught me to do - to think on my feet - to take charge of the situation. Looking back on what I did, I would have to say it was wrong. That's why I take full responsibility for my actions. I'm willing to take any punishment that you deal out if you could just find it in your heart to forgive me and to let me go to California." Patrick tried his speech a second time.

225

"Save it. It's hard for me to believe that after what you put us through tonight, you have the audacity to even ask us such a thing!" Mr. Baker was becoming visibly upset at his son's insolence.

"Now, wait a minute, honey," Mrs. Baker interrupted her husband, "this *is* a once in a lifetime opportunity. Maybe we could postpone his punishment until he gets back. Jennifer, what do you think your mother will say?"

"I think she'll say that this is a once in a lifetime opportunity, just like you did."

Patrick smiled. For some reason, he now had Mom on his side, as he often did when his father started yelling.

"Well, let's just give her a call and see what she says," Mrs. Baker babbled on, not giving her husband much of a chance to interject his feelings or opinions.

"Go ahead, do what your mother says. Just don't blame me when you grow up and land in jail because your mother didn't punish you when you were young."

"Thanks, Dad, you're the best!" Patrick said, giving his father a patronizing smile and a pat on the back.

"We should be good to go in about twenty minutes," Mr. Montgomery reported back to his entourage of passengers which included Jeff, Jennifer, Patrick, JC, Agents Scott and Bryce, and Coach and Tara.

He presented Coach with an affidavit from the governor of California which came in over the executive lounge's fax machine. It pardoned Jeff from any wrongdoing and authorized John and Tara to obtain custody of the children until legal details could be worked out. And it was signed by Byron Long, Governor of the State of California.

Chapter Twenty One

All systems were go, or so it seemed, until an unexpected announcement came over the public address system. "Attention all travelers, due to a sudden snowstorm which has moved into the area, we regret to inform you that the Cincinnati International Airport is closed for the remainder of the evening." A unanimous roar of disappointment could be heard throughout the terminal, as well as inside of the executive lounge when the statement was made. "We hope to resume regular operations in the morning, and we apologize for the inconvenience."

"What do we do now, Father?" the young JC asked.

"I suppose we find ourselves a hotel, spend the night there, and wait for the weather to clear," the senior JC reasoned quite patiently.

"Sir, I'm afraid that may be a problem," announced Mr. Montgomery's private pilot who had just entered the room. "I'm one step ahead of you. All the hotel and motel rooms are filled. When I heard the news, I started phoning all over town and I can't locate even one."

"No room at the inn, eh? Well, I suppose we're not the first ones to have something like this happen so close to Christmas," Mr. Montgomery speculated.

"There's plenty of room at *our* inn," Coach offered the weary bunch. "We'd be happy to have you come and spend the night there. Only we'd better get going before the highway department decides to close the roads."

"Excellent idea," Mr. Montgomery agreed. "If Jeff, Patrick, and Jennifer know the way, they can ride with us and show us where you live," he said to Coach. "And I suspect you'll be driving your own car home," he said to the Bakers, who nodded positively. "Very well, we'll have our trusty pilot, Michael, secure the plane for the evening and we'll see you there in short order."

Once the pilot had taken care of business, he joined the agents, the kids, and the Montgomerys as they piled into the limo once again and made their way back to the Webbers' mammoth inn where the out of towners spent a comfortable night in the makeshift motel.

By 8 o'clock the following morning the skies were clear and the winds had died down enough for air traffic controllers to declare flying conditions favorable once again. However, the roads to the airport were still in rough shape and the highway department issued a travel advisory to anyone brave enough to venture out.

But again, no one in the party seemed to mind very much. Mr. Montgomery was overwhelmed with the architecture of the mansion in which the Webbers lived and he spent an hour with Coach going from room to room and elaborating on how this could be restored or how that could be refurbished.

"All it takes is money," Coach Webber joked with the billionaire who seemed unable to grasp the concept of a lack of funds being a real issue in the restoration process.

It wasn't until around 10 a.m. that everyone seemed to have regrouped and prepared to once again pile into the limo and head to the airport.

Finally, they were off, flying in their own private friendly skyliner, with the world literally at their feet.

By the time they arrived in Los Angeles, it was still early afternoon as they had gained three hours in flying from the eastern time zone to the Pacific time zone. Again Mr. Montgomery paid for John and Tara Webber to rent a fully equipped Suburban to make the five to six hour drive from the LA airport to the small town where the Johnsons lived. Jennifer, Jeff, Patrick, and the Webbers were to make the trip alone as the two agents were officially relieved of their duty and the Montgomery men decided to spend the afternoon in LA getting to know each other again over a round of golf.

Out in the quiet town where the Johnsons lived, Sarah, Jamie, Harry, and the Johnsons had just returned home from an early Christmas Eve candlelight service and children's pageant. Sarah and Jamie had both been angels and in spite of their weary little feet, they danced around the living room, flapping their wings, while Harry, who had been a shepherd, attempted to prod them with his shepherd's staff.

228

"It's time for all little angels and shepherds to get ready for bed, so that Santa will come by to fill your stockings," Mrs. Johnson reminded the children.

"He won't come if you're not in bed," Mr. Johnson added.

Jamie tugged on Mrs. Johnson's shirt and asked mildly, "Don't we need to put out some milk and cookies for him?"

"Oh, that's right," Mrs. Johnson answered, suddenly remembering the holiday tradition. "Let's see what we have here. I think we may have some sugar cookies left in the cupboard." She opened a holiday tin with Santa's face on it and removed three cookies from it, placing them on a plate.

Harry was way ahead of the rest of them, grabbing a half gallon of milk from the refrigerator and splashing it into a large glass, filling it all the way to the top.

Sarah stood on a chair and whispered into Mr. Johnson's ear, "I'm not really into this Santa Claus stuff, but I'll just go along with it for the younger kids."

"You don't believe in Santa Claus, Sarah? Why not?" Mr. Johnson asked with a disheartened look on his face.

"When I want something, I don't waste my time asking those fake beards at the malls, I go to the one who can really give me what I need." She pointed upward.

"Very good!" he chuckled. "I knew you had it figured out."

After all three children had finished hanging their stockings over the fireplace, Mrs. Johnson accompanied them to the bedroom where they hopped into their beds and shivered beneath the icy sheets.

"Sarah, would you like to say the prayer tonight?" Mrs. Johnson requested.

"Sure," Sarah answered matter of factly. "Dear God, thank you for today, and for tomorrow being Jesus's birthday. Watch over Jamie and Harry, and Mr. and Mrs. Johnson, and me."

"And Santa Claus," Harry interrupted through chattering teeth.

"And the waindeer," Jamie added sleepily.

229

"Okay, whatever," Sarah acknowledged, anxious to get on to more important matters. "And watch over my brother tonight, wherever he is. And if it's at all possible, I pray that you would bring him back to me really, really soon cause I really, really miss him. Amen."

"Good night little angels, and little shepherd boy," Mrs. Johnson whispered, giving them each a kiss on their foreheads. She then switched off the light and closed their door, only halfway, so that they wouldn't be submerged in total darkness.

Jamie was out like a light almost immediately. It had been a big day for this three year old. Harry, on the other hand, was fidgety, and seemed to rustle around just enough to keep Sarah from falling asleep.

Just as both children were almost asleep, two bright headlights beamed through their window and then suddenly went black.

"Santa Claus!" Harry gasped with renewed enthusiasm.

"Those were headlights. Santa doesn't drive a Chevy," Sarah murmured and rolled over to face away from the window. She figured it was just some friends of the Johnsons stopping by to say hello.

Four car doors slammed and then there was singing. It was very off key, but it was singing. It got louder and louder as it neared the front porch, so much so that both Harry and Sarah jumped out of bed and ran into the living room where Mr. and Mrs. Johnson were just opening the front door.

Bewildered looks came over the Johnsons' faces as they eyed each one the auspicious strangers who continued singing chorus after chorus of "Jingle Bells."

There was, however, one character in the crowd, who was outlandishly unidentifiable. He was wearing a flaming orange ski cap with a bright green neon fleece scarf wrapped around his face and neck, dark sunglasses, a navy blue, fleece lined parka, jeans, and leather gloves. To top it off, he wore a white straw cowboy hat over the ski cap and carried an oversized sports bag over his shoulder. He hung his head low, revealing only the top of the white cowboy hat to the curious onlookers and seemed to only mumble the lyrics to the song being sung.

Harry and Sarah cowered closer and closer to the Johnsons who appeared to be ready to dial 911 at a moment's notice. But as the next carol, "Away in a Manger," began, the oddball character stepped inside the doorway and began to disrobe - first taking off the cowboy hat and then the gloves. Then, just as he was about to unwrap the scarf, Jamie woke up and toddled into the room. She seemed to be enjoying the singing and strolled right up to the mysterious intruder.

"Jeffie," she smiled sleepily and tugged on his coat.

Sarah's eyes opened as wide as frisbees as Jeff removed the rest of his disguise. Her big brother was standing there and she flew into his arms like metal to a magnet.

They hugged for a long moment, and then released their holds just long enough for Jeff to ask Jamie, "How'd you know it was me?"

"Your coat and da bag," Jamie answered, pointing to the fleece lined jacket that Jeff had worn for the past year and the ragged duffel bag that he was still toting around.

"I should have known those would give me away." He squeezed Jamie and Harry, too.

"What's going on?" Mrs. Johnson asked, tears welling in her eyes. "Is everything okay?"

"Everything's unbelievably okay!" Jeff went on to make introductions and to tell the story of how all of this had come about. "And Coach and Tara offered to take us back to live with them. Isn't that great, Sarah?"

All along Sarah had known that if Jeff's plan to live with Uncle Frank worked out, she would someday be leaving the Johnsons. But in her heart, she had been hoping that when Jeff returned, the Johnsons would adopt the two of them and life could return to normal. Now, the reality of what Jeff's return meant, leaving the Johnsons, was beginning to set in.

"I guess so," Sarah answered somberly, confused about her own reaction to the situation, "but what about Mr. and Mrs. Johnson and Jamie and Harry? I'm going to miss them."

"I know, Sarah, but trust me, you're really going to like living with Coach and Tara," Jeff tried to assure her. "They're really nice and they've got a really big house..."

Tara approached Sarah for the first time and kneeled down beside her. "Hi Sarah," she whispered. "My name is Tara. I know you don't know me, but your brother told me all about you on the ride here and you sound like such a wonderful little girl. I know how you feel. I've had to say goodbye to people that I've loved, too, and I know it isn't easy. But in this case, you won't be saying goodbye forever. I promise that if you decide that you want to come back here to live or just to visit, I'll personally bring you back here myself, anytime, because it won't be any good for any of us if you aren't happy."

Mrs. Johnson, too, knelt down to try to console her little angel. "Sarah, if you give it a try and you want to come back, we'll still be here. You can always come to see us, and we can come to see you, too. I've never been to Ohio. You just remember, we'll never be too far away. And you can call us anytime you want. Sarah, you know, this may be the answer to your prayers."

"Maybe," Sarah answered more optimistically after reflecting on what Tara and Mrs. Johnson had said. "Okay," she agreed, "I'll give it a try."

Since it was too late to make the long drive back to LA that night, the Johnsons pulled out the sofa sleeper and the sleeping bags to accommodate their guests. Mr. and Mrs. Johnson gave up their room to the Webbers and joined Jamie and Harry in the bedroom with the bunk beds. Jennifer and Sarah slept on the sofa sleeper while the two boys bedded down in the living room in the bags.

"See, Josh, I mean, Jeff," Patrick reflected when the house was quiet at last, "God causes all things to work together for good."

"Patrick, did you just do what I think you did?" Jennifer asked, somewhat stunned by his remark.

"What? What did I do?" Patrick asked ambiguously. "If you smell something, it wasn't me!"

"No, not that. You just quoted scripture!" Jennifer stated, euphorically enlightened by her cousin's revelation.

"I did what?" he asked again.

"You said something from the Bible," Sarah explained dryly, as if this was common knowledge.

232

"I did? I didn't know that. It's just something that's embroidered on that one pillow on my grandma's couch," Patrick blurted out in self defense. "Isn't it on that one pillow at Grandma's?"

They all laughed at Patrick's innocent, yet heartfelt proclamation as Jennifer explained, "Yes, it is and it's a good thing, Patrick. You don't have to apologize."

"It *is* all good, you know," Patrick continued, in spite of his critics. "Who would have ever thought we'd all end up here together on top of a mountain in California on Christmas Eve, singing Christmas carols to people we don't even know, having flown here in a leer jet that just happens to be owned by the Wizard of Oz?"

"I know, who would have thought? Who'd have thought that a guy like me from Wyoming, would end up posing as a rich kid from down under and pulling off this whole kangaroo conspiracy thing?"

"Excuse me, but I think you should give *me* a little credit for having pulled off this whole kangaroo conspiracy thing," Patrick interrupted. "After all I did come up with the nickname and the plan to steal the kangaroo, along with covering for you when you didn't have a clue as to what you were talking about."

"Okay, you're right. But anyway, what I'm trying to say is, who would have thought that I would end up in Ohio meeting you guys, my two best buds in the whole world? Who would have ever thought *that* would happen?"

"I'm just glad it did," Jennifer admitted.

"And I'm just glad that you didn't forget about me and that you came back to get me," Sarah interjected. "So, was it fun being a rich kid ?" Sarah wanted to know.

"It was nice to be able to buy things without having to worry about how much they cost. Like we bought some toys for some foster kids one day and that was cool. But other than that, it was no big deal."

"Hey, hey, speaking of being a rich kid, I've got a joke for you guys." Patrick was at it again. "Two cannibals are munching on a rich kid. One cannibal says to the other cannibal, 'does this taste *spoiled* to you?' Get it? Does this taste *spoiled* to you?"

Dull groans emerged from the sofa sleeper as well as from Jeff's sleeping bag as Jeff, Sarah, and Jennifer tried to dismiss Patrick's most recent attempt at humor.

"Don't you get it? Rich kid? Spoiled? Do I have to explain all of my jokes to everyone?"

"You wouldn't if they were funny," Jennifer responded, beaming with cynicism.

"Oh, I get it," Sarah finally admitted dryly. "A rich kid, spoiled." She thought for a moment and shook her head. "Yeah... still not funny."

Jennifer and Jeff chuckled at Sarah's remark.

"How *did* you happen to meet this guy anyway?" Sarah asked her brother when it was quiet again. "I mean out of all the people in the world, how is it that you were lucky enough to find a friend who tells such good jokes - jokes that I haven't heard since I was in kindergarten?"

Again, all three friends laughed at Sarah's candor.

"God only knows," Jeff surmised, answering his sister's question as he rolled over and closed his eyes. Then, releasing a contented sigh, signifying that he had finally found the peace that he'd been seeking for so long, he repeated, "God only knows."

The Rest of the Story

Hey, hey, don't close the book. It's me - Patrick, you know the good looking one with the fuzzy blonde hair. I got permission from the author to tell you the rest of the story - like what happened after we surprised Sarah and all returned to our happy homes in Ohio.

First of all, remember how Mr. Montgomery fell in love with the old mansion that Coach and Tara lived in, and how they didn't have the money to fix it up? Well, on the plane trip back to Ohio, Mr. Montgomery and Coach worked something out. I don't know all of the details, but I think they worked out some kind of partnership where Mr. Montgomery gave Coach a lot of money to turn it into a bed and breakfast. They did a whole big remodel job on it, putting on an addition and everything so that now Coach, Tara, Jeff, and Sarah have attached, but separate living quarters from the bed and breakfast. And since Coach already had a full time job, guess who they hired to help do the remodel and then to act as caretaker on a full time basis? Jethro.

That was a relief to me since I had this whole guilty conscience thing going on about Jethro losing his job at the zoo because of the kangaroo kidnapping. Speaking of the kangaroo kidnapping and guilty consciences, Jeff and I eventually came clean about that, too. Luckily, Coach's reaction to our confession was pretty similar to my rationalization. He said that it wouldn't have amounted to any more than the two of us borrowing the kangaroo if Bull and Pudge hadn't come along and stolen it. He also said that the 100 hours of community service that Bull had to do was probably good for him.

As for what has become of the young JC Montgomery, I think he's doing okay these days, maybe spending a little more time with his dad than he used to. Since neither Jeff or I really ever got to know him, we never hear from him or anything, but we did see a photo of him and his dad in a magazine, dressed almost identically in khaki pants and white polo shirts, each holding a titanium golf club in his hand. The caption underneath read, "Wizard of Oz and Mini Me Make Quite the Par." Don't blame me for this one - I didn't make it up, that's really what it said.

You're probably wondering how we finished up the season in basketball. Well, we did end up winning the league championship. Our record ended up being 9 and 1. I'm sure you're familiar with the game that constituted the 1. However, when we went to regionals, we lost in double overtime by one lousy point. It was a heartbreaker, but we just figured there's always next year.

Which brings me to where we are today. We're in high school now. Yeah, it's pretty cool, except that we're freshmen and that pretty much puts us at the bottom of the food chain all over again. The older guys commandeer all of our women, so we virtually have no one to go out with for the whole school year. That is, unless we go for the older chicks, which I'm not opposed to doing, at this point.

It's been almost a year since Jeff first came to Westbrook. In some ways, it feels like it was only yesterday, but in other ways, I feel like I've known him my whole life. He's still my best bro and he and Jennifer still have it going on. It doesn't seem to phase her that just about every guy in the high school would like to go out with her. And luckily, Jeff isn't the jealous type, so I think they'll be all right.

Jeff seems to be doing really well, now. He seems to be getting on with his life. He doesn't obsess over things like he used to, although I do hear him and Jennifer talking about stuff, you know, stuff that they don't think I'm deep enough to relate to. But that's okay with me.

As for Bull, it's like I said before. He may win some, but he'll still always be a loser. Unfortunately, I do have to put up with him again, as he moved back in with his mom. But he seems to be a little more humble this year. Maybe it's because he's a freshman and he knows that the guys on the varsity football team will kick his butt if he mouths off. Come to think of it, that may be why I'm a little quieter this year, too.

As for little Sarah, she is doing just fine, still as sarcastic as ever when it comes to my jokes, but I admire her savvy. Sarah called Tara and Coach, Mom and Dad for the very first time last week, Jeff told me. Jeff and Sarah's adoption by the Webbers should be final soon.

It was hard for Sarah at first, leaving the Johnsons and all, but she's doing really well, and she got to stay with them this past summer when the Webbers, Jennifer, Jeff, and myself took a little side trip of our own to Wyoming.

You see, as it turned out, Jeff's parents had already bought the lot that they were on their way to see when they were smashed by the boulder. (Sorry to be so blunt). It took the state awhile to track Sarah and Jeff down, but when they did they told them that they owned real estate in Wyoming. So, guess what we did? We called up Mr. Montgomery and asked him for a loan to build a log cabin there. And he said yes.

I swear I felt like I was in the movie, Heidi out there, you know the old one in black and white with Shirley Temple, where Peter, the goat boy, comes up to visit her and her grandfather. Well, I felt like Peter, the goat boy, trudging up those hills. Carrying those logs about killed us. But we did it. We built a log cabin. Jeff and Sarah decided to rent it out for now and then they'll either sell it or move back there someday. I'm hoping we can go out there over Christmas or springbreak to do some snowboarding. The mountains are like nothing I've ever seen before. They look like they're just painted in the sky.

All in all, it's been a good year, an interesting one compared to all of the rest in our tiny town. Basketball season will be starting up soon. I'm going to miss having Webber as my coach, but he'll still be around to give us pointers since he'll be my best bud's dad. As a typical red blooded American kid, I'm also looking forward to getting my license next year, so that I can drive. Legally, that is.

As for me? What can I say? I still look in the mirror everyday and ask myself how I can be so darn handsome. And I still fight with Amos at the breakfast table every morning and at dinner every evening. I still tell my share of jokes that, as Sarah says, she hasn't heard since kindergarten. And as I settle into a new routine, even as low man on the totem pole as a freshman in high school, I am happy to report that I can still look at life and say, "It's all good."

To the Jackson Hole High School Class of 2001

When I first set eyes on you many years now previous,
You were wide eyed, innocent and kindheartedly mischievous.
But you welcomed me with warmth and enthusiastic praise
Into your classes where I'd spend many days.

Over the years, I watched as you grew
Taller, wiser and more passionate, too.
All part of one entity, but yet each one unique
Finding yourselves in new ventures you'd seek.

And as you grew older, I grew younger at heart.
Feeling blessed to have played even a minuscule part
In celebrating a triumph or suffering a woe
Side by side with the individuals I had gotten to know.

I watched you say goodbye to those who moved on
To new destinations and to adventures beyond,
You felt joy, love, and laughter, you met heartbreak and sorrow,
Grieved the losses of friends, helped each other face tomorrow.

At times it was hard seeing what you went through
And I wished I could erase, or rewind and redo.
But there's no going back, the past, it is gone.
You can only let go; you can only move on.

You grew up too quickly as all children do,
Grew apart or grew closer to the people you once knew.
Played a part, scored a point, rode a board, dared to try.
You let yourself laugh and you let yourself cry.

Now when I see you, each unique and quite gifted,
I look back on those days and my spirits are lifted.
Though the years will go on and the memories will fade,
You'll never quite know the impression you've made.

So, I dedicate this book to each guy and each girl,
To thank you for welcoming me into your world.
I pray that the future holds the best for each one
Of my special friends in the class of 2000 and 1 !